JOURNEY TO THE
CORE OF CREATION

Borgo Press Books by BRIAN STABLEFORD

JOURNEY TO THE CORE OF CREATION

A ROMANCE OF EVOLUTION

BRIAN STABLEFORD

THE BORGO PRESS

MMXI

JOURNEY TO THE CORE OF CREATION

FIRST EDITION

Published by Wildside Press LLC

www.wildsidebooks.com

DEDICATION

For Minwen,

Who provided a light in the darkness
when I really needed it.

CONTENTS

AUTHOR'S NOTE

Although this story is complete in itself, occasional passing reference is made to earlier stories in the series to which it belongs: "The Legacy of Erich Zann" (in the Perilous Press volume *The Womb of Time*), *Valdemar's Daughter* and *The Mad Trist* (published as complementary halves of a Borgo/Wildside Double), *The Quintessence of August* and *The Cthulhu Encryption* (both issued as Borgo/Wildside novels). The full text of Benoît de Maillet's *Telliamed,* complete with the marginal notes to the manuscript, to which Auguste Dupin has privileged access in the present story, was published in English translation by the University of Illinois Press in 1968, translated and edited by Albert V. Carozzi. The fundamental idea of the "Thierachians" featured in the plot is borrowed from Jean Richepin's novel *L'Aile* (1911), translated into English as *The Wing* (Black Coat Press 2011), but I have embellished it considerably in equipping the imaginary nomads in question with an entire new mythology.

"I believe that I have sufficiently demonstrated," the philosopher continued, "the probability, if not the truth of the theory that terrestrial animals originate from marine ones, and which also established the natural formation of the latter in the sea, by the seeds with which its waters are impregnated, whether such seeds are assumed to be eternal or whether they exist by creation.... It is thus easy to imagine the manner in which all sensitive or vegetative things could be generated in a globe, whether it is being repopulated, or whether it has never been populated previously."

Marginal note to the manuscript of
Telliamed by Benoît de Maillet
(written 1692-1718)

I demand of you, and of the whole world, that you show me a generic character...by which to distinguish between Man and Ape. I myself most assuredly know of none. I wish someone would indicate one to me. But if I had called man an ape, or vice versa, I should have fallen under the ban of the ecclesiastics. It may be that as a naturalist I should have done so.

Carl von Linné (*alias* Carolus Linnaeus),
letter to J. G. Gmelin, 1747

If these different organisms are compared with one another and with what is known concerning man; if they are contemplated, from the simplest animal organization to that of man, which is the most complex and the most perfect, the progression exhibited in the composition of the organization, as well as the successive acquisition of different special organs and, therefore, of as many new faculties are developed organs; then it becomes perceptible how needs, initially reduced to a minimum and increasing gradually in number thereafter, have produced a tendency to actions appropriate to satisfy them; how actions that become habitual and energetic occasion the development of the organs that perform them; how the force that excites organic movements can, in the most imperfect animals, be located outside them and yet stimulate them; how, eventually, this force is transferred into the animal; and finally, how it there becomes the source of sensibility, and eventually of acts of intelligence.

Jean-Baptiste de Lamarck,
Philosophie zoologique, 1809

CHAPTER ONE
THE REVELATION

No matter how mild a winter might be, one is always glad to see the return to Paris of spring, which is said—not without reason—to be the city's best season. No matter how much delight lovers of darkness may take in the long nights of winter, they eventually become wearisome. To tell the truth, as Auguste Dupin and I got older, the particular fascinations that had united us in the early days of our acquaintance, including our fascination with darkness, began to fade somewhat. Even though fate continued to deliver us into dark places on occasion, we became increasingly glad to find or create light within them as time went by.

I cannot say that, before the spring of 1847, we had suffered any personal revolution in anticipation of the political upheaval that was shortly to arrive, nor even that we had changed in any essential way—the notion of Dupin changing seemed absurd, given that his character seemed only to have hardened as a result of all our bizarre adventures—but I think we had become less emphatic in our commonplace idiosyncrasies. As for less commonplace idiosyncrasies...well, those remain emphatic by necessity, if not be definition.

The perversity of my own temperament had left me in considerable doubt as to the so-called joys of spring in my youth, even though the changing of the seasons was sufficiently well-marked in Boston, where I spent much of my early youth, and noticeable even in Virginia, where I spend the most significant fraction of my adolescence—although Virginia, in particular, had nothing of the exaggerated changes in the relative duration of light and dark enjoyed by Paris. It is, however, entirely in keeping with the principle of perversity that a man who has avoided such follies when they might have taken fruitful effect should begin to feel something of a special zest at the advent of the season of renewal, once he in his forties and no longer likely to express that zest in any fashion remotely connected to procreation.

The one problem with the equinoctial season in Paris, however, is the changeability of the weather. There are bright days, to be sure, but there are also rainy ones, often in abundance. The vegetable world needs both, of course, to fuel the sudden rise of its saps, but rain, especially when it comes in near-deluges, can have a singularly dispiriting effect on a human spirit that has only recently been buoyed up by emergence from winter torpor.

It was raining heavily on the strange evening in 1847 when I learned more about Auguste Dupin's history in a matter of hours than I had contrived to winkle out of him in more years than I had fingers to count. There must, I suppose, have been dozens of people in Paris who had been acquainted him when he was authentically young, including at least three whom I saw on a regular basis, but they never talked about it any more than he did. His discretion was contagious, to a remarkably insistent degree.

I say "authentically young" because it was very difficult to judge Dupin's age. When I had first met him he had seemed younger than I was, but I had soon learned to doubt that judgment; for a while I had thought him much older, and then had changed my mind again—but all my attempts to determine a exact chronology of his birth and education had been met with a conscientious vagueness that had begun to seem irritating. I suppose that it was necessary for me to encounter someone who had known him a quarter of a century before but had not seen him since, thus avoiding the contagion of discretion, in order to discover any reliable information.

Dupin had come to dinner that evening, with the understanding that we would spend the evening together, chatting as we had in the early days of our acquaintance, but we had not even finished dessert when a messenger came from the Prefecture begging him to come, in order to offer his advice on a matter of urgency. For once, even Dupin seemed annoyed by the rudeness of the summons.

"I'll come back," he promised me. "Within an hour, if possible—two at the most."

As an unusually scrupulous man, he did not like to make promises he could not keep, but I knew better than to take that one too literally. Even so, I told him that I would wait up, at least until eleven o'clock.

Inevitably, two hours passed, and almost three. When the doorbell eventually rang, I assumed that it was a messenger from the Prefecture, come to tell me that my friend had been delayed, and would be busy all night with whatever mystery some bewildered inspector had been obliged to pass up the chain of command until it claimed that attention of the Prefect himself. I allowed Madame Bihan to answer it, sticking to my armchair, where I was reading through the sections of *Le Constitutionnel* that I had not bothered to peruse in the morning.

When she came in to the smoking-room, however, it was not to deliver the expected message.

"It's a lady, sir," she said, "asking for Monsieur Dupin."

"A lady?" I echoed, more in puzzlement than surprise.

"Yes, sir," Madame Bihan confirmed, "and a child."

Had I echoed the latter item of information, astonishment would no doubt have come to the fore, but I did not. The drumming of the rain on the widows had reminded me that it would be extremely impolite, on a night like this, to leave a lady—let alone a child—standing on one's doorstep.

I hastened to the door without bothering to mutter any further response to Madame Bihan, and begged the lady to come into the hallway even before making any assessment of her appearance and quality. That would have been difficult, in any case, until she was within direct reach of the light of the solitary oil lamp hanging from the ceiling of the vestibule.

She was evidently grateful for the consideration; although she had presumably arrived in a fiacre, the short interval between stepping down therefrom and being admitted into the house had sufficed to soak her upper garments, for she had no umbrella. When she had removed her slightly-bedraggled hat I saw that she was mature—not quite as old as the century, but not far off—but still very handsome. Her eyes were a piercing blue and her brown hair was only just beginning to display flecks of gray. Her clothing was not cheap, but not aristocratic either, Parisian in its tailoring but provincial in its style. It was evidently a traveling costume, and gave every indication that she had come a long way. Her complexion was not excessively sunburned, but her skin was beginning to show evidence of the inevitable stress exerted on Norman delicacy and pallor by a long sojourn in the south.

I confess that I hardly glanced at the child, who was a girl approximately twelve years old. She seemed somewhat vexed by the rain, although her broad-brimmed hat and capacious cloak had saved her from its worst effects, but she was sufficiently well brought-up to stand meekly by, half-hidden behind her mother. The family resemblance between the two left no doubt in my mind that the lady was, in fact, the child's mother.

"Is Monsieur Dupin here?" the lady was quick to ask, with a rather un-Parisian carelessness regarding the formalities of introduction.

"No, Madame," I relied. "He dined here, but he was summoned to the Prefecture. He promised to return, but...."

Still showing no respect or etiquette, she cut me off. "The Prefecture?" she queried.

"Yes," I said. "He is often summoned, as a...consultant."

The lady's lips pursed slightly. "Lucien," she said, more to herself than me, as if the explanation of Dupin's absence had suddenly occurred to her. Evidently, she knew—or had once known—Paris's Prefect of Police well enough to think of him in first name terms.

"I'm sorry," I said. "As I said, he promised to return, but...."

Again, she cut me off, this time rather paradoxically, to say: "I'm the one who owes you an apology. I really should have introduced myself. My name is Madame Guérande, and this is my daughter Sophie. I'm very sorry to call on you unexpectedly like this, at such an unsocial hour, but Amélie told me that Monsieur Dupin was here, and assured me that it would be acceptable to look for him here."

It took me half a second to realize that she not only thought of the Prefect of Police in terms of his first name, but that she thought of Madame Lacuzon, Dupin's concierge and guardian, in the same informal way. That was by far the more remarkable of the two facts, all the more astonishing because Madame Lacuzon, who protected Dupin's privacy with all the fierce determination of a dragon, had made the remarkable exception of telling Madame Guérande where he might be found, and assuring her that it would be perfectly acceptable to seek him out at my house.

For the time being, however, politeness demanded that I try to make my visitors a little more comfortable. The only fire that had been lit outside the kitchen—which doubled as the servants' parlor—was in the smoking room, but the windows had been open earlier in the day and I had been saving my pipe until Dupin returned, so the atmosphere was not as toxic as it might have been, and it seemed to me that their greatest urgency was allowing the two visitors an opportunity to relieve the chill of their sudden dampness. While Madame Bihan took their mantles away in order to dry them by the kitchen stove, I brought two more armchairs to the hearth and sat them down. I offered the lady a glass of brandy, which she refused, asking instead for some warm milk for Sophie. I gave the order to Madame Bihan, who accepted it with no more complaint than a world-weary sigh.

Sophie sat down meekly in the chair I had moved for her, but Madame Guérande did not accept my invitation immediately.

Instead, she moved around the room curiously, inspecting it with what seemed to me to be unnecessarily minute care. The walls were, of course, lined with books, which she was not content merely to scan with a glance. She was actually inspecting the titles—those which could be read on the spines in spite of the uncertain light—as if attempting to measure me by my reading habits.

A full half minute passed before she suddenly turned to look me in the eye and said: "Your name would not be Poe, by any chance?"

I suppressed the shock of the question, and all the possibilities raised by the fact that it had been asked. "No," I replied. "Mr. Poe was a close friend of mine once upon a time, and we still maintain a correspondence, although it has become a trifle desultory of late. It was from my letters that he drew the information on which he based a number of stories in which Monsieur Dupin figures as a character, but I never had his literary talent. My name is Reynolds: Samuel Reynolds." I felt a curious thrill as I articulated the syllables of my name, and realized that Dupin's contagious discretion had affected me to such a degree that I rarely pronounced them any longer.

"Are you from Virginia?" she asked, point-blank.

"I'm originally from Boston, Massachusetts," I told her, a trifle stiffly. "I lived in Virginia for some years in my youth, and met Mr. Poe at university there. I traveled a good deal before settling in Paris, and no longer feel myself to be a native of anywhere in particular. I have not entirely lost my appetite for travel, but Monsieur Dupin is a reluctant tourist, and...."

This time, she did not interrupt, but I left the sentence dangling of my own accord, not entirely sure how to explain the fact that Dupin's reluctance to leave Paris somehow functioned as an anchor restraining my own excursions.

Madame Guérande did not seem surprised to learn that Dupin was a reluctant tourist, but a shadow of doubt passed over her face, which was then in the lamplight, and I immediately jumped to the conclusion that she had some interest in breaking that habit.

What she said, however, was: "I'm glad that he has a friend. He needs society, although he is probably still reluctant to recognize or admit it. I'm sure that you're good for him."

I was sure of that too, although I was by no means sure exactly why it was the case. "Have you known him long?" I asked, mildly.

Madame Bihan brought in a tray, which not only had Sophie's warm milk but a bottle of red wine, already uncorked, some bread, butter and a selection of cheeses. I could tell be the glint in the lady's blue eyes that the sight of the food and wine was by no means unwelcome.

The cook positioned the tray carefully on an occasional table, and then stood back, as if to check that I had arranged the armchairs appropriately. She nodded briefly, and returned to the kitchen after the briefest of glances in my direction.

Instead of answering my question, or taking her seat, Madame Guérande suddenly reached out to a bookshelf and plucked a book out of the array.

"*Telliamed!*" she said, with a slight hint of delight. "I once gave Auguste a copy of this...." As she spoke she opened the volume and glanced at the flyleaf—and her features suddenly changed. "*This* copy, in fact." she added. She seemed disconsolate—as if the idea that Auguste Dupin might have given away a copy of a book of which she had made him a present was difficult to bear: a more than commonplace betrayal.

I hastened to redeem my friend's reputation. "Monsieur Dupin was resident in the house for a while," I said. "His own apartment is so cramped and cluttered that he moved a considerable number of his books on to what were then almost empty shelves. There is a sense in which he still divides his residence between the two locations; there is a room upstairs that I still call 'Dupin's bedroom,' and there are a great many books here that are most definitely 'Dupin's books.' That is one of them; I have never opened it...or even heard him mention it."

The lady finally condescended to take her seat. I poured her a glass of wine and invited her to cut some cheese. She did so, painstakingly, with an exaggerated delicacy that suggested deliberate delay. She was thinking hard—and so was I. It was evident that we were both building up a considerable pressure of curiosity, but I did not want to ask another question that would probably be ignored, or begin another statement that would probably be interrupted.

She handed the first plate bearing bread and cheese she had cut to her daughter, who raised her eyes for the first time to look at me. "Thank you," she said. Sophie Guérande was obviously well brought-up, although shy by Parisian standards.

The lady took some bread and cheese for herself, and then a sip of wine, with evident caution, but seemingly not without a keen appetite. She was obviously a self-contained person—and had brought up her daughter to conduct herself with a similar reserve—but I had a strong impression that she was making more effort than usual to contain herself, because she had more than usual to contain.

Madame Guérande finished her meager meal some time before the little girl, but she had wine to wash it down, while poor Sophie only had milk.

"Has Monsieur Dupin ever mentioned me to you?" Madame Guérande eventually asked, belatedly picking up the thread of my last remark, and the suggestion carefully concealed within it.

"Not that I recall," I confirmed, leaning forward slightly, in the hope that I might be able to read the inscription in the book, which she had picked up again, after placing it face down on her knee still pen at the fly-leaf.

For a moment, I thought she was going to close it again, but she must have realized the futility of such a gesture. Instead, she held the inscription up to the light, in order that I might read it.

"Julie," I remarked. I did not cite the remainder of the inscription, which referred to both love and affection.

"Julie Maret, as I was then," she said, evidently hoping that Dupin might have mentioned her in that guise, if not by her married name.

He had not—but the surname at least, was not unfamiliar. "Might your father, perhaps, be Achille Maret?" I asked. "The late geologist, who was once a close friend of the Chevalier de Lamarck?"

"Yes," she relied, colorlessly. "Achille Maret was my father." She still seemed disappointed that I had not recognized her own name. "Monsieur Dupin has, at least, mentioned him?"

"Occasionally," I confirmed. "But only once did he mention, *en passant*, that he had been personally acquainted with Professor Maret—and even then, he did not go into detail. If I were to hazard a guess that he had known him in his student days, it would only be a guess. I am not even certain—not absolutely, at least—that Dupin was once a Sorbonnard, or, if so, when. I have not the slightest idea what degrees he holds, if any, or even how he qualified for the red ribbon of the Légion d'honneur that he never actually wears. Indeed, after all the years I have known him, and all the hours we have spent in seemingly free-and-easy conversation, I can still say that Dupin's past, before the day we met, is as much a closed book to me as the one you are holding in your hand."

She took that aboard, slowly and carefully, and eventually said: "Ah!" She seemed to be wondering whether, in the circumstances, she should say any more, lest she reveal some nugget of information to me that Dupin had been carefully hiding from me for more than a decade. Eventually, however, she seemed to come to the conclusion that she was entitled to some revenge for Dupin never have mentioned her, even to the close friend that she felt entitled to be glad that he had.

"Auguste was one of my father's students, for a while," she told me. "It was in the years immediately before and after 1820. I suppose that I was little more than a child, although I felt very much a young lady, entirely ready for society...perhaps something of a coquette—what an American such as yourself would probably call a *flirt*. My husband was one of my father's friends, then: one of a little coterie of Lamarck's disciples, headed by my father and Étienne Geoffroy Saint-Hilaire, which met once a week in our drawing-room, in a fashion that always seemed to me to be that of a secret society, although I hardly understood then why the ideas we discussed were considered so dangerous that I was forbidden to mention them even when I went to confession. The Chevalier was still alive then, and still working on his magisterial catalogue of invertebrate species when I knew him, although his health and eyesight were beginning to deteriorate. He was still lecturing to the public at the Jardin des Plantes, although his academic situation had been compromised and he was subject to virtual ostracism by all sectors of society but ours... principally because of the Restoration, you understand...."

She paused, looking at me inquiringly. I nodded. I did understand. Lamarck, like many other pillars of the various branches of the University of Paris, had enjoyed a rocky ride, in terms of his vocation and his career, as the Revolution had produced the Convention, the Convention the Directoire, the Directoire the Consulate, the Consulate the Empire, and so on. His father had been a Baron, but he had become an Encyclopedist even before the Revolution, and had finally nailed his colors too firmly to the Bonapartist mast to be regarded as anything but a traitor to the Bourbon crown after the Restoration. He had clung on to a marginal position in Parisian Academe, and remained popular with the public who attended his open lectures, but the number of people who still counted him a genius in 1820, on account of his *Philosophie Zoologique*, could probably have fitted into a single room—Achille Maret's drawing-room, presumably.

"I had not known that Dupin was one of Lamarck's...disciples," I commented, for want of any better observation to make.

"He wasn't, quite," Madame Guérande replied. "Not in their reckoning, at least. He was certainly very sympathetic to evolutionism, including the supposedly-blasphemous aspects of which my father and his friend spoke in whispers, but he had too much independence of spirit to be anyone's faithful disciple, and he had ideas that my father considered heretical, without being aware of the irony of that judgment. Auguste was interested...very interested...in a great many subjects. He and my husband were close friends, for a while, and Claude was certainly interested in Auguste's heretical notions, in spite of my father's disapproval but...the matter became complicated. Auguste could not bring himself to speak as diplomatically as Claude, and my father was not a man to tolerate overmuch dissent from his students...."

By this time, of course, my imagination was conjuring up all kinds of wild fantasies. Throughout the time I had known him, Dupin had shown even less interest in the opposite sex than I had, and had always seemed to me to have cut himself off conclusively from all emotions of that kind. I had never quite been prepared to take it for granted that the sole reason for that exclusion was his devotion to the cause of study and rationality. I had always wondered whether his excessive commitment to dispassionate logic might have been, at its inception, a reaction to some wounding experience. Now, the notion that he might once have been in love with Julie Maret, but had lost her, in a context of parental disapproval, to an older rival he had initially counted as a friend, and then as a betrayer....

I had to remind myself, sternly, that real life does not normally bear overmuch resemblance to a *feuilleton* in *Le Constitutionnel*.

"At the risk of being indiscreet," I said, glad for once to be an unrepentant gambler, "may I ask why you want to see Monsieur Dupin so urgently."

"I want to ask him, rather urgently, for his help," she said, bluntly. After a moment, during which she challenged me with her eyes, she added: "You don't seem surprised. I presume that Lucien isn't the only person who solicits his aid on a regular basis."

"Indeed not," I murmured. I could not resist the temptation to add: "But Madame Lacuzon turns most of them away, with a ferocity that has become legendary. I have never known her to reveal his whereabouts to anyone."

"Amélie always made an exception for me," was Julie

Guérande's curt but revealing reply. In a sense, I supposed that "Amélie" had always made an exception for me, too, but never with a conspicuously good grace. The gorgon evidently understood that I was in some sense essential to Dupin, and therefore to be tolerated, but it seemed, if I were reading the implication correctly, that Julie Maret had not been merely tolerated, but actively welcomed. Julie Maret had evidently grown used to thinking of the old witch as "Amélie"—a name that even Madame Bihan, her cousin, hesitated to pronounce.

It was possible, of course, that Madame Lacuzon had not been a "gorgon" or a "old witch" in 1820, but a mere middle-aged woman of much milder character—but somehow, I doubted it, Dupin might have been young at heart then, but not the concierge.

"If she did not guard him so closely," I admitted, "he would be besieged. He lives semi-reclusively, but his reputation has nevertheless spread. I suppose that is partly my fault—or Poe's, for not observing the convention of changing names to protect the innocent. Eddie assumed that his stories would never filter back to France, and would not strike a chord if they did...but even in the absence of translations, the tales have somehow been communicated. The steamships that have regularized communication between the continents have facilitated a freedom of information that Eddie, in spite of being an unusually far-sighted man, had not quite grasped imaginatively. Even without that excessively lurid account of the murders in the Rue Morgue, however, Dupin's adventures in detection and the solution of strange mysteries would have generated rumors. Even the wizards of modern Paris take Dupin for a magician as great as themselves; at least one of them firmly believes that he is a reincarnation of John Dee—which goes to show how rare logic and erudition are in today's world."

Madame Guérande did not laugh at the half-hearted witticism. She weighed the book she was holding in her hand, and then glanced around the shelves again. "Has Auguste abandoned his more esoteric interests, then?" she asked, curiously. "I did not see his once-precious copy of *Les Harmonies de l'enfer* on your shelves."

"Oh, he keeps his shelf of forbidden books in his own apartment," I told her, laconically. "They might not be safe here, without Madame Lacuzon to guard the threshold."

She looked at me strangely, apparently wondering how serious I was, or ought to be. Then she nodded her head, almost imperceptibly. It was not a communication, but a faint reflex.

"Has the reason you want his help something to do with the Harmonies of Hell?" I asked, tentatively.

"Not in the sense that the silly book in question means the phrase," she assured me, "although there is an underworld involved, and strange legends concerning it—but it's more a matter of disharmony than harmony. There's nothing truly supernatural involved, so far as I can tell."

"If there's one thing I have learned in my acquaintance with Dupin," I said, with a slight sigh, having taken note of the cautionary *truly*, "especially in recent years, is that one never *can* tell. He is very adamant in saying that everything that happens is natural, but if he is right...well, the bounds of the natural are not what I once thought them to be."

Again, there was an imperceptible nod, as if she were taking note of another echo of the distant past. "That was one point of faith on which all the members of my father's secret society agreed," she said, softly. "Everything that had ever happened was natural: the origin and progress of life; the origin and progress of humankind. They took reverent delight in private speculation and deduction on such subjects, all the more so because their mouths were routinely sealed in public."

I had discussed similar issues many times with Dupin, and had always been struck by the idiosyncrasy of his attitude when he mentioned certain matters. The majority of intelligent men, he had once told me, had believed ever since Carl von Linné published his taxonomy of species, that humans were a natural product of evolution, closely related to the great apes—but none had dared say so in their writings, and some had even resorted to vehement denial, for fear of the disapproval of the Church. I had been in Paris long enough to know that the Revolution of '89 had not put an end to the power of that disapproval, especially in the upper echelons of Academe, which still retained the legacy of its one-time domination by the Church.

Madame Guérande looked at her daughter, who had fallen asleep in the armchair. Gently, she removed the empty plate from the little girl's knee and set it down on the tray.

"Have you come far?" I asked, innocently—but with an extensive hidden agenda of my own.

"From the Ardèche," she said, casually.

"That's a long journey," I observed, although I had only the vaguest notion of where the Ardèche was.

"It was very long the first time I made it," she agreed, "but now that the railway from Paris has reached Chalon...within three years, or five at the most, it will stretch all the way to Lyon, perhaps to Marseilles....unless a new Revolution throws the country into chaos again."

"The one thing about which there is no political dispute is the necessity of expanding the railways as rapidly as possible," I said. "On that matter, the king and Monsieur Thiers are in complete agreement, and have no need to seek a *juste milieu*. The most hardened Legitimists and the most radical Anarchists are similarly besotted with railways, even if they disapprove of the role played by the Bourse in their instigation. No one can any longer imagine how we could once have been content with canals. You traveled by train, then, all the way from Chalon to Paris?"

"Yes. Have you traveled by railway yourself?" What she wanted to know, I presumed, was whether Dupin was amenable to railway travel. In spite of my enthusiastic little speech, she and I both knew that there were people in the world who had sworn that they would never step into a railway carriage, either for fear of accidents or love of horses.

"Only as far Rouen," I told her. "It was an experience. If you're correct about the speed of the network's extension, I may one day be able to overcome Dupin's resistance to tourism."

"I'm convinced of it," she replied.

"You're hoping to persuade him to travel to the Ardèche, then?" I queried.

"The word I used," she pointed out, with a little smile, "was *convinced.*"

"I'm delighted by your conviction, Madame," I said, permitting myself a hint of over irony. "I've never been to the Ardèche."

Her blue eyes bored into mine like gimlets. "Do you go everywhere with Monsieur Dupin nowadays?" she asked.

"Everywhere," I assured her.

This time, she nodded more conspicuously—and much more dubiously. "I suppose we shall get to know one another better, then," she said.

"I hope so," I said, mildly. "If I am to be allowed to accept your invitation too, might I enquire as to the nature of the urgent problem with which you intend to confront him? You mentioned strange legends—which have become a particular fascination of Dupin's of late, and mine too."

"That's a peripheral mater," she said, "and rather conventional, I fear. The house that my husband inherited from his father shortly after our marriage—in which we took up residence almost immediately—is situated at the bottom of a mountain. The mountain is meager by comparison with the larger peaks of the Central Massif, which lie to the west on the other side of it, and it has a rounded top that soothes its outline, but it seems impressive enough when viewed from the valley floor. It is known in the valley as Mont Dragon, because local folklore says that there is a dragon sleeping underneath it, whose breathing can be heard and felt every spring, when it always comes close to waking—but fortunately never quite does. The mountain is part of a range of long-extinct volcanoes, however, and the prolonged geological effects of fire and water have left it honeycombed with caves. When the winter ice that forms in the outer layers of the mountain soil and the superficial fissures of the rock breaks down, and the melt-water begins to drain away, it generates sounds that reach the surface as muted hisses and groans. Occasionally, there are slight earth-tremors. There's nothing supernatural about it, although I must confess that the phenomena began early this year, and seem more striking than usual—circumstances that seem to have added to an anxiety that seems to have gripped the whole valley, and prompted me to an action that I have contemplated several times before but never undertaken."

"It must be an interesting location for a geologist," I remarked, "Your husband spends a good deal of time in the caves, I imagine."

She hesitated, but then decided that she might as well continue, given that Dupin would presumably tell me anyway, once she had confided in him.

"Far too much, in my opinion," she confessed, "and he spends all winter fretting, waiting for the thaw in order to gain access again. It's become something of an obsession, reaching an unprecedented fever pitch in the last two weeks. He has made discoveries there—indeed, he told me long before we married, swearing me to secrecy from the other members of my father's coterie, that he had first gone into the caves as a child, while his father was away at war, and found something wonderful there, about which he was anxious to send a *mémoire* one day to the Académie—but nearly thirty years have gone by since he told me that, and no *mémoire* has been forthcoming. He keeps on saying that there must be far more to find, which he would find, if he only had a little more time—but I know little more now about what it was he found as a boy than I did when he first confided that news to me, even though I have seen the specimens he has brought out. Whenever I ask him about what still remains inside the mountain, he merely mumbles that it is immovable, and that he has not yet discovered the whole of it. I have often had to fight a powerful temptation to go into the caves to see for myself, in spite of the danger."

I did not imagine that she meant danger from the dragon, or any other phantom of folklore. She seemed an eminently commonsensical person, sufficiently well-controlled to suppress the agitation that she must be feeling. She seemed glad of an opportunity to talk—and perhaps glad, too, that she had an opportunity to talk to someone else before renewing an old acquaintance with Dupin that would inevitably stir up echoes. I wondered how much she had confided to Madame Lacuzon—and how much Madame Lacuzon had confided to her.

I filled the lady's wine-glass again. She took a long sip, and relaxed slightly.

"I can understand why your patience has worn thin," I observed.

Her lips formed a wry curve that I could not honestly describe as a smile.

"I have often suggested to my husband that we should invite people that we had known in Paris to visit us—especially Auguste," she remarked, distantly. "He always agrees in principle, but always puts it off."

"But this time," I said, probing gently, "he finally agreed?"

"Yes," she said. "He agreed."

I had the strong impression that her husband had been given little choice—that the agreement had been forced. I also took the inference that the lady had not paused after obtaining that agreement, lest it be rescinded. Otherwise, she would surely have written to notify us of her arrival...unless, of course, she was also anxious that Dupin, too, might be inclined to procrastination, if given an opportunity to object.

"Perhaps I have said too much," the lady suddenly remarked. "I beg you to let me put this matter to Auguste in my own way, in my own time."

"Of course," I said.

I heard the front door open then, as if one cue. I knew that it was Dupin; he was the only person in the world who was entitled to do so without ringing. The Bihans always used the back door, as befitted the dutiful servants they took an altogether un-post-Revolutionary pride in being.

I gathered myself together in anticipation of Dupin's surprise, and my enjoyment thereof...and, of course, of the further revelations that were still to come.

CHAPTER TWO
DUPIN SURPRISED

By 1847 I had already seen Auguste Dupin confronted with some exceedingly strange things—things far stranger than I had once been able to imagine—without flinching, or even condescending to seem surprised. I had never, in all the years of our acquaintance, seen him look "thunderstruck" or "flabbergasted"—but those were the two words than came into my mind when I saw his eyes settle upon Julie Guérande as he opened the door of my sitting room that evening.

Perhaps I am exaggerating, and my own anticipation had added more than its fair measure to what I saw—briefly, it had to be admitted—but I remain convinced of the impression. Dupin was more disconcerted by seeing that old acquaintance of his student days than he had been when he had looked through a window between the dimensions and had seen the Crawling Chaos on the threshold of invading our sector of the Universe.

As I said, the effect was brief. It only took a few seconds for his gaze to register the sight, take account of the shock and repress the overt reaction of astonishment. Then he glanced in another direction—toward the sleeping girl—for a slightly longer interval, collecting himself all the while.

Finally, he bowed politely, and said: "I see that we have visitors. Forgive my startlement, Madame Guérande—I'm a little tired, having spent the last three hours racking my brains over a strange puzzle."

"How is Lucien?" the lady inquired. "I haven't seen him since the day when I last saw you, at the *Messageries*—although news of his good fortune has reached us, even in the Ardèche. Prefect of the Parisian Police!" Her tone was slightly unsteady now, and she was obviously nervous, although she had been quite self-composed a few moments earlier.

I poured the dregs from the wine-bottle into a spare glass and handed it to Dupin. Madame Bihan appeared, as if by magic, carrying another bottle, already uncorked, and set it down. She it was, I think, who indicated to Dupin with her eyes that he would be welcome to slice some cheese from any of the fragments she had brought. I had assumed that he would not want any, and was mildly surprised to see him pick up the cheese-knife. I suppose that he wanted some task with which to be busy, other than drinking wine—and perhaps some reason for prevarication, in order to get his thoughts in order, even before answering a question as innocuous as the one she had asked.

I hastened to get up and move my chair in order to make room around the hearth for a fourth. Madame Bihan stirred up the fire and used the tongs to place two more small logs on it—but Dupin did not sit down immediately. He began murmuring as he cut himself a slice of cheese and picked it up, but suddenly seemed to realize that he was speaking too softly, and raised his voice lightly, in order to make himself heard without running overmuch risk of waking the child.

"Monsieur Groix is very well, considering," he said, before taking a bite of the cheese—a Saint-Paulin, I think. Then he stopped in order to chew.

Neither I nor Madame Guérande had to ask "considering what?" Revolution was in the air, and the political division of the various police forces of which Lucian Groix was in nominal control—a division with which Dupin remained scrupulously uninvolved—was extremely busy detecting plots against the regime and filling the prisons with dissidents.

When Dupin has finally swallowed, he did not have to hurry in order to add: "Is this your daughter, Madame?"

"It is," the lady confirmed. "Her name is Sophie. She's twelve years old. I'd introduce you properly, but the journey has tired her out, as you can see."

"My friend has introduced himself, I suppose?"

"Oh yes—Mr. Reynolds and I are the best of friends already."

A slight shadow seemed to pass over Dupin's face as she said that, but I could not believe that it was jealousy. It was more likely to be anxiety, caused by not knowing what Julie Guérande might have told me while we were waiting for him to return.

"And how is Monsieur Guérande?"

"Claude is not so well, I fear," the lady countered. She seemed to have tired of the forced conventional manner of conversation, and wasted no further time. "That, as you will undoubtedly have deduced, is why I am here. I'm sorry that I did not write to warn you that I was coming, but I had left it too late. I kept hoping that the winter would cool the fever that overwork brought upon Claude last year, but instead, his impatience has become corrosive. I hoped too, that spring might bring an amelioration, but it has not. Now, on top of everything, vague threats are being made of legal action against him—entirely unnecessarily— and that seems to have brought his anxiety to boiling point. He needs a calming influence, Auguste, and I cannot provide it."

Dupin feigned puzzlement. "I'm not a lawyer, Madame Guérande," he said. "If and when I lend assistance to the Prefecture, it is in the capacity of a logician."

The lady had barely restrained herself from cutting him off in mid-sentence. "The legal issues are a mere irritant," she said. "The last straw, so to speak. What is crucially at stake, in Claude's eyes, is the research that he has been carrying out in the caves close to the house he inherited from his father—with or without proper legal authority. It is in that respect, I believe, that he needs an understanding ear and some wise advice. I wish that he would trust me sufficiently to discuss the matter with me—but he does not consider that I was a true member of my father's salon, and the older members of the clique are all dead. Lucien is not the only one to have put such matters behind him, but even if there were veterans of the salon still in the heart of the Sorbonne...you will understand well enough, Auguste, why I thought of you...."

"You want me to renew my friendship with your husband," Dupin stated, in a tone so neutral as to seem quite dead.

"More than that, I fear," the lady replied. "The matter is urgent. Now that the spring has come, the caves will become accessible again—and *they* will return in a matter of days...."

This time, her hesitation was very obviously planned for effect. She was being deliberately tantalizing. She might not have seen him for twenty years and more, but she knew her man. She knew how to manipulate Auguste Dupin, even—perhaps especially—when he was in an atypically refractory mood.

"They?" Dupin queried.

"The Thierachians," she supplied, ready to follow up once he had taken the bait—but only so far.

Dupin condescended to arch an eyebrow. Then he moved around the armchair that I had positioned for him, between my own and the lady's, and sat down.

He put his wine-glass down on the occasional table, and then looked up at me, as if to remind me that I was still standing. I sat down too. I understood the symbolism of the gesture; he was accepting his part in the drama that the lady had scripted, agreeing to take an interest in her problem—not because he had once been a close friend of her husband's, and perhaps an admirer of hers, but because she had mentioned something odd, something intriguing, something strange.

"Given that you spoke of their returning," Dupin said, "I take it that you mean Thierachian in the specialized sense, rather than the people resident in the vicinity of the city of Guise. You're referring to the nomads who are sometimes known by that name?"

"Yes," said Madame Guérande. "Bohemians, the locals also call them, or even Romani—but all the labels are incorrect, in a deeper sense than the one that merely attributes them a false geographical origin."

Dupin nodded, approving of the pedantry—which had, indeed, caused her to sound, just for a moment, exactly like him. "And how has Monsieur Guérande contrived to irritate the so-called Thierachians?" he asked, mildly. "They normally keep very much to themselves, even more so than the Romani."

"I can't explain that here and now," the lady replied, still deliberately tantalizing. "It would take too long, and it's very late. As you can see, poor Sophie needs to be put to bed, and I'm very tired myself. I need a clear head in order to give you a full explanation. Will you come to my hotel tomorrow...alone?"

I did not take offence at the final word. I could think of any number of reasons why the lady might want to talk to Dupin without a third party being present—even one that she had already identified as a friend

Dupin glanced at the little girl as mention was made of her, but then his gaze was suddenly caught by the book on the lady's lap, which a movement of her left arm—deliberate or accidental—had only just revealed. "I shall very pleased to make your daughter's acquaintance when she wakes up," he murmured, with deliberate irrelevance, before his tone sharpened. "That, if I'm not mistaken, is the copy of *Telliamed* you once gave me. You must have keen eyes, to have seen it on my friend's shelves in this weak light. Has he explained to you how it comes to be there?"

"Your friend has explained that you count it among your less precious books, which you keep here because your apartment has become overcrowded with others dearer to your heart."

I wanted to protest but did not dare.

Dupin did not even glance at me. "I can assure you that any diminution of the importance I once attributed to it is due entirely to its censorious editing," he said, evenly. "I have since acquired copies of the remainder of the text, which was omitted even from the third posthumous edition, and of the marginalia attached to the manuscript by the author, which flesh out his thoughts considerably. By comparison with the watered-down version that his so-called friends published, after Maillet's death, in fearful anticipation of difficulties with the Church, the whole dialogue is very interesting. It's a great pity that the Chevalier de Lamarck was never able to see the full text. Monsieur Guérande might have been interested, too. But then, the forbidden parts of forbidden books always are interesting, when they touch upon matters of our own interest. I'm flattered that you should come all this way to seek my help, Madame, but don't you think that you might have done better to seek out a physician, with regard to your husband's health? As for legal difficulties, the Dordogne is a long way from Lucien's present jurisdiction, of course, but if the Prefect of the department is reluctant to involve himself, Monsieur Groix is certainly in a position to provide a sharp spur—and I'm sure that he remembers you just as fondly as I do."

Dupin was playing games, I knew. He had been tantalized, and was now tantalizing in his turn, after his own fashion—but I saw the ghost of a genuine smile on Madame Guérande's lips, and knew that she knew it too. She was satisfied. His willingness to play the game of pretence told her that he was well and truly hooked.

"Perhaps he does," she countered, a trifle coquettishly. "But when *he* is confronted by a vexatious puzzle, it seems, he comes to you. My instinct led me in the same direction—and Amélie told me where to find you."

That was a powerful point, I knew—and Dupin knew it too. "Amélie always made an exception for you," he murmured.

"Yes," she repeated. "And it's not from the Dordogne that I've come, as you know perfectly well, Auguste, but the Ardèche. Obviously, you have not had news of us for a long time, but you know perfectly well where we are. You mustn't try to tease me—I'm no longer seventeen, and you're no longer...how old were you when we met, exactly? Twenty-two? Twenty-three?"

"I often get the southern départements mixed up," Dupin said, mendaciously—and blatantly ignoring her question regarding his age. "They're so far away from Paris, and seemingly still resentful of the Cathar crusade. I never visit them."

"You should," she countered, not in the least deceived. It was in a hardly-audible voice that she added: "You must."

"Madame Guérande wondered whether I might be Edgar Poe when she first arrived," I put in, not because I wasn't enjoying the cut and thrust of the dialogue, but because I felt a little jealous, and didn't want to be left entirely on its sidelines. "I think she has read 'The Murders in the Rue Morgue'—in English, obviously. She has never heard of me, of course."

"Of course," Dupin echoed, more brutally than dutifully. He never took his eyes off the lady. "You do understand, Madame Guérande, that the story in question is a work of fiction, which only employs my name mischievously? The incident on which it is based was much more trivial than my friend's American correspondent made it out to be. My friend has melodramatic tendencies—he was probably infected by the contagion when he knew Mr. Poe in their student days. Fortunately, his own fever has slackened, while his correspondent's seems to have worsened considerably. You might imagine that Paris is far more conducive to such miasmas than New York, where Mr. Poe seems to spend a deal of time nowadays, but apparently not."

"I'm sure that your sane presence has helped to calm Mr. Reynolds' metaphorical fevers considerably," the lady suggested. "I hope you might be able to do the same for another who was once your closest friend." Her tone now was bantering, with a comfort suggestive of something long dormant but easily reborn. Was this, I wondered, how they had "flirted" twenty-five years ago?

Dupin was less comfortable with the sudden timeslip than our guest. He did not reply to the prompt.

"It's true that Dupin has had a salutary effect on me," I said, this time genuinely trying to be helpful. "While I keep close company with him, my infection of melodrama is somehow held within bounds, in spite of everything."

Dupin gave the impression that he would rather I had not included the last phrase—and, indeed, that I had kept my mouth shut. The great logician had finished his wine, and poured himself another glass. He offered Madame Guérande another, which she declined. I accepted when my turn came.

"You're right, Madame," he said, as if making a great concession. "Claude was my closest friend. If he wants my help, I owe it to him."

A slight shadow crossed Madame Guérande's face. "Claude needs your help," she said, stressing the verb slightly, and making it clear that she was the one who was asking, even though she had been careful to obtain her husband's permission for the invitation.

"I have no influence with Thierachians," Dupin said. "If I were a diplomat expert in soothing disputes, Lucien Groix would surely retain me here, to unpick all the old quarrels that are seething under the multilayered surface of Parisian society. Nor am I a physician with any expertise in calming fevers, in spite of what my friend says." He was not refusing his help, but merely warning her that he was not optimistic as to the probability of success. She understood that.

"But you *are* an antiquarian of great distinction, Auguste," Madame Guérande countered. "You have not lost your interest in ancient artifacts—antediluvian artifacts, some would say, although you and I...you and Claude...know better than into use such terminology. The hunt for explanation of the puzzles they embody must intrigue you still. Do you remember the discussions you and Claude used to have in my father's drawing-room, about the kinship of species, the possible origins of life and humankind, and the various rival schools of monogeny and polygeny? I was not allowed to be party to such discussions, of course—my father had too narrow a view of a woman's place—but I was allowed to be present, by way of decoration, and I listened, Oh, how eagerly I listened...if only because it was so casually assumed that I would not understand."

"I remember," Dupin said, perhaps with a hint of uncustomary nostalgia—a nostalgia to which our visitor was now making manifest appeal.

"You were quite the heretic then," she went on, still probing with her eyes as well as her delicately-judged words. I had no doubt at all that I would soon be packing my trunk for an expedition to the Ardèche, perhaps as early as the impending morning—which was almost upon us, now that the clock's hands were marching toward their midnight rendezvous.

"Having no beliefs," Dupin said, rather dully—as if he felt obliged to live up to his reputation for pedantry, although, for once, the zest was not there, "I was incapable of heresy. I still am. I question all firm-set convictions, as everyone should. How else can we ever determine our mistakes?"

There were potential double meanings in that remark, which I would have been very interested to see unraveled, but Madame Guérande was still very conscious of the hour.

"It's late," she said, decisively. "I really must get Sophie to bed. We need to return to our hotel. You will you come to see me there tomorrow morning, won't you, Auguste? I would like to give you a fuller explanation of why Claude and I need your help, but that will take time, and I would prefer to do it in private. Even if you and Mr. Reynolds are nowadays inseparable, there are things that I can only say...you *will* come, won't you? It's the Hôtel Marco Polo—on the nearer end of the Rue Vaugirard, close to the junction where the Luxembourg Gardens are."

I couldn't help making a note to the effect that she had referred to the Gardens rather than the old Palace. Sorbonnards accustomed to walking there always did that. No one in the Latin Quarter ever felt truly qualified as an intellectual until he had acquired the habit of walking and reading the Gardens on sunny days—and it was one of the few places in Paris where women from all levels of society came and went freely, sometimes without chaperons. The Gardens played a key role in almost all student love-affairs.

"Of course I'll come," Dupin answered, thus making a firmer promise by far than the one he had made to me when he had promised to return in two hours, at the most. "Madame Lacuzon would never forgive me if I did not, and I dare not risk upsetting her, now that she is so vital to my peaceful existence."

The joke, if it was one, fell flat. Madame Guérande rose to her feet and leaned over to shake her daughter awake.

"I'll send Bihan to get you a cab," I said. "You must not step outdoors until it's as close to the door as it can get. The weather seems mild enough, but that's when the danger of catching chills is at its maximum. I shall lend you an umbrella—you should not be abroad in Paris at this time of year without one"

"Thank you, Mr. Reynolds," she said.

It took Bihan a full fifteen minutes to find a fiacre and bring it to the front door of the house, but Madame Guérande had said all she had to say for the time being. She thanked me effusively for my hospitality, and apologized almost as effusively for having disturbed me. She instructed Sophie to thank me too, which the little girl did, mechanically. When she left, the lady shook my hand, as the French always seem to feel obliged to do when they bid farewell to an American, but she only nodded her head to Dupin—who replied to the gesture with a formal bow.

CHAPTER THREE
DUPIN INTRIGUED

When the door had closed behind the unexpected visitors we returned to the smoking-room. Dupin sat down again with unusual heaviness—and not, I judged, simply because his excursion to the Prefecture had tired him out. He picked up the copy of the book that Julie Guérande had left on the seat of her own chair, opened it—not at the fly-leaf but half way through the pages—and stared at the print as if he had momentarily forgotten how to read.

Then he looked up again, and said: "How much did she tell you?"

I sat down, and relied: "Little more than she told you, about her husband's tribulations. Doubtless she'll give you more details tomorrow. About you, no more than she said in your presence—that you used to attend salons at her father's house, where some kind of Lamarckian cabal used to meet in the dark days of the Restoration."

"There's little more to say," he murmured. I did not believe him.

"What are Thierachians?" I asked him, thinking that it was as good a place as any to start, given that that was the bait that seemed to have prompted him to take the lady's hook.

"Thierache," he replied, in his most pedantic manner, "is a region overlapping the border between France and Belgium, in the foothills of the Ardennes massif. What the inhabitants of other parts of France often mean by 'Thierachians,' however, is a population of nomads—known as the Hescheboix in Thierache itself—who follow a way of life similar to the Romani, but who seemed to have arrived in Thierache at a much earlier date, before spreading out from there to the rest of France...or Gaul, if you prefer."

"And why are you interested in them?" I asked.

"They are a puzzle," he said, as if that were explanation enough. "Indeed, they seem to delight in making themselves a mystery—indulging in secrecy for secrecy's sake. The Romani seem to have similar inclinations, but they're recent arrivals by comparison, first appearing in the fifteenth century, and some of them, at least, have consented to adapt to French custom, many having converted to Catholicism, albeit of an odd stripe, adopting Sainte-Sarah-la-Noire as their patron saint. The arrival of the Thierachians in Thierache certainly predated the influx of the Franks, and even the attempted invasion of the Huns, who were deflected southwards by an alliance of the Romans and the Catalauni. No one—including the Thierachians, I assume—knows for sure exactly how long ago their first excursion into what is now France occurred. I would have to go to the Bibliothèque Nationale to find out more about them, but I have a vague memory that their own religion, or mythology, claims that they preserve the true blood and the secret knowledge of the original human race, which dispersed from its cradle in Central Asia an exceedingly long time ago."

"Long before Adam, I presume," I observed. I understood now why the word had caught his attention. He knew perfectly well that any "secret knowledge of the original human race" had to be a fiction, but it was the kind of fiction that fascinated him, as an evolutionist as well as an antiquarian

"Indeed," Dupin agreed. "Their legendry, it seems, is more closely akin to the time-scale of the world's affairs imagined by the Comte du Buffon and Geoffroy Saint-Hilaire...though not quite on the scale imagined by Maillet." He lifted his hand to confirm his reference to the book he was holding.

I was aware of the fierce dispute raging between Biblical

chronologists, who dated the creation of the world to the year 4004 B.C., and contemporary geologists, whose analysis of the various strata of the Earth's crust had convinced them that the upheavals in the Earth's surface recorded there must have extended over hundreds of thousands of years, perhaps millions. Indeed, I knew that the English geologist James Hutton, in founding a new school of "uniformitarian" geology, to rival that of the "catastrophists" who attributed the epochs of nature to violent events such as deluges and volcanic eruptions, had boldly declared that the evidence of the Earth's crust displayed "no vestige of a beginning, no prospect of an end."

"And what sort of time-scale did Monsieur de Maillet envisage?" I asked, meekly accepting the invitation that Dupin had issued.

"Monsieur de Maillet studied the geology of North Africa—particularly that of Egypt—while he was a diplomat in that region," Dupin said. "His analysis of the strata persuaded him that the Earth is at least two billion years old."

"Two *billion*?" I echoed, with all due respect. "But he surely does not think that human history extends over more than a tiny fraction of that span."

"Indeed not. He was an evolutionist before Lamarck and Geoffroy Saint-Hilaire, and would now be recognized as a genius of their stature had his friends, careful of his reputation, not censored his work before its posthumous publication. Only a handful of people—of whom I am privileged to be one—have seen the full text, which he compiled between 1692 and 1718, complete with its annotations. The published version—there were three editions, the second and third slightly augmented—has the bare bones of his thesis, which suggests that behind the various upheavals affecting the Earth's surface there has been a slower and more measured process, in which a world that was once entirely covered by the sea has gradually given birth to continents as the sea's level has declined. Much of what was left out of the published versions concerns the evolution of vegetable and animal life by adaptation to the new milieu. According to

Maillet, all land-dwelling species are ultimately descended from sea-dwelling species, and have continued to evolve as new species have gradually appeared to exploit the changing resources of the land in its various aspects. Similar processes of evolution, he believed, must have taken place under the sea, but he remained conscientiously agnostic with regard to whether the ultimate origin of species was Earthly or other-worldly."

"Other-worldly?" I queried, sensing a reference to Dupin's theories about leakage between the parallel worlds filling the space that seems empty to our senses.

"As soon as Maillet became a pioneering evolutionist," Dupin said, a trifle absent-mindedly—as if he had other matters still on his mind, "he ran into a problem that still vexes evolutionism today: if all living cells derive from other living cells, and all Earthly species from earlier species, how did the process begin? Wanting to leave God out of the picture—although the omission was not something he wanted to advertise too conspicuously—he wondered whether life on this planet might have begun from seeds that fell to earth from interplanetary space, with the corollary possibility that the pattern of Earthly evolution might be a recapitulation of one that had already unfolded elsewhere, perhaps many times."

Again, I thought: *No vestige of a beginning, no prospect of an end. An infinite process, with no need of a first cause.* As rhetoric went, however, it looked suspiciously like cheating to me.

"Do you believe that?" I asked.

"It's not a matter for belief," he said, sharply—and inevitably. "We can only speculate."

"But you do believe that all life on Earth ultimately had a single point of origin in some kind of primal cell," I pointed out.

"That's a different matter," he said. "The patterns of related-ness between species, scrupulously catalogued by taxonomists like Carl von Linné and the Chevalier de Lamarck provide strong evidence to that effect. To begin with, Linné and Buffon tended to map the relationships in series of circles placed in varying degrees of proximity, but that conceptual geometry is now being replaced by a diagrammatic 'tree of life,' in which phyla, orders and genera are represented as branches from a single root-stock. Polygenists, of course, believe in a more generous mechanism of continuous creation or spontaneous generation, which is still ongoing, with respect to primitive organisms, but the monogenists have the upper hand now."

"I see," I said, although I was now out of my depth. As usual, when he saw me out of my depth, Dupin hastened to explain—with the inevitable effect of dragging me into even deeper intellectual waters.

"Polygeny is the thesis of multiple origins, as opposed to monogeny, which proposes a single point of origin. As Madame Guérande mentioned, it was one of the principal axes of debate in Achille Malet's salon. If we had had Malet's full text available to us then, it would have added an extra dimension to the debate—although our discussions usually focused on the corollary issue of the origin of man, which also gives rise to polygenist and monogenist arguments. Modern monogenists, who believe that the human species had a single point of evolutionary origin, tend to place it in Central Asia—with which Maillet would have agreed—but their estimates of the timing of that origin vary considerably. Polygenists, of course, attribute separate origins to the various human races now extant, some even disagreeing as to the nature of the ancestor-species that preceded the human."

"Apes, that is," I said, eager to show that I understood something.

"That's the most common opinion," he agreed, "among those who dare voice an opinion at all. Linné and Lamarck both regarded it as obvious, although they would only admit to the conviction in private—but I have heard seals mentioned, and pigs too. The polygenist is, of course, free to accept all three as hypothetical possibilities, although the monogenist is forced to choose."

"And that was the sort of thing you used to debate in Professor

Malet's salon?"

"Among others. We thought of ourselves as very bold free-thinkers—as, indeed, we were. Nor was our secrecy unwarranted. The spies thronging the Sorbonne might have been paid by Monsieur Fouché—who contrived to keep his post as Minister of Police even after the Empire's fall, just as Napoléon had been forced to recall him to it because he knew too much to be left out in the cold—but their reports reached the Church as well as the Crown, and those members of the salon who had salaried positions in the university still had something material to fear from accusations of heresy."

"It sounds to me more like metaphysics than biology," I confessed, "and it surely has no relevance to whatever problems Monsieur Guérande has with his problematic research in the caves of Mont Dagon, legal disputes over the ownership of the land and Thierachian nomads."

"It's difficult to imagine how it might," Dupin admitted. "The probability is that Julie plucked the book off the shelf because she recognized it as one that she had given me, rather than because it struck any chord with regard to her mysterious problem. She has not changed as much as I might have expected, given that she is a quarter of a century older than when I last saw her, a dutiful wife and doting mother. She has not lost her taste for temptation and teasing."

"She referred to her old self as a *flirt*," I told him, "although that was for my benefit, as an American—she was, I think, flirting with me, ever so slightly."

"Doubtless she was," Dupin said, dryly. "Even at seventeen, she thought that she could twist us all around her little finger—including poor old Lamarck, while he was still able to attend our gatherings. She had known him for years by then, of course. And she was right—about being able to twist us all around her little finger, that is. The adorable Julie, we called her."

That, I knew, was a quotation, referring to the star of some eighteenth-century salon, about which Molière had written a famous satire. I could not quite recall the salon-keeper's name, but I had a vague memory that her daughter—the "adorable Julie"—had kept her multiple suitors dangling for fourteen years before finally condescending to become a Duchesse. But Dupin's Julie—or, to be strictly accurate, Monsieur Guérande's Julie—had obviously not strung things out to that extent, and evidently had not granted herself, in the end, to the suitor with the highest-placed rank in the peerage...not that the peerage had counted for much in the 1820s, in spite of the Restoration.

Perhaps, I thought, science had its own peerage now, and perhaps Julie Malet had accepted the proposal of the most promising young scientist in the Lamarckian clique: the man most likely to carry evolutionary theory forward to its inevitable triumph over superstition. If so, that promise did not seem to have come to fruition. I could not imagine, however, that anyone would have considered Dupin to have been a better catch, given the manifest eccentricity of his own interests and exploits. Lucien Groix, on the other hand....

"I was surprised to learn that Monsieur Groix was a member of Achille Mallet's coterie," I observed, curiously.

"He wasn't, quite," Dupin replied. "He was a regular in the salon, for a while, but his commitment to the Lamarckian doctrine, as preached by Malet, was even weaker than mine. His primary interest was the professor's daughter, I suspect—and if so, he was not alone in pretending a greater interest in science than he actually had, in order to gain entrée to the circle. On the other hand, he might simply have been Fouché's spy, at the very outset of his glittering career as a policeman."

"You're not serious?"

"Perfectly serious. Fouché had spies in every significant salon in the capital. They were the richest source of information he had. Monsieur Groix has kept up the tradition and his successors will doubtless do likewise. It is, after all, through salon society that ideas circulate at their greatest and most careless ease, and where they thrive in their natural environment. Do you imagine that Louis XIV's lieutenants of police did not collect regular reports from the Marquise de Rambouillet's drawing-room?"

The Marquise de Rambouillet, I remembered then, had been the mother of the original "adorable Julie."

"But Malet and Geoffroy Sainte-Hilaire were pillars of society," I said. "They were men of science, among the glories of the nation in an Age of Enlightenment. They surely posed no danger whatsoever to the interests of Louis XVIII."

"With the aid of hindsight," Dupin admitted, "we can probably conclude that they did not—but monarchy, in the final analysis, derives its privileges from the myth of divine right. Evolutionism was seen then—and is still seen, in certain quarters of society—as a dangerous threat to that notion, inherently supportive of the belief that all men are essentially born equal, and that aristocracy is merely a form of unjustified oppression. Had Malet and Geoffroy not been so diplomatic in the assertion and promulgation of their convictions, they really might have given Church and State alike cause for concern. Lamarck can certainly be considered a martyr of sorts, his crucifixion only a little less painful for being slow and subtle."

He was in full flow by now, his earlier absent-mindedness conquered—but his gaze, even as it was reaching for intellectual infinity, was suddenly captured by the clock. He suddenly sat back in his chair, almost as if he were wondering what he was doing in it, when he ought to be elsewhere.

"I must go home," he said, abruptly. "I need sleep."

"Shall I pack my trunk with a view to an expedition to the Ardèche?" I asked.

He looked at me sharply. "I have little idea, as yet, what Madame Guérande is going to tell me tomorrow. Perhaps it would be as well not to be precipitate."

Perhaps it would, I thought—but I decided to pack anyway. I had not made a specific study of Madame Guérande's little finger, but I suspected that its potential as a bobbin was by no means exhausted, and the lady had certainly seemed to me to be in a hurry.

CHAPTER FOUR
COMPLICATIONS

I waited all day for Dupin to return. I expected him before noon, and when he had not turned up by one I assumed that Madame Guérande must have drawn out her explanation of her predicament to extraordinary lengths, perhaps in pursuit of some hidden motive. By the time the clock chimed four—long after my preparations for travel had been completed—I began to wonder whether Dupin had decided to break with hallowed precedent and actually leave me out of the affair.

By half-past six, when the doorbell rang, I was in a state of high anxiety. Assuming that Dupin was standing on ceremony for once, I ran to open it, avid for news of our impending departure—which might still be possible that evening, if we really did intend to travel by railway, given that "sleeping cars" were fast becoming normal for the convenience of southward-bound passengers.

It was not Dupin who had rung the bell, though; it was Lucien Groix.

It was not the first time that the Prefect had come to call in person, but he usually sent messengers, even when matters of considerable delicacy were concerned—and he rarely went abroad without a bodyguard when he did consent to run his own errands. This evening, he was alone.

"I'm afraid that Dupin's not here," I told him. "I've no idea where he is."

"He's at the Bibliothèque Nationale, delving in the Archives,"

Groix told me, coming into the house with such perfect assur-
ance of authorization that I stepped aside without giving thought
to the possibility of keeping him at bay.

"He's been to see you, then?" I queried, reflexively, assuming
that Groix must be here at Dupin's request.

"No," the Prefect retorted.

"How do you know where he is, then?" I asked, intemper-
ately. "Are you having him followed?"

Bihan had appeared, and made as if to take the visitor's
hat and coat, but the Prefect would not surrender them. Groix
brushed the servant off as if he were a stray piece of lint and
strode into the smoking room; it was not until the door was shut
that he condescended to answer.

"Don't be ridiculous," the Prefect said. "Dupin's the only
man in France in whom I have perfect trust, just now. Even
so, I happen to know that Madame Guérande came to see him
yesterday, and I know that he went to see her at the Marco Polo
this morning."

I was still puzzled. "But if you know he's at the Library, and
haven't arranged to meet him, why did you come here?"

Lucien Groix fixed me with an authoritarian stare. Someone
more sensitive than I was to his position would probably have
been intimidated, but to me he had always been a man who
occasionally asked my friend for help rather than a figure of
awesome power and influence. "Can I trust you, Mr. Reynolds?"
he demanded. It *was* a demand—he was certainly not looking
for a negative answer, or an expression of doubt.

"Of course," I said.

"The Bibliothèque is a public place," he said, "Had I gone to
see Dupin there, our meeting would have been noticed. Had I
summoned him to the Prefecture, we would most certainly have
been observed. I have reason to suspect that he might go haring
off to the south at any moment, and that the possibility of fixing
some kind of secret tryst before then was exceedingly thin. I
thought it best, therefore, to have a quiet word with you."

"About what?" I asked, quite mystified.

"You're an American," he said, obviously not so pressed for time as to avoid beating around the bush. "You've had occasion to observe the aftermath of your own Revolution. Are there still parts of the nation stuck in a pre-Revolutionary past—and pasts even remoter than that?"

"And how," I told him. "America is full of immigrant communities who came in order to live as they wished, and still insist on doing so, with no more regard for the Federal Government than they had for the British—and that's not to mention the indigenes. We may be one nation under God, but we're a very strange patchwork, beneath that ostensible surface."

"Exactly. You probably think of France as being very different, but it is not. Our recent past of Revolutions, Empires and Restorations has created a new kind of temporal chaos, but there are regions far from Paris that have never fully emerged from the Middle Ages. We too are a patchwork, more tightly knitted than the sprawling Union, but all the more vulnerable to friction for that. There is a sense in which petty disputes in places like the Ardèche are utterly irrelevant to the nation as a whole, but they can, on occasion, supply sparks that ignite fuses, which lead...but I'm sure that you get the picture. I, of course, am merely the Prefect of Police in Paris, a very minor member of the Administration, and have no business interesting myself in the affairs of the Provinces—but things sometimes come to my attention, of which I take note *en passant*, before passing them on to other sections of the government. Sometimes, I come to know things, almost by accident, that it is not my business to know, let alone act upon...."

"I see," I said, although I wasn't entirely sure that I did. "Something's going on in the Ardèche that you want Dupin to know about, but you don't want anyone else to know that you've tipped him off about it?"

He didn't seem entirely pleased with that way of putting it, but his embarrassment was understandable. He didn't know me very well, and one or two of our meetings had not shown me in a very good light.

"I've no intention of trying to dissuade Dupin from getting mixed up in this business," the Prefect went on, "but it would be as well if he were aware of certain facts before he goes barging in—and you can't deny that he does have a tendency, occasionally, to *barge in*. What I have to tell you is for Dupin's ears alone, of course. Do we understand one another?"

Utterly mystified, I nodded my head. The Prefect sat down, in the chair I thought of as Dupin's. Madame Bihan appeared on cue, ready to supply anything that we might need, but before she could ask whether we wanted anything, I told her to make sure that we were not disturbed and sent her away. Then I sat down in my turn.

"I don't want to be mixed up in this," Monsieur Groix told me, bluntly. "I have more than enough on my plate with Paris seething with Republican fervor. Quite frankly, residues of the last white terror in the Midi don't interest me in the slightest—but the Prefect of the *département* is a weakling, under the thumb of the local clergy, who have persuaded him to petition the king on Tibère's behalf. The king! Have they any idea what kind of a man Louis-Philippe is? No, of course not. But these things get handed on and on...and if they go awry, the eventual mess always ends up on my plate, because I'm supposedly Fouché's reincarnation: the man with the magic wand. If Dupin's going to get involved, that's fine—but he needs to know that he'll be dabbling in politics if he does, and will have to tread carefully."

"Politics?" I queried, completely out of my depth. "Are you talking about the Thierachians."

"The Hescheboix," Groix corrected, showing off his own talent as a pedant by making the unnecessary substitution. "Yes—they're likely to end up as the victims if things go awry. It's come to my attention, indirectly, that there's a dispute between Guérande and the Comte de Tibère, who owns the land—or thinks he does—in which the caves are situated, and on which the Hescheboix establish a summer camp every year that's important somehow to their religion. Tibère still thinks he's living under the *ancien régime*, if not in the Golden Age of feudalism, and his temporary dispossession in the wake of '89 has only made him all the more determined, since the Restoration handed him back his château, to recover what he believes his ancestors once had. He doesn't seem to understand that we're no longer living in a world where he can just send a dispatch to the court demanding the issue of a *lettre de cachet* that will have poor Guérande banged up in the Bastille. He's only a petty Comte, for Heaven's sake, not even a *pair de France*! That's irrelevant, though—the real point at issue is that he seems to be supported in his delusions of obsolete grandeur by Philippe Aignan, the Bishop of Viviers, who apparently considers himself a spiritual descendant of Simon de Montfort. The Tibères have been at odds with Guérande's family for at least forty years—the fathers before the sons—and at odds with the Hescheboix even longer, and the Prefecture at Privas has had some difficulty reining them in, ever since the last white terror gave them reason to think in terms of violence."

"What's a white terror?" I queried, helplessly.

Groix frowned, but then remembered my American origin, and the fact that Dupin rarely, if ever, discussed politics. "The first white terror was a backlash against the so-called Red Terror instigated by the Convention in the early 1790s," the Prefect explained. "When the Jacobins fell from power, the aristocracy took the opportunity to pay them back in the currency of blood, wherever they still retained the power to do so. The same label was transferred to the further backlash against the old revolutionaries that followed the overthrow of the Directoire, and the third that followed the Restoration. Such outbursts are always messy, providing opportunities for paying off old scores, and indulging petty hatreds.

"The central power always clamped down on such massacres as hard as it could, but in the provinces—especially the southern provinces—respect for the central power has always been grudging. At present, for reasons I don't have to spell out to you, the last thing the crown needs is another flare-up of that sort, even in a backwater like the Ardèche. The Church ought to be backing us to the hilt, but the Church is Legitimist through and through, and...well, suffice it to say that Aignan fancies himself as a Machiavellian careerist, who would love to have an excuse to take stern action against some easy victims he's able to represent as dangerous heretics: the Hescheboix. He seems to be trying to take advantage of Tibère's animosity against the Guérandes to stir up trouble, and might well succeed, notwithstanding the fact that the Hescheboix and Guérande don't like one another any more that he likes them.

"I wish I could say that Aignan's as much an embarrassment to the Church as Tibère is to the Crown, but he has his supporters—and whether you're aware of it or not, the Church has begun to cast a slightly jaundiced eye upon Dupin. You and I know that he and that idiotic *poseur* Falleroux—the man you probably know as the Comte de Saint-Germain—are chalk and cheese, but the Church can't tell the difference, and the recent antics of the Harmonic Society have sent a distinct whiff of sulfur into the cloisters of Paris. At any rate, it would be a bad idea, not merely from my point of view but his, if Dupin were to inflame the situation in the Ardèche in any way at all. It's in everyone's interests to see that no one—and I mean *no one*— gets unduly upset. It won't matter who turns to violence first: there's a powder-keg waiting to explode down there, just as there is in Paris. The last thing anyone needs just now is some idiot launching a new crusade, whether against the Hescheboix, against evolutionism, against Tibère's former tenants or against any other imagined agent of anarchy."

"I don't understand any of this," I confessed.

"It's probably beyond human understanding—even Dupin's. The point is that he has to be careful. He needs to understand that, if he can't steer clear of Tibère and Aignan, he has to handle them with kid gloves. The mere fact that he's from Paris might give him the apparent status of a representative of one or other of the powers-that-be, and he can't simply deny the responsibility. Please ask him, on my behalf, not to do anything that might tip Tibère and Aignan over the edge. If he can actually calm them down, so much the better. In the great scheme of things, they're utterly unimportant, but the situation in France is so delicate that we really can't afford the tiniest example of apparent repression making headlines in Parisian newspapers. You read *Le Constitutionnel*—you know how the pettiest of incidents can nowadays be inflated into a national scandal. Teaching the masses to read was supposed to be progress, but... well, you know how the argument goes. By the way, they'll probably tell him at the Bibliothèque, but in case they don't, tell Dupin that some lawyer from Lyon has been rummaging through the Archives searching for documents relating to Tibère's old fief, from the Convention's confiscations all the way back to the Crusades. I don't know whether he's working for the Comte or for Guérande, but either way, my esteemed colleagues in the Administration would far rather that the dispute could be settled quietly."

"I'll tell him," I said. What else could I say? I failed, however, to resist the temptation to add: "Dupin is a wise man. You really can trust him."

"I do," Groix stated, with conviction. "Except that...well, he might be the greatest logician in the world, but he really does seem to attract trouble. You have no idea how much difficulty I had putting a lid on that affair with the blunderbuss at Dupotet's soirée. Dupin sometimes needs to be reminded that curiosity kills cats—and they have nine lives. As Prefect of Police, I'm very keenly aware of the fact that there are times when it really is best to let things remain uninvestigated, at the risk of unwittingly stirring up a hornets' nest."

That was an opinion that Dupin was never going to endorse. "I still can't see why Madame Guérande's husband and these Thierachians, Hescheboix, or whatever are in dispute," I complained. "What's so important about these caves?"

"All nonsense," the Prefect said, dismissively. "Sleeping dragons and the like. Guérande used to talk about some discovery he'd made there back in the old days, always in whispers, making a big mystery out of it—personally, I thought he was just trying to impress Julie. At any rate, he hasn't sent any *mémoires* to the Académie as yet. Aignan probably thinks that Guérande's sacrilegious theories are part and parcel of the Hescheboix's pagan ideas about the original humans emerging from some underworld in the Himalayas, created by some kind of godlike entity of flame and song. Utterly harmless, of course—unless you're an aspirant cardinal who wants to strike a manifest blow against the Devil Incarnate, or at least his faithful idolaters. Personally, I couldn't care less who owns the caves or why the Hescheboix and Guérande are so fascinated by them—but I'm duty-bound to care about the possibility of Aignan stirring up trouble. If Dupin can soothe things over for once, I've got friends and colleagues who'd be grateful. Tell him that, will you."

It occurred to me that Monsieur Groix seemed to know a good deal about something that was supposedly not his affair. I suspected that matters concerning Monsieur and Madame Guérande still attracted his keen attention, more than twenty years after he had last seen either of them. "I'm sure that he'll do his best to oblige you," I assured the Prefect.

"Of course he will—but if he gets carried away playing the white knight, I'm relying on you to remind him that there are complications in this matter that the adorable Julie isn't able to reveal to him."

"He used that phrase," I murmured, reflectively.

"*White knight?*" Groix queried.

"No—*the adorable Julie.*"

"It's an old joke—but I'm not surprised that he remembers it."

I knew that I was being criminally reckless, but I simply couldn't resist temptation any longer. "Were you in love with her too?" I asked. "Or were you simply Fouché's spy, keeping watch on Achille Malet and the Lamarckian cabal?"

Lucien Groix stood up abruptly, and replaced his hat on his head. "You mustn't trade too much on the reputation Americans have for bluntness," he said, a trifle harshly. "This is Paris, and you've been here long enough to know that there are certain questions that one simply does not ask."

He had made his exit, and the front door had closed behind him, before it occurred to me to wonder whether he had meant my first question or my second—or both.

He had only been gone ten minutes when Dupin finally arrived.

"Lucien Groix was here," I told him, unceremoniously. "He says that there's more to this business in the Ardèche than meets the eye, and wants me to impress the delicacy of the situation upon you—although it isn't his business, officially."

Dupin frowned, perhaps more in puzzlement than annoyance. "Was he alone?" he asked.

"Yes," I said, "but his bodyguard was probably lurking outside."

Dupin nodded, a trifle uncertainly. "He could have sent word by his customary messenger," he said, reflectively. "If he came in person...what did he say, exactly?"

I summarized the significant elements of the conversation as best I could, omitting any mention of the final questions and their curt response. "I can't imagine why he's concerned, or even interested," I said. "Surely the follies of a provincial Bishop are of no consequence in the great war between Monarchists and Republicans."

"Perhaps, "Dupin admitted, cautiously. "But the Church is notorious for making much out of very little, and has its own hand to play in the current war of words. The fact that its hierarchy is not only on the side that seems to be losing, but is isolated from Louis-Philippe by the Monarchists' own internecine squabbles, increases its desperation. Even old dogs can be dangerous when cornered, and with Revolution very much in the air...while there's a real danger that the socialists might try to seize power any day now, the Church is bound to feel threatened, and heresy-hunting has always been good publicity in times of stress. The Thierachians might be a small target, but they're an easy one, and a colorful one."

"I never heard of them before last night," I said. "I can't see that there's much publicity to be gained by attacking them."

"That depends how far the contagion of wrath might spread, once roused. These are anxious times, my friend, and in anxious times, strange panics sometimes find purchase that they would never grip in times of stability and plenty—especially in regions like the Ardèche, where the accumulation of history doesn't follow the same swift and sweeping pattern that it does in Paris. Is your trunk packed?"

"Yes."

"Then we'd best summon a cab, pick up the luggage that Madame Lacuzon will have packed for me, and then collect Madame Guérande and her daughter from the Rue Vaugirard. She assures me that the late sleeper will give us a more comfortable ride than the best of mail-coaches on the driest of roads."

I left the summoning of the cab and the loading of the trunk to Bihan, although I couldn't help feeling a pang of anxiety at the possibility that there might be to opportunity to dine at the Gare before the train pulled out on a southward journey that could not, as yet take it any further than Chalon.

As soon as we were ensconced in the cab, I asked Dupin why he had gone to the Bibliothèque Nationale and what he had learned there.

"I learned that French law is in a terrible mess," he said, "so many new laws having been passed since 1789 without anyone bothering to repeal the old ones."

"That's hardly news," I observed. "There's a whole legion of advocates making a fat living out of contests between the dictates of conflicting laws. What specific statutes did you have in mind?"

"Those relating to the restoration of properties seized during the '89 Revolution to their previous owners. The particular tangle that I contemplated from without concerns the property rights to various parts of the Comte de Tibère's old estate—and, for that matter, his title. The title isn't one of those that go back to the crusades, but it has still been confused in the past with claims and counterclaims of bastardy, alienation of property rights, and God only knows what else. Put simply, this is one comtal crown that rests rather uneasily on the head that wears it.

"Claude Guérande doesn't care a fig for such things as *particules* and titles, and would never dream of making a claim on the title or the château—so Julie says, and I see no reason to doubt her—but that doesn't prevent the present Comte from being direly anxious that his right to retain them might be challenged. He has the backing of the Church, of course—the Bishop of Viviers in particular—but that automatically ensures that he lacks the backing of other would-be powers within the land...or, to be more specific, the socialist Mairies of the region. The local Republicans, while not overly pleased, in principle, to have another lord of the manor in his place, would love to be rid of Tibère. The locally-held copies of the documents that might potentially disprove his entitlement have all been lost or destroyed during the upheavals and conflagrations of the last sixty years, and the copies held in Paris are buried in archives that are by no means easy to search, but, as the Prefect told you, someone has recently been searching...a lawyer from Lyon named Arnauld Lebrun."

"Do you know who he's working for?" I asked.

"Not Claude Guérande," Dupin stated, decisively. "Presumably the Comte, although the local farmers, who were Tibère's tenants before the Revolution and are anxious not to be under his thumb again, also have an interest. At any rate, the archivist believes that the man from Lyon found something relevant to his cause. He had notarized copies made of several documents, apparently, both recent and ancient."

Dupin had to pause then, in order to leap down and collect a valise from Madame Lacuzon, who was waiting outside her lodge. As soon as he had hopped back up he resumed his tortuous and rather murky explanation: "Although he's uninterested in the title, Claude Guérande is necessarily interested in the land on which his own home stands, and certain other lands once attached to the Tibère estate—specifically, in a tract that has attracted little interest in the past because of its derelict nature. Although there are a number of cottages there, which used to be farms and whose tenants still keep herds of sheep, the rents they brought in before '89 in were trivial by comparison to those of the farms in the eastern reaches of the valley. Until recently, no one seems to have cared very much who owned the land adjacent to Guérande's property, but since the Comte has begun complaining about Claude's activities and trying to heat up old hostilities against the Thierachians, Claude has felt obliged to make enquiries about the possibility of obtaining title to the land himself—purely because of the scientific value of what he's found, I assume. He won't be glad to learn that someone has already investigated the National Archives, presumably on behalf of another interested party.

"The fathers of the local farmers, who regarded the Comte as a bad landlord, were Jacobins through and through when it came to seizing his property in the wake of '89, but now they're proprietors, their sons are anxious not to have it taken away again. The Thierachians, however, seem to regard the very notion of ownership in land as fictitious, and to them the important point is that the caves have a mystical significance within their traditions. According to Madame Guérande, they don't approve of Claude conducting his research in the caves—but that doesn't make them ready allies of Tibère, who would be their enemy even if the Bishop weren't pouring poison into his ear regarding their dangerousness as heretics."

The fiacre pulled up outside the Hôtel Vaugirard. Madame Guérande was waiting in the lobby, with her daughter, and baggage far lighter than any Parisian lady would have deigned to carry on such a long journey. It was easy enough for the four of us to squeeze into the cab, and the other cases fitted neatly enough around my cumbersome trunk on the rear luggage-rack.

I had known, of course, that the lady was in a hurry, and had observed that she had communicated that haste to Dupin—and, at second hand, to Lucien Groix—but even so, I was surprised by the urgency with which the cab was loaded and instructed to set off once again. We had a train to catch, of course, but there was something more: a physical agitation that had been communicated from Julie Guérande to Dupin, and was beginning to affect me too—and Sophie, for all that her careful education had trained her to be meek and quiet.

It was all entirely natural, of course...but as I had told the lady, I was no longer certain exactly where the boundaries of the natural lay.

CHAPTER FIVE
THE INDEFATIGABLE RAILWAY

As I watched Madame Guérande supervising Sophie's accommodation in the cab I realized that Dupin's casual reference to her as a "doting mother" was fully justified. The child, who obviously thought that she was too old to be fussed over, and well able to act on her own behalf, seemed embarrassed by the intensity of maternal concern, but was obviously too well trained in being "*sage*" to make any objection in front of strangers. I tried to express sympathy with my expression when I caught her eye, but she was obviously too well brought-up even to respond with a grimace.

To Sophie, of course, Paris had to be a source of great fascination—but to her mother, it now seemed a source of unease. It must have been hard for the adorable Julie, I thought, to have been taken away from the city in which she had grown up to an alien environment like the rural Ardèche, and then to be confined there for such a long period. The eventual arrival of a daughter must have broken the monotony, and given her a new focus for her attention, but she did not seem, as yet, to have accepted Sophie as a companion; she was still treating her as a baby, in constant need of that solicitous attention.

When we set off again, Sophie made every effort to crane her neck out of the window, to get a better view of what as going on in the streets through which we passed, but her mother continually pulled her back, almost as if she did not want the little girl to know what attractions Paris had for someone curious about the life of civilization.

I half-expected Dupin to start his explanations all over again for Madame Guérande's benefit, but there was obviously little enough in what he'd learned at the Bibliothèque that she didn't already know, and the rest of what he had just told me had come from her. Whether for that reason or another, he didn't bother to recap, and actually needed some prompting to resume his discourse. Once I had provided the prompt, however, once we were all as comfortably settled as we were ever going to be, the pent-up flow was released without difficulty.

"Very little is written about the Thierachians, or the Hescheboix," he said, now speaking to Madame Guérande as well as to me, "because they don't seem to have a written language of their own and are very secretive by nature. *Hescheboix* is no more their own name for themselves than *Thierachians* is—it is merely a mangled version of French terms signifying 'ax' and 'wood' although it would probably be more accurate to describe them as "woodcarvers" rather than "woodchoppers." Such art as they have seems to be largely confined to the making of wooden figurines representing animals, although they're also very adept mixers of pigments, and often sell paintings of animals made on roundels of wood or pieces of slate.

"In much the same way that everything we know about the ancient Druidic religion of Gaul comes from observations made by outsiders like Julius Caesar, who was both ignorant and hostile, what little that modern scholars think they know about the nomads' religion is based on observations made in the past by Christian monks, who regarded the nomads' worship as intrinsically diabolical. Reading between the condemnatory lines, however, the likeliest interpretation of their beliefs is that they address their reverence to spirits inhabiting an underworld: not the shades of the dead, but physical beings composed of some kind of primal fire, which they consider to be the ultimate parents of the vital spark animating all organic life, as well as the creator of human consciousness.

"Even friars, who are usually very free with accusations of

human sacrifice and cannibalism, don't accuse the Thierachians of such horrible crimes, although they do level the more commonplace charge against them, as against all nomads, that they frequently steal children. It's possible that there's some confusion of Christian reports of the Thierachians with folk-tales relating to the fairy folk, who are also deemed to be occasional child-stealers and are often said to inhabit an underworld of sorts. At any rate, there can be no doubt that the Thierachians have long considered the caves in which Guérande is interested to be important to their religion."

"What has the sleeping dragon to do with it?" I asked.

"I don't know," Dupin confessed. "How the local folklore of the permanent residents connects with the Thierachians' mythology, if it does, is anyone's guess. Some overlap is to be expected, but the two are essentially separate. If dragons of the sort featured in the Golden Legend or other Western sources have a role to play in Thierachian belief, there's no obvious record of it—but the records are very sparse indeed."

Dupin was not trying to hide the fact that an opportunity to find out more about Thierachian beliefs would be very welcome to him, as an antiquarian. There is nothing an antiquarian likes better than an opportunity to correct and fill out unreliable records.

"Unfortunately, Monsieur Dupin," Madame Guérande put in, speaking very formally, presumably for Sophie's benefit, "the Thierachians might be reluctant to talk to you, as a guest in our house. They always seem very reluctant to speak to anyone, but this year, in particular, when the phenomena caused by the thaw are more exaggerated than usual...." She left it there.

"Madame Guérande is afraid that their long-simmering conflict with Monsieur Guérande, consequent on his explorations in the caves, might finally boil over this spring, once it becomes possible to gain easy access to the caves again," Dupin said, this time speaking directly to me, although he doubtless had the presence of the mother and child very much in mind. "In winter, water trapped by superficial ice floods some of the entrance tunnels, but the annual thaw has already begun the process of clearance." He glanced at Madame Guérande as if for permission to continue.

"There's no need to add anything more, Monsieur Dupin," she said to him. "Your friend already knows about the legend of the sleeping dragon, and will not be intimidated by any sounds that he hears in the house."

Dupin nodded in his turn, but for once, didn't seem very sure of himself. I suspected that it wasn't permission to mention the legend of the dragon that he had been seeking. He had probably wanted to say something more about Claude Guérande's troubles, but there were limits to what he could say in the presence of the man's daughter.

I thought I could understand why, for once in his life, Dupin was unsure of himself. Claude Guérande evidently knew that his wife had come to fetch Dupin, and must have consented to her doing so—but that didn't mean that he approved of her action, and it was certainly no guarantee of the warmth of the welcome that he would offer his old friend. Guérande might not see Auguste Dupin as a neutral party, at least where his wife was concerned, and might not be at all ready or willing to confess secrets to him that he had kept for so long, or listen to his advice even if he did confide in him. That was not an opinion I could broach in the lady's presence, however, so I kept quiet. Mercifully, because I was sitting opposite Sophie, I did not have to look the lady in the face while I felt the awkwardness increase. I concentrated on smiling in a kindly manner at the little girl, although I dared not go so far as to start pointing out monuments as we trotted through the streets leading to the new Gare de Paris—an edifice still too young to be considered a monument, but which would doubtless become one soon enough.

I confess that I was glad to get down when we arrived, hoping that the railway carriage would be considerably more spacious than the interior of the fiacre.

Someone—Madame Guérande, I presumed—had already

reserved a first-class compartment on the train, plus two double sleeping-berths. I was disappointed that we had to board directly, having arrived at the station with only a quarter of an hour to spare before the scheduled departure time, but my disappointment eased when I discovered that the train was actually equipped with a restaurant car, by way of substitution for the coaching inns that sometimes made a long-distance journey by diligence seem slightly less hellish.

I cannot honestly say that the dinner served in the restaurant car was good, but I had eaten far worse, and there was nothing at all wrong with the wine that accompanied it, even if it was the produce of the vineyards of Seine-et-Oise rather than those of Bordeaux or Bourgogne.

Over dinner, as convention demanded, we talked about other things than the reason for our journey. I learned more than I could ever have wanted to know about Sophie's history, from the day of her birth, and infinitely more than the poor child could possibly have wanted me to know. Had she been living in Paris she would doubtless have been lodged in one of the better *pensions* by now, but that was not how things were done in the wilds of the Ardèche. She had a governess, however, named Madame Cormontaigne, who had attended a Parisian *pension* herself, and had followed as many open courses at the university as she could. Madame Cormontaigne evidently had cause to bless the legacy of '89, which had opened the door to such innovatory possibilities.

"She knows little or nothing about science," Madame Guérande explained, "but that does not matter. My father educated me in elementary mathematics and chemistry, and I have picked up more than a smattering of natural philosophy; I can pass that intelligence along to Sophie myself."

"And her father can teach her geology," I put in, trying, as always, to be helpful.

"He has said that he will," the lady answered, with more than a trace of skepticism, "when the time is right." Immediately, she changed the subject. "Well, Monsieur Dupin," she said, "what do you think of railway travel. Is it not the ultimate proof of the doctrine of progress?"

"The tracks on which the locomotive and the carriage run are certainly smoother than a rutted road," Dupin admitted, "and the train's speed is impressive. Unlike the horses that pull carriages, the locomotive is presumably indefatigable, and the tracks, being parallel, even more indefatigable, in conformity with the Euclidean boast regarding their potential infinitude and their immunity to the muddying and freezing that often make roads impassible in winter. On the other hand, it is a trifle noisy, and rather smoky—inevitably, I suppose, as the output of the locomotive is routinely swept backwards to swathe the carriages. On the whole, I'm prepared to grant that it is a considerable improvement on road and river transport, and I have no doubt that it will provide a useful spur to the development of telegraphy."

"Telegraphy?" I queried. "Why telegraphy."

Madame Guérande knew the answer. "Efficient signaling," she said. "At present, the network is in its infancy, but when it is much elaborate and traffic has multiplied ten or a hundredfold, the ability to send electrical signals along the track much faster than the train will become vital."

"Ah!" I said. "Progress indeed. It will not be long, you know, before the east and west coasts of America will be linked, and then we shall see the automated conquest of the frontier—complemented, I don't doubt, by the advent of dirigible airships. A new era in the transportation of goods...and armies."

"Oh no!" said Madame Guérande. "We shall soon see the end of war, if dirigible airships enable bombs to be dropped anywhere and everywhere, with no possible defense against them." She glanced at Sophie, more for my benefit than her own; she was trying to indicate that I ought not to talk about the possibility of war in the girl's presence. The girl seemed annoyed by the warning glance; again, I tried to express my sympathy with a smile.

"I doubt that," I said, thinking that the nobility of the impulse encouraging me to side with Sophie gave me a license to defy the mother's censure. "Much bloodier wars, I'll grant you...but we are a bellicose species. The horrors of war, however mani-fest—and they are certainly very manifest now that newspapers have begun to report their progress—have never deterred their perpetrators or their combatants. In that arena, progress is a double-edged sword—if you'll forgive the play on words."

She did not specify whether she forgave it or not. "But I was born and brought up among evolutionists, even though I was never fully admitted to their inner circle," the lady said, affecting a jocular tone, although her lips were a trifle tight. "I firmly believe in progress, and human perfectibility, in terms of Monsieur de Lamarck's philosophy if not the Marquis de Condorcet's. Every living organism is engaged in an eternal and insensible quest to improve itself physically—and intellectually too, in the case of human beings, who have already come a long way from mere brutishness, He dared not say so explicitly in his books, but I sat on the Chevalier's lap when I was younger than Sophie is now, and heard from his own lips his conviction that humankind was on the threshold of a great moral leap forward."

I performed a quick mental calculation, and estimated that Lamarck had probably said that to little Julie before Bonaparte's crashing fall and the completion of his own professional ruin. I could not help but wonder whether he would have repeated it afterwards, even when speaking to a beautiful and curious child. I looked at Sophie, pensively, and wondered what reas-surance regarding the world's future I would dare to give her, if ever I were to find her on my lap, looking up at me with her bright blue Norman eyes. She was not looking at me now, though, but staring out of the window, putting on an appearance of not listening to us

"What do you think, Monsieur Dupin?" the once-adorable Julie demanded of Dupin, stressing the name very slightly, as if she wanted to make it clear that she would rather be calling him "Auguste," but felt it inappropriate to do so in her daughter's hearing.

"I would like to believe in the philosophy of progress," Dupin said, mildly, "but mere desire is not sufficient grounds for doing so, and I fear that there might be many a backward step before our society finds a secure balance in its forward momentum. Figuratively as well as literally speaking, we have not yet abandoned the horse for the steam engine, and might find the transfer more problematic than we hope. Nevertheless, I do dare to hope that obstacles we find in our path will not be insurmountable, and that Sophie's children and grandchildren will come to adulthood in a kinder and more prosperous world than ours."

"You haven't changed a bit in twenty years, as regards your painstaking pedantry," the lady remarked. "You haven't even aged as much as I have. Perhaps the wizards of Paris are right to consider you the greatest of their company."

Dupin gave me a sharply critical glance, which almost caused me to wince. I remembered that I hadn't passed on what the Prefect had let slip about Saint-Germain's real name, but I had no opportunity to insert the information into the conversation.

"There is no wizardry involved," Madame," Dupin replied to the lady's remark. "Chance alone has maintained my appearance—but I can assure you that I have aged internally, perhaps more than you suspect."

"I can believe that," Madame Guérande replied, in a pensive fashion suggesting that she was probably thinking about her own internal aging, or perhaps the lack of it. "You seem to have led a peculiar life since we last met."

That was a deliberate provocation, but Dupin warded it off. "Oh no," he said. "It has been a very quiet and orderly existence, as befits a scholar. You're doubtless familiar with the tendencies of the scholarly temperament, having never known men of any other sort." His tone was very mild, but there was a hidden accusation in the words themselves. Even Sophie knew that, and turned to look at the interior of the carriage for once.

The lady was careful not to react sharply to the remark, although I got the strong impression that she might have done so once, while she was still "the adorable Julie" and the jewel in the crown of her father's Parisian salon, rather than the good and patient wife of a provincial antiquarian. "I have, indeed, known a great many clever men, Monsieur Dupin," she said, "but I am not at all sure that they were of exactly the same sort. You and Claude still seem to have much in common, but there are differences in your mentality as well as your physique—and there were other members of our little circle, like dear Lucien, who were evidently marked out for different destinies. I believe that I was able, even at seventeen, and certainly by the time I turned twenty-one, to make sensible discriminations between men."

She did not add *and rational choices*, but the words certainly seemed to me to be implied. She was definitely making the point that she did not regret the choice that had led her to become Madame Guérande—but it was a point that she had no alternative but to make, sincerely or not. There was something else I sensed behind her words, however, which I could not quite define: an uncertainty, perhaps, as to whether she really had had as much choice as she had assumed. I suspected that she did not know, any more than I did, whether Auguste Dupin had really been in love with her or not, back in 1820.

I wondered, too, whether Dupin knew the answer to that question himself. It is not unknown for men who are exceptionally wise in some respects to be utterly blind in others. Besides which, he had been young then, and callow...or had, at least, appeared so to the world. The adorable Julie's estimate of his age was based on the fact that he had been, or appeared to be, a student, not on any inspection of the record of his birth.

Dupin did not seem at all disturbed by the sudden tension that had crept into the conversation. It was his turn now to turn to look at Sophie, as if to remind everyone that she needed some protection from adult matters. "I don't doubt, Madame," he said, "that you were capable of wise choices. The fact that you have such a beautiful and intelligent daughter confirms that you made an excellent choice of husband."

It was flattery, and Sophie knew it; there was no conspicuous gratitude in the way she returned Dupin's gaze.

"Yes," the lady murmured, "I sometimes forget how intelligent she is becoming, being distracted by maternal affection, but you're right: she is beautiful, and also bright, like a luminous flower beginning to blossom."

That was flattery enough to make a saint blush, but Sophie reacted to it in a slightly peculiar fashion, almost as if there were a mystery in what had been said, and a hidden implication that troubled her slightly. Then she remembered what a good girl she was supposed to be, and favored her mother with a smile that suggested, very clearly, that a talent for winding the male of the species around a little finger was hereditary, in the distaff line of her family.

CHAPTER SIX
THE SLEEPING DRAGON

I had vaguely imagined Chalon to be three-quarters, or even four-fifths, of the way to "the south of France" but my appreciation of French geography was vague in that direction. I found, somewhat to my dismay, that Chalon was only about half-way even to the Ardèche, which is situated to the east of the Massif Central, in a region descending from the Monts de Vivarais. The region's principal town, Privas, lies in the eastern plain, but the district for which we were headed was in a much hillier region whose most prominent landmark was a peak known as the Gerbier de Jonc. The Ardèche River now runs a long way to the south of that peak, but has not always followed its present course, having once flowed considerably further to the north— so Dupin informed me, in his capacity as a scrupulous know-it-all.

The Auvergne, to the west of the Ardèche, was once a region of active volcanoes, but the old conical peaks have been extinct for a long time now—far longer than human memory, or at least the memory of the Vivarais. There is a ruined temple to Mercury in one of the range's largest craters, which nowadays seems a monument to the crater's antiquity as well as to the obsolescence of the old gods of Rome. Even at its ragged edges, the mountainous mass thus piled up is full of ravines and gorges, most of which have streams flowing through them, but relatively few broad valleys attractive to intensive cultivation. At least, that was true of the region in which we finally arrived, after two further days and nights of travel beyond Chalon, in the last of several hired coaches.

Mont Dragon seemed far milder than the mountains further to the east, having no peak to speak off, nor even steeply conical slopes. Had it been smaller it would have been a gentle, round-topped hill, but its sheer mass gave it a certain majesty as it loomed over the plain extending eastwards from its foot, bounded to the north and south by ragged ridges but gradually broadening out along the meandering course of the stream, which grew into a small river as it was fed by numerous tributaries, into a confusion of shallow dales. In that fruitful region, the hamlets typical of the splayed foot of Mont Dragon seemed to swell, along with the stream, into veritable villages. As we came down the slope from the northern ridge I counted four visible church steeples, but by the time we crossed the stone bridge at the land's lowest point only one still peeped over the woodlands aggregated on and between the hilltops by the line of sight.

Although it was an old manor, whose foundations probably went back to the eleventh century and its main structure to the seventeenth, the house in which Claude Guérande lived seemed a relatively modern and comfortable building by comparison with the isolated cottages on the mountainside and those in the nearby hamlets—and even more so by comparison with the old Château de Tibère, which was perched on a spur of rock—almost a crag—to the south. Although not much bigger than the Guérande house, the château bore a much closer resemblance to a Medieval edifice, with thick walls and towers, which would have needed nothing but jagged battlements and a severe portcullis to turn it into a small fortress. The château would have appeared to be a mere five kilometers from the Guérande house on a map, but it seemed to my eyes that the third dimension of the terrain almost doubled that distance, and surely quadrupled the difficulty of transit for those heading upslope rather than down.

What struck me most about the landscape of Mont Dragon

itself was the relative dearth of authentic trees. Most of the French mountain regions I had seen in my travels had been heavily wooded, usually with sullen evergreens, at least up to a certain point, beyond which the bare rock was challenged in its possession of the summits only by mosses and lichens. In the terrain extending around and looming over Guérande's house, however, there were only a few clumps of thin-boled trees, save for the willows sporadically lining the meandering trickles of water that combined to form the stream. Instead of lofty trees, there were vast expanses of thorny bushes, and what seemed to me to be capacious stands of unusually tall bracken.

Although these dense thickets rarely rose to a man's height, they nevertheless gave the impression of providing an insurmountable obstacle to human progress, save for occasional twisting paths cut through them at eccentric angles. The relative smoothness of the mountain, as viewed from a distance, was obviously not replicated at a more intimate level, where the ground was very uneven. The vegetation, although abundant, failed to conceal numerous outcrops of bare rock when the slope was viewed at close range. At first glance, I could not see any caves opening into the hillsides, and had to assume that their entrances were concealed by the bracken and the thorn-scrub—but it occurred to me soon enough that the eccentric paths must have some objective in mind. Julie Guérande's commentary on the landscape, as the horses drawing our carriage toiled away, seemingly no more comfortable on the downward slope than they had been on the upward one, confirmed that guess.

Where the land on the hillsides had been cleared, it was used for grazing rather than planting; there were more sheep than cattle even on the valley floor, and they would have had sole possession of the higher slopes had it not been for a number of goats and donkeys roaming free. The scattered homesteads were meager, small central buildings being surrounded by squat outbuildings where geese and poultry were kept, and milking goats tethered—but all of that seemed distant, when seen from Guérande's house, when we finally arrived. The house then appeared to belong to the mountain rather than the valley, in spite of its low elevation and proximity to the stream. It had once had a farm surrounding it, where attempts seemed once to have been made to set out fields for plowing and planting, but all that was left of it now was a glorified kitchen garden and a single barn used as stables, for a small company of donkeys as well as the horses charged with pulling the family's carriage and carts.

Inside, it was even more obvious that the house was not a conventional rural dwelling, primarily devoted to the coordination of agricultural endeavors. It seemed to me to be more like a fragment of a town, or even a city, magically displaced into the middle of nowhere. It was well-equipped with books and other apparatus of study, and the core members its domestic staff were uniformed, like those of a town house in Paris, almost genteel in their appearance. There were old military memorabilia on the walls, in abundant quantity, which readily revealed, even to an inexpert eye like mine, that Claude Guérande's father had fought proudly with Napoléon's *grand armée*, in Egypt, in Italy and in Spain, and that his grandfather had seen service too, both before and after the Revolution, fighting first on behalf of the Bourbons, and then for their usurpers—but always, of course, for France, even if her enemies were sometimes within her frontiers.

I could not help making a careful count of Claude Guérande's staff, and the proportion of it that might be potentially capable of bearing arms. He had fourteen servants, not counting the cook's two children, aged five and eight, and the governess. Eight of the servants were male, but only five were in the prime of life. In a battle, I thought, they were unlikely to be able to hold off a Bohemian horde—not that I had seen the slightest sign of a horde, or even of a lone Bohemian. No Thierachians, it seemed, had yet arrived in the valley in the course of their estival wanderings.

Claude Guérande was a tall fellow, who certainly did no dishonor to his military ancestry, in spite of being very slenderly built and having defected to the cause of science. Although he appeared to be as near to sixty as fifty, he was a good five inches taller than Dupin, and better-looking, at least in a conventional sense. His bronzed complexion suited him, given his black hair—which showed less trace of silver than his wife's—and his dark eyes. It was easy enough to imagine him twenty-five years younger, and to understand how a naïve Parisian coquette might have found him a much more attractive suitor than Auguste Dupin or Lucien Groix, in spite of the fact that he was more than a decade older than either of them. The combination of his height and slimness must have allowed him to dress and pose very elegantly in Paris, although he was very simply dressed now in a while blouse and moleskin trousers, and had not even put on a jacket to greet his visitors.

In spite of my fears, the manner in which Guérande greeted Dupin can only be described as effusive. He seemed genuinely delighted to see him, and also welcomed me with as much bonhomie as could possibly be expected.

"I wish that we had kept in touch, Auguste," he said, as he ushered us into a drawing-room whose furniture and decor would not have been out of place in the better parts of the Marais, if not the more pretentious reaches of the Faubourg Saint-Denis. "I continued to correspond with the professor, of course, and with Étienne Geoffroy too. I'm still in touch with Isidore Geoffroy, Étienne's son—you must know him, I suppose—but one makes more effort to keep in touch with one's mentors and peers than one's younger colleagues. How is Lucien, by the way? Prefect of Police! Who would ever have thought it? If rumor can be trusted, you still work with him occasionally as a consultant, when you are not buried in your antiquarian studies...not that I believed that rubbish about the murders in the Rue Morgue for a moment. Gentle creatures, orangutans, not given to violence at all."

Dupin weathered this verbal flood with ease, and seemed perfectly comfortable as he settled into the chair pulled out for him. He too must have been relieved by the enthusiasm of the welcome. Madame Guérande had not come into the drawing-room with us, but has hastened away with Sophie, after murmuring a brief apology

"I know of Isidore Geoffroy's work," Dupin said, mildly, in reply to Guérande's confused speech, "but I don't know him socially. When Étienne Geoffroy died I hadn't seen him for twenty years. Lucien is a very good Prefect of Police, in my estimation, although I fear that he will fall from grace, along with the government and the king, within a matter of months. Unlike Fouché, he has no treasure-chest of blackmail material that would enable him to keep his title even under a Socialist administration. He's mortally afraid that he'll be put in jail when all the political prisoners that his colleagues have put away are released, and I suspect that he has good reason to be anxious. He won't resign, though, let alone disappear abroad or into some hospitable monastery. He'll face whatever comes, courageously."

"And the orangutan?"

"Innocent, as you supposed. The story made a better melo-drama told that way, however. I hold nothing against Mr. Poe on my own account, although I do regret the publicity he gave to the Valdemar case, which had unfortunate repercussions in Paris. But what about your own situation? You promised us a *mémoire* about your discoveries twenty-five years ago, but if the Académie has had any correspondence, it has not been published in the Proceedings."

"Your own publications are hardly profuse," Guérande retorted, evidently having nursed that shot for the occasion. "You will understand, I think, better than anyone, how time drags on when one is searching for the further details that will make a report as conclusive and dazzling as one wants it to be. My wife would rather I had rushed into print long ago, but she did not inherit her father's scientific turn of mind along with her mother's beauty. You will sympathize, I know, with my desire to complete the picture before applying the varnish."

Dupin had no alternative but to concede the point, given his own reluctance to commit his awesome knowledge to paper, for lack of a few final details. "You have had some difficulties, I understand," he said, delicately.

Guérande made a dismissive gesture that was a little too sweeping to be sincere. "Mere trivia," he said. "Nothing that need worry you. I want you to regard this as a purely social visit—a holiday from the turmoil of Paris. I'm sure that you need a vacation, given the hectic pace of life in a capital city, and the perennial political disputes raging there."

"Of course," said Dupin. "But however trivial they might be, some report of your troubles has reached Paris. Lucien has heard of them—although there are precious few whispers that don't reach his ears, one way or another."

"Has Julie seen Lucien, then?" Guérande asked, in a perfectly level tone.

"She did not have time—but I'm in regular contact with him." Dupin did not elaborate on that slightly deceptive point, but went on: "The Comte de Tibère is making difficulties, it seems, and the Thierachians do not approve of your explorations—although I notice that they haven't returned to the valley as yet."

"Oh, they'll be here. They're not the magicians they claim to be, but they do have a remarkable sensitivity to the weather. They'll know when the way into the deep caves becomes clear again, as the summer sun dries the land from above and the melt-water from the winter snows runs away into mysterious underground seas. I've done my level best to befriend them, over the years, and persuade them that there's no conflict of interest between us, but I can't get through to them. Like orangutans, though, they're essentially placid. Their disapproval has never turned to violence. The Comte is an old fool, living in the past, who can't forget that his father quarreled with my grandfather... he's threatening to go to the law to claim the land on which the house stands, and the eastern slopes of the mountain, but it's all bluster. There's nothing much the Bishop and his Dominicans can do to help him, no matter what he might think. I'm not worried—just impatient to resume work in earnest."

"Dominicans?" Dupin queried, effortlessly picking out the one datum that was unfamiliar to him.

"Yes—Julie doesn't know about them, yet; they arrived after she left. The Bishop of Viviers is spending a month or so as the guest of his old friend the Comte de Tibère, and he has come with a guard of honor, made up of black friars. Mercifully, the days of warrior monks and the Inquisition are long past, and all these fellows can do, if they're inclined to do anything at all, is preach to deaf ears. If they hope to convert the nomads, or to rouse the indigenes to form a mob to march against the nomads, they simply don't know the people they're dealing with. The only man in these parts whose fundamental philosophy isn't 'live and let live' is the Comte."

"Except, perhaps, for Arnauld Lebrun," Dupin put in, obviously interested to know whether Guérande had heard the name.

Apparently, Guérande had not. "Who's he?" he asked, bewildered.

"A lawyer from Lyon who has been rummaging through the National Archive, searching for documents related to land tenure hereabouts."

Guérande laughed. "From Lyon!" he said. "A foreigner! And what do the documents moldering in the National Archive matter, since the Revolution? We're all free now, to own the land we work, or on which our houses stand—and there's surely no Tribunal anywhere in France that would even dream of trying to turn the clock back to 1788, let alone the Middle Ages."

While he was speaking, Madame Guérande had come into the room to join us, presumably intent on telling us that dinner would shortly be served, but she could not help reacting to what her husband had said, and is dismissive manner

"The ownership of the land on to which the caves open might be a different matter," she observed. "Tibère is capable of attempting to claim that just to strike another blow in the ancient family feud—and the Bishop is perfectly capable of attempting to strike a blow against the Thierachians' supposedly-diabolical worship, if only in a spirit of showmanship."

The dissent put a distinct dent in the tall man's ebullience, but he was not about to concede defeat. "Nothing will come of it," he insisted. "In any case, I've come too far to stop now. The things I've seen and the scraps that I've collected are sensational in themselves, but there's more—I *know* there's more. All I need is a little more time."

"Sensational in what sense?" Dupin asked, mildly.

This time, however, the verbal spring occasioned by the unusual fact of having guests to impress had run abruptly dry. After a pause, and in a more hesitant tone, Guérande said: "I haven't even discussed that with Julie. I trust her implicitly, of course, but the servants don't have her education. Silence has been my armor against misunderstanding. I've drafted half a dozen *mémoires* to the Académie over the years, not to mention letters to Isidore Geoffroy outlining my finds and the deductions I've made therefrom, but I've always torn them up, because I'm not yet ready. Once the search is completed—once I've found what I *know* there is to be found...."

"You must show me the caves tomorrow," Dupin said. "The entrances, at least." I immediately took the inference that he wanted to talk to Guérande in private: in the open air where there was no possibility of their being overheard, and where secrets might safely be imparted, if anyone had a mind to impart them.

Did Guérande have a mind to impart them, though? And if he had, would he deign to impart them to Auguste Dupin, rather than to some old acquaintance at the University, the Jardin des Plantes or the Museum. There was no man in France whom Lucien Groix trusted more—but that was because there were so few men in France who trusted Lucien Groix, and Dupin's reputation as the Prefect's confidant might well work against him here, as it doubtless did elsewhere.

"I must certainly show you around," said Guérande. "Indeed, I'll be glad to take you into the caves, once we can gain proper access—I'd be grateful for the impression of a fresh but educated eye."

There was no emphasis on the word "fresh," but I interpreted it as the foundation of a pretext. Guérande was not going to let Dupin in on whatever secret he was keeping from his wife—not yet, at any rate. Dupin did not let his disappointment show, but Julie Guérande pursed her lips, defiantly. She had not lost faith in her little finger, but she knew that she still had work to do, and that its expertise in twisting might yet be tested.

We went to the dining room, where we were introduced to Madame Cormontaigne, a lady not much younger than Madame Guérande, who did not seem to me to be the kind of person in whom Sophie might find a companion, any more than she could easily make friends with the cook's much younger children. Positioned at table between her mother and governess, the poor girl seemed flanked by protective but nevertheless forbidding guards.

The food was understandably rustic, and did not have the evident freshness that is traditionally supposed to compensate for lack of culinary sophistication in the provinces, but I reminded myself that the staff had not had any notice of the exact time of our arrival, and had not been able to make special preparation for it. Tomorrow, when Madame Guérande's housekeeper had had a chance to go the village—even if it were not yet market day—the standard would doubtless improve.

After dinner, rather than waiting to see whether it was conventional even in the Ardèche for gentlemen to retire to the smoking-room, I announced my intention to go straight up to my room, pleading exhaustion—and I was, in fact, quite exhausted. Three days of travel had worn me out, and the headache I had developed on the last and most arduous stage of the road journey had not been cleared by the water and wine I had drunk with the meal. Had I thought that a late night conversation might lead to further revelations. I might have forced myself to stay up until Dupin announced an intention to retire, but in view of Guérande's reserve, I thought it safe to take the initiative. In fact, Dupin took his cue from me, and seemed glad of it, so the entire household dispersed. Although it must have been a trifle early for Guérande, he too seemed a trifle relieved to be able to postpone the continuation of his reunion with this old friend until the morning.

"I'll send one of the servants up to your room with a bowl of hot water and a towel," Madame Guérande promised, aiming the remark at me as well as Dupin. We both thanked her.

In view of that promise, I did not begin to get undressed immediately, but merely lay down on the bed and closed my eyes. When there was a knock on the door, I did not bother to open them, but merely called: "Come in." I heard a bowl being set down on the side-table, and felt obliged then to make some gesture of thanks, so I opened my eyes and sat up.

I found myself looking into Sophie's blue eyes.

"I offered to help," she said, by way of explanation of her presence.

"You're a good girl," I told her. "Thank you very much."

She didn't move. She wanted something—but I had no idea what it might be. I waited, nonplussed.

Eventually, she said: "Is my father in danger?"

"I don't believe so," I replied, honestly enough.

"Nobody tells me anything," she said, "but I listen. They know I listen, but they still don't *tell* me anything."

It took an effort of memory, but eventually, I was able to say: "That's quite normal, even on the far side of the Atlantic. Well brought-up children are taught to be seen and not heard. Their parents don't tell them anything—they leave that to their schoolteachers, who never tell them what they want to know. I expect that it's the same with governesses."

"My mother's frightened," the little girl stated, flatly.

"She's a little anxious," I conceded, "But I don't think she's *frightened*."

"*I'm* frightened," she said.

"Of what?" I asked, gathering myself to do an adult's duty and offer her reassurance.

I fully expected her to say: "The dragon"—or perhaps "The

Thierachians"—but she didn't.

"I don't know," she said. "It would be easier if I did."

It was at that precise moment that I heard and felt "the sleeping dragon" for the first time. In the silence that followed her remark, I heard a faint but quite distinct groan, and I felt the house quiver, as if echoing the noise.

"Of *that*, you mean?" I said. "But you know what that is: it's just water, released from the mountain slopes by the spring thaw.

"I know *that*," she said, implying that she had meant something subtly different. "but there are other things in the caves."

I wasn't sure what she meant. Obviously, she knew that her father had made discoveries of some sort in the caves—but if that was what she meant, what did she imagine that they were?

"What things?" I queried, hesitantly.

"People say that there are flameflowers," she said. "They say that they look beautiful...but that it's not what they look like that matters. They say there's a song as well—a song that it's dangerous to listen to."

I paused for thought, by only momentarily. "Have you ever been into the caves, Sophie?" I asked, as gently as I could.

"No," she answered, "but I hear people talk. Nobody tells me anything—but I listen."

"And who talks about flameflowers? The servants?"

"No."

"The Bohemians?"

"I don't understand what they say to one another—they only speak French to Papa."

"The local farm-laborers, then?" I guessed, having run out of other possibilities.

"Yes—and the people in the village, when we go to the market. I've asked Mama and Papa, as well as Madame Cormontaigne, but they just tell me that there's nothing to worry about, that it's just fairy stories. But Mama and Madame Cormontaigne are frightened—and so is Papa, just a little."

"They're a little anxious," I corrected her, once again, "but it has nothing to do with *things* in the caves. There are arguments about who owns the land hereabouts, that's all. It's not a matter of life and death, by any means."

"Is there really going to be another Revolution?" she asked, suddenly changing tack. Obviously, her own anxieties were compound. I felt slightly flattered that she had come to me for clarification—that my attempts to establish some sort of rapport had not been completely ignored. I didn't have to reflect long and hard to figure out that there was no point in lying, given what she must recently have overheard while no one was telling her anything.

"Probably," I admitted. "But you don't have to worry about that. If it happens, there'll be barricades on the streets of Paris, but nothing bad is likely to happen here. You'll be perfectly safe here."

"What about the white terror?" she asked. Evidently, there were some things she'd heard about that I hadn't, until very recently.

"Not this time." I said. "In the last century, things were very bad—but it's different, now. For fifteen years, the parties in Parliament have been trying to find a *juste milieu*. Even though they haven't quite managed it, that's the frame in which everyone is thinking and working. Nobody wants to see massacres again—the memories are still too raw, even for people like your mother and father, who weren't alive in the '89 Revolution, and missed out on the Parisian disturbances of the July Revolution too. This time, it will be restrained. There won't be any Red Terror and there won't be any white terror to follow it." I hoped to God that I was right, for my sake even more than hers.

She nodded her head, as if sagely. "Thank you, Mr. Reynolds," she said.

"You can call me Sam," I said, for the first time in my life. "In fact, you can even call me Uncle Sam, if you want to."

She didn't see any joke, if there had, in fact, been one to see. She nodded again, and left, closing the door quietly behind her.

The conversation had served to dispel some of my tiredness, and when I lay down on the bed again I could hear the rumblings inside the mountain. They were not continuous, but were frequent enough to leave a sense of anxious anticipation in the silent pauses. They really were disconcerting, and after twenty minutes or so I decided that I had best seek distraction and try to "read myself to sleep." With that aim in mind, I picked up a book I had brought with me to read: the copy of *Telliamed* that Julie Malet had once inscribed so affectionately to Dupin, by way of innocent flirtation.

CHAPTER SEVEN
THE CAVES OF VIVARAIS

I didn't sleep well, although there was nothing wrong with the bed. Just like Sophie, I knew exactly what the sounds inside the mountain were. I even knew that they were too close at hand, in spite of their apparent distance, to be the stirrings of a dragon sleeping in the heart of the mountain, even if there had been any such thing. They were just water, recently liberated to drain away from the subsurface layers, which would replenish the springs and the streams of the valley as well as the deep aquifers beneath its fertile soil. I preferred to think about "deep aquifers" rather than "subterranean seas," because it sounded less melodramatic, and I really had outgrown my youthful taste for melodrama—because, rather than in spite, of the "everything" that Dupin hadn't wanted me to mention to Madame Guérande.

What one *knows*, however, even for certain, is only ever part of the story. Sophie had grown up with the noises that haunted the Guérande house on a seasonal basis. They were familiar to her. She was able to muster contempt for them, whether they were draconian or not, simply because they had always been there and never done her any harm. She was more worried about mythical flameflowers, which no one had ever seen, and songs that were rumored to accompany their flamboyance and render them even more mysterious.

I, on the other hand, had never heard the stirrings of the imaginary dragon before. To me, the sounds were alien and unprecedented. I had been in supposedly haunted houses before; I even had some reason to suspect that I had been haunted by expert phantoms, but I could not help, nevertheless, likening the hissing and groaning sounds to the troubled breath of a hypothetical sleeper, as countless people must have done before me, on hearing it for the first time—and sensing, too, by means of some subliminal intuition, that the sleeper in question might be on the point of awakening, and might actually do so *this time*, even though it had never done so before, while thousands or hundreds of thousands of vernal equinoxes had arrived, and given gradual birth to hot and somnolent summers.

I promised myself, when I got up, that I would do better the next night. I owed it to myself to make that petty conquest.

After breakfast, Guérande, Dupin and I set off together on an expedition that was intended to take in not merely the entrances to the labyrinthine cave-system within Mont Dragon, but also the other "sights" of the neighborhood, such as they were—excepting the Château de Tibère, which we would only observe from a respectful difference, looking up with due or undue reverence.

Forewarned that the going was sometimes likely to be hard, I had put on my stoutest boots and trousers, and gloves that ought to have armored me against the fiercest thorns. I had my stoutest walking-stick in my hand, and my oldest felt hat on my head. I would have looked like a scarecrow in the Boulevard Saint-Germain, but I did not feel self-conscious at the foot of Mont Dragon, even though Dupin had contrived to retain something of his urbane elegance in his own costume.

As we ascended the slope, we did not stray from the paths that had obviously been cleared many years or decades before, and were evidently still maintained by periodic human traffic. The wear and tear inflicted on my clothing was nevertheless greater than I might have expected from a year of fighting my way through the crowds of Paris. Dupin, of course, somehow contrived to move with an eel-like suppleness that kept his own coat and trousers out of harm's way. The President of the

Harmonic Society would doubtless have called it magic—but the President of the Harmonic Society called almost everything Dupin did "magic."

I had always thought of bracken as harmless stuff, but it turned out to be coarser than I had expected, and not as monopolistic in its empire as much have been hoped. Quite apart from the hostile vegetation—which became even more hostile among the brambles and the hawthorns—the ground was strewn with small stones, and there were hidden projections everywhere.

The first cave entrance that Guérande showed us was a dire disappointment, seemingly little broader than the opening of a badger sett, and the second one was a mere slit, so narrow that I had to be convinced that a man of Guérande's size could actually slip through it—but he proved that he could.

Dupin did not pester our guide with questions, evidently feeling that there was work yet to be done to earn his trust. Guérande did not take long, however, to recover the volubility engendered by the rare gift of having visitors—especially visitors from Paris. The higher we went as we zigzagged up the seemingly-interminable slope, the further he relaxed.

"Did you know Cuvier, Auguste?" Guérande asked, enthusiastically. "I always thought it a pity that he and Malet had quarreled—he would have been useful addition to our salon, would he not?"

"I met him on several occasions," Dupin admitted. "Brogniart too, who was his collaborator on his initial analysis of geological strata. Indeed, I saw Brogniart only last year, although he's in his seventies now, and has not changed his catastrophist views. Cuvier never changed his mind either, in spite of the number of fossil bones he collected and the number of complete models he built with the aid of his anatomical theories. Faith had too strong a grip on him to allow him to meet Malet and Lamarck in free debate. He recognized change, grudgingly, but not *development*."

"No," said Guérande, with a sigh, "he was no evolutionist—and he provided a model for many others, who had no alternative but to accept the evidence while still denying the implication. Do you know Boucher de Perthes, who seems to be making interesting finds related to early humans?"

"Yes—in fact, I've seen some of the flints he has found, which show evidence of being worked by hand, although not the most recent ones, which he found at Menchecourt last year. I was present at the session of the Académie when the Somme Valley flints were first displayed, but the ones he has found in company with rhinoceros and elephant bones haven't been displayed in Paris as yet. He'll need more than that to convince the Academicians, though, let alone the clergy. Some admit that the flints might be older than six thousand years, but deny that they were worked by human hands. Other admit that they were worked by human hands, but deny that they can be any older than five thousand years. Malet's disciples are still few in number, and still discreet. I dare say that there are still salons akin to his meeting in the Latin Quarter, but they're as secretive as we were."

"But the evidence was already there in our day!" Guérande protested. "Can anyone still doubt that the whole of France has been covered by the sea more than once, long enough for the remains of marine creatures to become petrified into rock— into entire mountains? Can anyone doubt the relatedness of all earthly species, both plant and animal, and that countless species once alive have vanished, becoming petrified themselves? Is there anything in nature more obvious?"

"If it were not for the blindfold of Scripture," Dupin said, "perhaps it would be obvious—but while scripture blinkers the God-fearing, they will continue to interpret the evidence to fit their case. Until we have a reliable and undeniable means of dating rocks and fossilized bones, they will be simply be slotted or jammed into gaps in scriptural chronology. The first few days of creation might have been stretched by interpreters of *Genesis* so that every minute becomes a century, but the elastic will not break unless it suffers a ruder shock than anything that Professor Malet's intimate colleagues and favorite students have so far been able to administer."

"So far," Guérande echoed, as if he were about to follow that line of argument—but he switched tack, and said: "We might have done it already had not so many of the younger generation deserted the cause."

Dupin did not flinch under the tacit accusation. "Students are students, Claude," he said, gently. "They are, by definition, exploring possibilities, not adopting faiths. You can't and shouldn't expect students of science to behave like novices in the Society of Jesus, utterly committed to the Company from the age of five. It's a good thing that students of science go their separate ways, carrying what they've learned into distant provinces and other professions."

"Prefect of Police!" Guérande snorted, as if he could not imagine any lower vocation, thus making the high rank irrelevant. "And...what is exactly *is* your profession, Auguste?"

"My profession," Dupin retorted, calmly, "is to have no profession. I remain a student, in what I hope is the best sense of the word, still exploring, still hunting for pathways to enlightenment, steadfastly refusing to settle into any narrow specialization, in the admittedly-distant hope that I might somehow be able to grasp the whole."

Guérande did not seem convinced. "You weren't such a sophist back in the twenties," he said. "You were better for it, I think."

"The Sophists have had their reputation tarnished by the dogged followers of Socrates," Dupin remarked, "but they, like him, were seekers of the truth, who do not deserve to be crudely lumped together any more than they deserved to be summarily dismissed. If I am a Sophist, so be it—I am proud to be one. Are we not all Pythagoreans at heart, seeking keys to the harmony of the universe, trying to decipher its secret mathematics and arcane logic?"

"And the mystic streak is still there too," Guérande observed. "I always thought you were incorrigible, and here you are to prove it. But you do talk well, and that's something I've missed.

I have Julie, of course, who talks as well as any woman I ever knew, but it's not the same, is it?"

"I must confess that I do not see the difference," Dupin retorted, mildly. "I have the reputation of being a misogynist, but I honestly think myself less so than those men who claim to adore women. Personally, I talk to my concierge, who is one of the wisest people I know."

I was not entirely sure whether that was a mere stratagem or not. I could imagine Dupin talking to his gorgon—but I could not imagine her making any material contribution to the dialogue. On the other hand, it was not inconceivable that she might think the same about me.

Dupin was becoming distinctly breathless after the long climb, and his normal eloquence was being impeded. He did not seem unhappy that Guérande had let the conversation lapse, as the length of his natural stride carried him ahead of us. I wanted to compare notes with him, but it was not the right time.

The third cave-entrance we saw had a more generous opening, although it also seemed to exhibit an intimidating downward slope. Guérande's impatience was visible as he peered into it, and had we not been with him I feel sure that he would have plunged in, if only in order to check the further and narrower tunnels to see whether they were still blocked—but he did not want to do that while we were with him. For the time being, he was clinging to his deeper secrets in a jealous fashion. In order to distract himself he turned way to look back over the valley.

"There's no point in going any higher," he said, "so you might as well enjoy the panorama from here. The mist is still hiding some of the eastern villages, but they're really very much alike, repeating a familiar pattern. That near-rectangular clearing down there is where the Thierachians pitch their camp. I'm slightly surprised that the first caravans haven't yet arrived, and we might well see one or two creeping over the northern ridge on the way down. The view of the château is quite picturesque if you like that sort of thing, although there are much finer castles to the east, hidden by the bulk of Old Dragon. You can see the higher Alpine peaks in the distance, though, still covered in snow. There's not that much going on in the fields just now, but you can see some laborers at work, and traffic on the roads—the place isn't as dead as it sometimes seems, viewed from the windows of the house."

There was a slight edge to the last remark, as if he were replying to a grievance of his wife's. I wondered whether the idea had crossed his mind that she might not have returned from Paris at all...and might be more tempted to go back there more frequently, now that she had caught a further glimpse of it, stirring up all her old memories. He was presumably well aware of the fact that she was eagerly anticipating the moment when the railway line would connect Chalon to Lyon, and make it far easier to travel to the capital from the south, even from a relatively remote district like this one.

I would have been glad to pause a little longer, more to complete my physical recuperation than to enjoy the rather dull view, but once Guérande had decided that we had savored the landscape sufficiently, he set off down hill again, his mighty stride even longer now that the slope was in its favor. Dupin and I did our best to catch up, but we were both toiling, to the extent that we both seemed to be suffering a slight vertigo from the hurried descent.

Eventually, and mercifully, we paused by a spring to eat a little food that Guérande's cook had packed for us before we set out, and to rest our weary legs for a while. I felt quite exhausted, although we had covered no more than ten kilometers, and had taken three hours to do it.

"Why," I said, having taken a draught of water from the spring, "it's rather warm."

"Not uncommon hereabouts," Guérande told me. "Nor in the whole of the Auvergne, in spite of the fact that its volcanic peaks are infinitely quieter than Etna. The geology of the region is beautifully complex, with sedimentary layers of rock alternating with volcanic ones, often magnificently twisted by upheavals of one sort or another. There's nowhere else in France, perhaps in Europe, where ancient fire and water came into such fascinating conflict—and in keeping with the principles of geological uniformitarianism, the conflict is ongoing and everlasting. The fires beneath the Earth's crust have not burst forth here for tens of thousands of years—perhaps hundreds of thousands—but they still seethe below, and their heat snakes upwards capriciously, through countless galleries and fissures, to meet the water that is forever seeping downwards, etching the tunnels as it flows. The rain is eternal, but by no means consistent; hereabouts, its fall is markedly seasonal.

"There are many more caverns beneath our feet than I've so far managed to penetrate, and vast open spaces in which I've hardly set foot, which would take half a lifetime to explore properly. They extend in every direction. Some are always dry, still effectively possessed by fire; others are always filled with water, forming underground lakes and rivers. Every year, when circumstances permit, I go a little further, discover a little more—but the caves know how to tease and tantalize. They promise so much, but always a little further on."

My curiosity got the better of me, and I said: "Have you found human relics, then, like Boucher's flints?"

After a long moment's pause, he said: "Yes I have. Perhaps better than his, although I'd need an expert anatomist like Cuvier to confirm whether there are fragments of elephant and rhinoceros bones among those I've found—but Auguste is right. If I were to show off those I've collected and examined at the house, no one who is not already on our side would be convinced. I'll show them to you, and perhaps you'll be prepared to marvel—but they're not firm proof of anything, as yet. There's more evidence down there, which cannot be removed, but again, anyone who looked at it through the blindfold of faith would simply say that those aspects that are undeniably artificial cannot be very old, while those aspects that belong indubitably to remoter strata cannot be the work of human hands."

"To which category do the flameflowers belong?" I asked, whimsically.

I had no reason to expect the apparent depth of his astonishment, or the violence of his reaction. "Where did you hear mention of flameflowers?" he demanded, in a rude tone that immediately prompted me to protect my source.

"Is it not an item of local folklore?" I said, innocently. "Although I cannot compete with Dupin, I'm something of an antiquary myself. I'm sure that I've read tales in which venturers into caves in the south of France discover flameflowers and other unlikely vegetation. Surely there are similar tales from many regions of Europe?"

Guérande's expression cleared, and he turned to Dupin. "Julie said that you had been to the Bibliothèque Nationale to research Thierachian legendry," he said. "You found the rumors of their worship, I suppose—the rumors alleging that they worship creatures of light that dwell in the darkness of an underworld."

"I did come across references of that sort," Dupin supplied obligingly. "As my friend says, similar ideas are a commonplace of European folklore. Any folklore that imagines an underworld must imagine it lighted, for the sake of narrative convenience, and the ancient imagination could hardly supply it with gas jets or Davy lamps. Flameflowers are an expectable romantic substitute, and very useful to storytellers."

After another slight pause, Guérande said: "If only it were that easy. When the way opens up into the deep caverns where I've made my own discoveries, we'll certainly need Davy lamps, and every other asset that modern miners possess."

"When you refer to them as the deep caverns," I said, eager to change the subject, "I presume you mean deep in a more-or-less horizontal dimension—deep within the mountain—rather than deep in a vertical dimension."

"I mean both," he replied. "The flooding that creates barriers during the winter is superficial, caused by the blocking of narrow passages below the level of the valley by ice, which traps water in a series of chambers far above the mean level of the water-tables. When the ice melts and those chambers clear in their customary gurgling fashion, which happens very rapidly once a critical point is reached—and the effects of which you doubtless heard last night—access is reopened into the central labyrinth, where ice never forms because the rocks are heated from below. I know that there are huge chambers full of water far below, and other water-traps at various heights, but as one gets closer to the heart of the mountain, the temperature rises quite steeply, and I'm sure that there are ancient chimneys in and around the center that lead down to molten rock. Sometimes, the hot rock and the water come into contact, for the hissing sounds that accompany the rumblings and groanings sound very much like sudden evaporation, and the tremors that sometimes afflict the house and its foundations must surely be triggered by the build-up and release of pressure. The temperature of the warm springs varies; at the height of summer, they can become very hot indeed—seventy or eighty degrees—but only briefly. Sometimes, therefore, the fire must ascend within the mountain's core, perhaps to the point where the hot rock emits visible light in locations accessible to human eyes, thus giving birth to rumors of dragon's breath and flameflowers, and doubtless appealing to the mythology that the Thierachians brought to France from God knows where."

"It sounds like a dangerous environment," Dupin observed.

"Perhaps," Guérande replied. "It's not one that I'd advise a novice to venture into—but I've been exploring and mapping for twenty years now. I know the environment, and I know a dozen paths that are safe, once the initial barriers are removed, even for a man of my overgenerous size. I suspect that the people who navigated the caves in the distant past were smaller in stature, for there are openings that bear traces of human handiwork into which I cannot fit."

"What kind of human handiwork?" Dupin was quick to ask.

Guérande hesitated again, but then said: "Nothing spectacular—no pit props, hollowed steps or corridors widened by means of tools, but merely scratches that I take for guidemarks, still visible after centuries...or millennia. When I said 'paths' a little while ago,' I really meant *paths*. I'm not the first man to have walked them, although I might be the first to have walked some of them for thousands of years...except perhaps for Thierachian priests, if they have priests. Such evidence of recent penetration as I've found doesn't go very deep, but that might be because the Thierachians are discreet in what they bring into the caves, and in what they do there. They sometimes tamper with deposits I've made in the superficial caves, but the apparatus and tools that I've stored in the deep caves have never been touched."

"Are there 'paths,' then, that I might be able to explore while you cannot?" Dupin asked.

Guérande did not seem glad to be asked the question. "Height is not the most serious issue," he said. "It's more important to be slim than short. I doubt that you have sufficient advantage in that dimension to go anywhere that I cannot. Twenty-five years ago, perhaps—but most men, when they pass forty, increase their girth markedly. I've been fortunate that my height has always been correlated with slenderness...although it does cause me occasional difficulties in the mountain, which make me wish that I were a shorter man. It would be a shame, would it not, if the humans of the nineteenth century were to be barred from access to the treasures of their remoter ancestors simply because the species has grown larger?"

"It would be an unkind irony of fate, if it were the case," Dupin agreed.

I have to admit that this aspect of the conversation caused me some anxiety. I too was past forty, and although I prided myself on not having allowed myself to run to corpulence, I was no slimmer than Dupin. The idea of squeezing through a narrow slit like the one that Guérande had shown us further down the slope, only to get stuck in one that was even narrower further down, while my lamp ran out of fuel and the mountain hissed, rumbled and quivered, was the stuff of nightmares. The prospect of exploration began to seem a little less exciting, even with the lure of ancient human artifacts and legendary flameflowers to tempt me.

We set off again, heading down the slope. I hoped that we had completed our tour of the rough-hewn hillside, and that Guérande might have postponed his plan to take us further afield to the south and the north to see more "sights." We were heading back in the general direction of the house, moving through thickets of hawthorn along a path that was only wide enough for one of us to pass at a time. The conversation lapsed again as Guérande's long stride carried him into a lead of several meters and I dropped back to allow Dupin to precede me.

Fatigue was now beginning to put lead in my feet, and I had retreated into myself somewhat under the pressure of discomfort, so I was not paying due attention to what was happening ahead of me, and walked straight into Dupin when he stopped dead, bring an extremely uncharacteristic muttered curse from his lips. He, of course, had not committed the same error by walking into our host when Guérande stopped, at one of the many curves in the path.

Guérande had stopped because the way ahead was blocked by another party of three individuals coming in the opposite direction. They too had stopped, of course. It would not have been impossible for the two parties to pass without risking a severe scratching, but it would have required a certain amount of polite negotiation, at a distance that French cultural norms would normally consider too close for comfort. In a sense, we had reached an impasse.

CHAPTER EIGHT
THE BISHOP OF VIVIERS

Positioned at the back of our party, as I was, it was not very easy for me to see what was going on, and Guérande's slenderness did not seem to be making up for his height in terms of blocking the view, but with a certain amount of neck-craning, I was able to make out that all three of the individuals blocking our path—or, I suppose, whose path we were blocking—were wearing clerical garb. The two that I could barely glimpse seemed to be common monks. The one in the lead, although he was not wearing a heavy ceremonial cross, let alone a miter, was obviously a cut above his companions in terms of rank. It was he who overcame the general surprise and spoke.

"Monsieur Guérande, I presume," he said, in a tone that seemed surprisingly smooth and warm. "I'm very glad to make your acquaintance. I intended to call upon you on the way back to the château, in order to introduce myself. I'm Philippe Aignan, Bishop of Viviers. This is Brother Xavier, and the poor fellow you can hardly see is Brother Michael."

I have no idea what Simon de Montfort looked like, but Philippe Aignan did not conform to my notion of the kind of man who would launch a "crusade" against the land of Oc on the grounds that there were heretics lurking among its pious Christian citizens and merry troubadours, and, when asked how the heretics were to be identified, was content to reply: "Kill them all—God will know his own," or words to that effect. I will not say that Aignan looked like a kindly man, but he did have the appearance of a civilized one, and an intelligent one. His features were a trifle gaunt, but his once-slim body had acquired the same kind of extra girth, common to men in their forties, that I had, suggestive of a calm temperament and an adequate digestion, There was nothing angry or aggressive about the manner in which he was looking at us, even though we were manifestly in his way.

Guérande seemed as surprised by the friendly tone as I was, although he doubtless had the same suspicion that it was deceptive. "I'm Claude Guérande," he admitted, reflexively. I presume that his interlocutor must have possessed an effective interrogatory gaze, for he only hesitated briefly before saying: "This is an old friend of mine from Paris, the Chevalier Auguste Dupin, and his friend from America, Samuel Reynolds."

"A Chevalier of the Légion d'honneur!" said the Bishop, who did not seem to recognize Dupin's name at all but had taken due note of the slight stress Guérande had put on Dupin's honorary title. "I'm honored to meet you, Monsieur Dupin." He raised his voice slightly to add: "And you too, Monsieur Reynolds." Then he reverted to his normal tone to say: "This really is a most inconvenient meeting-place. Fortunately, once we have negotiated a practicable crossing of our paths, we shall be able to look forward to a better one. My good friend the Comte de Tibère has authorized me to issue an invitation to you, Monsieur Guérande, and your wife, to dine at the château this evening, and I am sure that he will not mind my extending the invitation to embrace your two friends from Paris."

If Guérande had been surprised before, he was astonished now. Invitations to the château were obviously exceedingly rare. He was certainly in no hurry to accept, but he did not seem quite able to refuse. He was, after all, addressing a Bishop, and even evolutionists cannot help feeling a certain awe in the presence of the luminaries of the Church.

After a few seconds, the Bishop said: "I understand your reluctance, Monsieur Guérande. My friend has explained to me that there has been a certain amount of bad blood between your two families in the past. I consider it a part of my pastoral duty to attempt to mend such quarrels whenever I can. I wish you would come. Neighbors ought not to be at odds, especially in regions where neighbors are so few and far between."

It seemed to me that if neighbors were going to be at odds, then being few and far between was their ideal situation, but it would hardly have been a diplomatic remark to make, even had I been in a situation to make it. Although Dupin was between us I could see the back of Guérande's head clearly enough, and it is surprising how much one can read from the back of a man's head when he is tense with frustration. I saw Dupin reach out to take his arm, trying to signal to him, evidently counseling caution and discretion—but he was a little too late.

"Will Maître Lebrun be there?" Guérande asked, gruffly.

By craning my neck, I could see Aignan's face, and the surprise thereon seemed genuine enough to me. A lesser man might have blurted out: "Who?" but all that the Bishop said was: "I fear that I am not acquainted with any gentleman of that name. There is no one staying at the château but myself and my companions."

Dupin's pressure on Guérande's arm became urgent and intimate, in spite of the fact that the two men hardly knew one another any longer. Dupin had obviously taken Lucien Groix's advice to heart, and was very enthusiastic to see the matter of the Bishop's involvement handled diplomatically, if possible. In any case, he was probably very curious to see the château and meet the eccentric Comte.

Guérande capitulated with the inevitable. "Thank you," he said, probably as warmly as he could. "My wife and I will be pleased to come. Monsieur Dupin?"

"My friend and I will be delighted to accept your invitation," Dupin put in. "It's very kind of you to include us."

"Excellent!" said the Bishop. "Shall we say six-thirty?" For Dupin's benefit, he added: "People dine earlier hereabouts than in Paris." Swiftly, he went on to say: "And now, I believe that if we turn our bodies sideways and extend a little Christian charity to one another, we might pass by without undue difficulty or injury."

About that, he was right, although I had to hold in my stomach, in order to avoid actual physical contact with the Bishop himself. Fortunately, the two monks were not nearly as rotund as the majority of their Parisian brethren. Indeed, their weather-beaten complexions and muscular build made them seem more like soldiers than idlers, and I could not help remembering the flippant remark about warrior monks and inquisitors that had passed without comment earlier, as well as my own reflections about Simon de Montfort's short way with suspected Cathars.

Once the passage had been safely negotiated, Guérande, Dupin and I waited until there was a good hundred yards between the two parties—by which distance the path had widened out somewhat and we had come back into the bracken—before any of us spoke.

"He's on his way to the caves," Guérande said, darkly. "Scouting the lie of the land, no doubt. He'll have difficulty finding them, though. If they do, I can only hope that they try to go in, and drown."

"It will be better by far if they do not," Dupin murmured.

"He didn't seem to know your lawyer from Lyon, though," Guérande said. "Is it possible that the Comte hasn't told him?"

"If he did recognize the name, he's a very good actor," Dupin admitted. "But he *is* a Bishop, and I doubt that one could rise to such a position in today's Church without being a skillful dissimulator. The Jesuits have set new standards for clerical cunning, alas."

Guérande was in no mood for witty banter. "I can't imagine why Tibère would invite us to dinner, if it isn't to gloat over some bad news," he said, grimly, "and what bad news could he possibly have to give us, if not some discovery relating to the land?"

"If it is the documents from the Archives with which the Bishop and the Comte wish to confront us," Dupin mused, "the probability is that Maître Lebrun was merely a clerk, sent to Paris by a notary whose name the Bishop would have recognized. Whatever the documents imply, though, they could do no more than initiate a problematic lawsuit that might be dragged through the court for years. You might have a more urgent problem on your hands, if the appearance of those two Dominicans is anything to go by."

"They certainly looked like soldiers," I said, skeptically, "but this is the nineteenth century—Bishops don't have private armies any more, and even Bohemians have the protection of the law."

"You didn't study their hands closely enough, my friend," Dupin said. "Those calluses are certainly not typical of men who routinely wield swords or fire muskets. I've seen their like before, though. Even the monasteries of Paris require continual upkeep, and since the monks resident therein have lost some of the artisanal skills that were once required, they import specialist laborers from the south when they require the aid of expert stonemasons."

"Stonemasons!" Guérande exclaimed. "You mean that Tibère has plans to renovate the château. What has that to do with the Church—or with me?"

"I suppose that it *is* a possibility that the Comte wishes to make repairs to the château," Dupin conceded, slightly wearily.

"I think that what my friend means, Monsieur Guérande," I interjected, helpfully, "is that the Comte and the Bishop are considering the possibility of blocking up the entrances to your tunnels—or *his* tunnels, as the Comte evidently considers them to be."

Guérande paled slightly—but only slightly. "They'll never find them all," he muttered. "Even if...."

"I think they might find the ones you judge most useful very easily," Dupin replied, "given that you and the Thierachians have left them so many indications by keeping the paths clear."

"The Thierachians will surely tear down anything they build, even if I can't," Guérande said, curtly.

"That might not be easy," Dupin said, thoughtfully. "Our notions of mechanical progress are focused on steam engines, railways and electricity, but there has been significant progress in many humbler crafts too, including the art of cementation. The recent invention of Portland cement in England has added significantly to the binding force of concrete. Although it is proverbially easier to destroy than to build, I think you might find that blocking tunnels, with the aid of modern methods, is a good deal easier than opening them."

"Would they really take the trouble, merely to frustrate scientific enquiry?"

"Probably not—but to frustrate heretics, perhaps. If the Bishop were to succeed in provoking the Thierachians to violence...which would be atypical of them, I know, but when matters of deep-seated tradition are at stake...and if you were to join forces with the Thierachians against the Church and the Lord of the Manor...well, if Lucien Groix's colleagues have caught wind of this possibility, I can understand his anxiety a little better. But what is the Bishop's pretext? He would surely need a far better reason for taking such strange action than the desire to provoke a violent reaction, and a more plausible one than any title deed moldering in the National Archives could possibly provide. There is something we do not know, Claude—and must try to find out tonight....unless, of course, the whole purpose of the Comte's invitation is to confront us with the surprise, in which case no cunning interrogation will be necessary."

Although we were heading in the general direction of the house, Guérande took yet another side path, heading northwards toward the head of the valley. I stopped again. "Do you think we might return to the house to rest for a while first?" I asked. "I'm a little tired."

For a moment, I thought that Guérande would tell me to go back by myself while he and Dupin continued, but the duties of hospitality immediately claimed the upper hand.

"Of course," he said. "Forgive me—I'm used to the terrain,

but city-dwellers...the Butte of Montmartre is steep enough, I suppose, but it's a mere hillock compared with the slopes hereabouts. There's nothing much to see where the Thierachians make camp, in any case, until they actually return."

We made our way back to the house at what probably seemed to Guérande to be a snail's pace, although it seemed very brisk to me, and were soon comfortably ensconced in his study.

Madame Guérande took the news of the dinner invitation very well, I thought; she seemed glad, if only because it would give Dupin a chance to weigh up one of her husband's two sets of opponents. Nevertheless, she took the first opportunity that presented itself to speak to Dupin in her husband's absence, prepared to ignore the fact that I was still with him.

"How does he seem?" she demanded.

"Claude?" Dupin parried, although she could not possibly have meant anyone else. "Quite well, I think—he is certainly physically fit. Perhaps he is a trifle anxious in his haste to resume the work that he was forced to suspend some months ago—but there are many scientists of my acquaintance who would have been far more feverish after such an interval. If you cast your mind back...."

"Yes, yes," said Madame Guérande. "Men of science are a breed apart, who cannot be measured by conventional standards of sanity. I know all that. You must go to the village when you can—with me, if possible—in order to see the signs of the more general apprehension. I do not say that I haven't seen it before, but it's more intense this year than last. Coming back from Paris, I found it almost palpable, especially in the house. Do you not feel it yourself, Auguste?"

"I did not sleep well last night," Dupin admitted. "I lay awake listening to the sleeping dragon—and for other sounds that might signify something disturbing. I did feel a trifle nervous, it's true, but that would not be unusual, in the circumstances, and you've said yourself more than once that nothing truly supernatural is happening here. On the other hand, I do feel a trifle relieved that the Bishop's bed is located on that high crag, where the sounds of the meltwater are far beyond the limits of aural perception."

"He's gone to the caves, though," I reminded him. "He'll be able to hear the hypothetical dragon from there—and if his faith is sincere, he's a man who can put his own dire interpretation on the phenomena."

"Perhaps," Dupin conceded. "Let's not anticipate, though. Even a man sincere in his faith might be capable of making an intelligent judgment of the situation. No matter how enthusiastic he is to persecute the Thierachians, he's probably too wise to believe that the Devil has any active involvement in their annual pilgrimage. In a way, it might be better if he were not, for if his intentions could be deflected in the direction of a harmless exorcism rather than violence against the living—especially if he could convince himself that it had worked, and quieted the source of evil...."

"You surely don't intend to try to persuade him that the Devil is responsible for the mountain's mutterings?" said Madame Guérande.

"No," Dupin admitted. "That would be dishonest, even if I had any confidence that it might work—but if, perchance, the Bishop's ideas are deflected in that direction of their own accord, I shall not try to talk him out of it at dinner tonight."

CHAPTER NINE
THE DIMINUTION OF THE SEA

As the day wore on, I observed that Dupin was still handling Claude Guérande very gently, respectful of his reluctance to speak freely about whatever discoveries he had made inside the mountain. I knew, though, that he was hopeful that time would wear away the resistance, and that the other would gradually slip back into the frame of mind that had once secured a close friendship between the two of them.

When Dupin asked to see the flints and bone fragments that Guérande had brought out of the caves, I felt sure that their examination would give Dupin the opportunity to winkle out the whole story—but when Guérande let us in to the room where they were stored, he left us there alone. "I'll be interested to hear your impressions," he said to Dupin, "all the more so since you've seen Boucher's specimens, and will be able to compare his finds with mine.

Dupin did not seem to mind the stratagem; he was, inevitably, exceedingly interested in the flints and bones alike, and he spent a long time examining each item one by one—especially the bone fragments, of which there were more than two hundred, as compared with only two dozen flints.

"Are there human bones among them?" I asked him, curiously.

"I believe so," he said. "I'm not an expert anatomist, but I'm reasonably convinced. More interesting, perhaps, are the animal bones that have apparently been worked by tools in order to sharpen them, and those which are charred, having presumably been subjected to cooking fires. Again, I cannot be absolutely sure, but I believe that some of these bones belonged to animals now extinct, at least in Europe—but there is nothing from which the most imaginative Cuvierist could construct a megatherium, alas. Most are the remains of sheep, goats, deer, cattle and horses, although some vary from the modern representatives of those genera. A skeptic, of course, might argue that the human bones might have been added to the ossuary at a far later date than the earliest animal bones, and that the use of stone tools on the bones might also have taken place long after the animals died, but even so, I wish that Guérande had presented this evidence to the Academy. The more specimens we accumulate, the more convincing the argument becomes."

"These are interesting too," I observed, picking up a piece of pumice stone that had been carved into an apparent representation of a horse's head, and a flat sheet of stone on which something that might have been an image of a bison's head had been scratched. There were half a dozen other items of a similar kind.

"Yes, indeed," Dupin agreed. "But those seem to be far more recent—that's not the work of a flint knife. The horse's head, at least, cannot be very old. My impression is that these remains were abandoned over a very long time span, but the presence within the collection of some items that are evidently recent, geologically speaking, would give succor to any creationist intent on arguing that they must all be post-diluvian."

"But Guérande will show us what is in the caves," I said. "That will surely make a stronger case—and three witnesses are better than one."

"Not to eyes blinkered by faith," Dupin said. "In any case, it is not to find out what is presently to be seen in the caves that Julie brought me here—it is to discover what Claude believes to be there that will not let him let up in his obsessive quest."

"Flameflowers?" I suggested.

It was as if the comment triggered a memory of something Dupin had intended to ask me. "Where *did* you hear mention of that word?" he wanted to know.

"Sophie," I told him. "I didn't want to tell Guérande in case he was angry with her. She seems deeply anxious about something, but I don't know what—and I don't believe she does either. She thinks her father is in danger, though—or perhaps will be, if he goes back into the caves. Have you heard of flameflowers?"

"Only from Julie—but I did approve of your improvised explanation. Similar ideas do crop up very often in folklore, which is as rich in underworlds as it is in dragons."

We completed our examination without our host returning to enquire about our impressions. In the end, we had to go in search of Guérande ourselves. We found him in his study. Dupin must have been a little annoyed with him, because he did not wax as enthusiastic about the bones as I had expected, and even put on a show of diffidence, in declaring them "less interesting as Boucher's recent discoveries at Menchecourt, alas." I guessed that he thought the tacit disparagement to be the most likely stratagem to draw Guérande out further, and spur him to boast about his other discoveries—but it did not seem to be working, for the moment, and Guérande retreated into sullen disappointment rather than responding to the challenge.

I felt that it was my duty to help the situation along, but also felt that it might be best to do so indirectly, by addressing questions to Dupin and hoping to lure Guérande gradually into the meat of the conversation.

"I took the opportunity to finish reading your copy of *Telliamed* before I tried to go to sleep last night," I said, by way of an opening, "but I could not find much in the published text regarding the evolution of animals. Perhaps Monsieur Guérande would also be interested to hear about the unpublished parts of the manuscript, to which you have recently had access."

Guérande nodded to concede that he would, indeed, be interested. His sulkiness did not disappear at once, but we certainly had his attention.

"There's much more in the manuscript than made it into print," Dupin said. "The crucial part of the argument is, of course, the notion that all terrestrial organisms are descended from marine ones—a probability that has become much stronger since Maillet's day, by courtesy of more comprehensive analyses of a larger range of fossils. There are, however, some interesting speculations regarding the manner in which that might have happened.

"The Chevalier de Lamarck's suggestions regarding the possible mechanism of evolution relies heavily on the notion of continuous and stubborn effort on the part of organisms to improve themselves. According to the Chevalier, all organisms are driven by some king of internal impulse, which ensures that they are all evolving, albeit imperceptibly. I always felt, even in the days when I used to participate in Professor Malet's salons, that there was something awkward about that notion, because it did not seem to me to account for the vast differences of complexity and sophistication that exist between living species. If simpler creatures have evolved into more complex ones—from monad to man, as the fashionable phase has it—over thousands or millions of generations by virtue of some universal impulse, why have some come so far while others have not even transcended the utmost simplicity. Claude will doubtless remember the various arguments that Achille Mallet raised to my objection, which I need not repeat.

"Maillet offers a different perspective. Imagining the level of the sea gradually diminishing, exposing more and more land, he suggests that the organisms left behind by that retreat would have been under tremendous pressure to adapt or perish. Most, he supposes, perished—but any that did contrive to adapt to the changing conditions with sufficient swiftness would then have had a whole new realm at the disposal of their progeny. Given that organisms vary naturally among themselves, Maillet imagines that certain individuals or families might have been equipped by the hazard of those natural variations to survive where other members of their species could not. In this view, the active efforts of the organisms to modify themselves, though not irrelevant, only come into play when changing circumstances provide a stern challenge—thus explaining why some ancestral lines remain unmodified, whereas others undertake great leaps forward in terms of complexity and capacity. It is, at least, an intriguing notion, and it is a great shame that it was lost to academic discussion for more than a hundred and fifty years."

"Geoffroy Saint-Hilaire broached a similar notion," Guérande reminded him, his interest evidently piqued.

"He did," Dupin admitted, "but rather tentatively—his notion of the remote past had been formed by Cuvier's description of the Epochs of Nature, which offered a more complex pattern of development that Maillet's singular retreat of the waters, even though Maillet did suggest that the process might have been reiterated, perhaps infinitely. Cuvier himself, of course, was convinced that each new epoch required a new creation, but Maillet's thesis is adaptable, provided that we think in terms of his timescale—which is to say, in terms of billions of years—rather than the hundreds of thousands that Cuvier was prepared to entertain."

"Can the Earth really be billions of years old?" I asked.

"Why not?" Dupin countered. "Once, we imagined that the universe was no larger than a series of crystal spheres in which the Earth was embedded, extending for a few hundreds of thousands of kilometers—but every estimate of distance that telescopic astronomy has allowed us to make assures us now that the stars are billions of kilometers apart. If that expansion of our notion of space were matched with a similar expansion of our notion of time, it would reduce human existence to a very small margin indeed—but why should it not be true?"

Dupin, I knew was convinced that our margin of existence was very much smaller than that, because he believed that there were an exceedingly large number of parallel universes filling what appears to our senses to be "empty space," but that did not seem to be relevant to the present discussion.

"It would, I suppose, require billions of years, if all life on Earth were to have evolved from a single monad," I mused. "But where did that monad come from?"

"Several writers, from Christiaan Huygens onward, have suggested that the seeds of life might be widely distributed throughout the universe," Dupin said, "and that they literally rain down to planets from the sky—a hypothesis to which Maillet seemed to be sympathetic, although he remained neutral. At some stage in the story, however, there must indeed have been a first monad, which emerged from inert organic matter by discovering the secret of reproduction. Personally, I find it easier to imagine that within the framework of Maillet's thesis—as a freak of chance—than within the framework of Lamarck's, which would invites us to imagine some kind of vital impulse in embryo in inert matter, prior to the advent of life itself."

"But whether the origin of life was a matter of natural hazard or mineral effort," I said, "one might surely expect it to have happened more than once, over a span of billions of years. In that case, the apparent kinship between living species—an important prop for your theory evolutionism—would surely show us more distinct kinship groupings resulting from several distinct origins. Isn't that what you called *polygeny*?"

"It's one version of it," Dupin agreed, nodding in approval. "We have to remember, however, that living organisms prey upon one another. If the descendants of one primal monad evolved more rapidly, or more variously, than the descendants of other monads, they might simply have consumed the early products of rival emergences."

"Making us the ultimate descendants of the fiercest and most gluttonous of the monad clans," I remarked. "That sounds plausible."

"It's not obvious," Guérande put in, thoughtfully, "that all the extant species we've described do descend from a single original monad. There are polygenists among the ranks of contemporary evolutionists, as you doubtless remember from the old days, Auguste. Nor is it obvious that we have yet discovered all the extant species that there are in the remoter regions of the Earth. In Maillet's thesis, as you've described it, the only kind of environmental challenge effective in shaping life on land was the gradual diminution of the sea, but when you add in the various kinds of upheavals imagined by Cuvier—which imagine crises of vulcanism as well as crises involving deluges and the subsequent retreat of waters—the possibility arises that monads of a very different kind might have arisen, in places inaccessible to our easy examination...beneath the earth's surface, for instance."

"It's an interesting hypothesis," Dupin agreed, in a carefully considered tone reflective—if only to my ears—of the success of our ploy, in drawing him out, "but I can see one obvious objection to it."

If he hoped to score a point by forcing his old rival to ask what that objection was, he failed. "The absence of light," Guérande said, confidently. "The ultimate powerhouse of life on the surface of the earth—and in the sea too, so far as we can tell—is the sun. Sunlight fuels plant growth, and plants provide further fuel to animals. In the darkness, life cannot develop...not, at least, the kind of life that we find on the surface of the Earth. But there is energy of a different sort far below: the energy of heat. Suppose monads were to emerge in the planet's core that took their fundamental fuel from heat rather than light, converting it into vegetable flesh—or something akin thereto—which could, in its turn, provide fuel for organisms akin to animals."

"Again, an interesting hypothesis," Dupin admitted—but did not follow up with a question, evidently hoping to draw Guérande out more subtly.

"Then again," I said, letting the idea out as it occurred to me, "if there were monads deep in the earth capable of reproducing themselves, they might be able to convert heat into light as well as flesh, just as herbivorous mammals produce their own internal heat with the aid of vegetable flesh. Then there really might be flameflowers, as legend suggests."

"There are luminescent organisms," Dupin added, swiftly, perhaps to deflect attention away from the specific term I had used. "Fireflies, and certain deep-sea fish."

"If you're trying to tempt me to admit you that I'm searching for evidence of that kind of life in the labyrinth on Vivarais," Guérande said, a trifle resentfully, but with a sigh, "I'll gladly admit that I would love to find something of the sort—but I repeat that I have seen no flameflowers, and have no strong reason, as yet, to think that Thierarchian legendry regarding creative lights beneath the earth is any more than legend."

"Have you persuaded them to talk to you about their legends, then?" Dupin asked.

"No," Guérande confessed, after a momentary hesitation. "I've tried hard, but...."

"You've found some other source of information about their beliefs, then, inside the caves," Dupin deduced. "Immovable artifacts of some kind. Carvings, of course...and paintings? Murals on the walls of the caves? Murals depicting animals... but also depicting mysterious luminous entities, which might conceivably be flameflowers?"

Guérande shook his head, dolefully. "Half a day," he murmured. "I remember now Auguste, how clever you used to be in penetrating secrets. For twenty years, I've kept my secret from everyone but the Thierachians, who know full well what I've seen in the caves—but in half a day, you've wormed it out of me, without even seeming to make an effort. There's something of the magician about you, Monsieur Dupin."

"Not at all," said Dupin. "My logic was perfectly clear, I believe—and anyone could have followed it, had they had the inclination. Am I correct, then?"

Guérande sighed again. "Insultingly correct," he said. "Not a single mistake...and virtually no omissions. I must be a great deal more transparent than I thought...or Julie must have deduced far more than I ever told her explicitly."

"It was simple logic," Dupin insisted. "Anyone could have done it. Are you sure that Tibère and Aignan have not made similar deductions?"

"I'm perfectly sure that they haven't read *Telliamed*, let alone the unpublished sections of the manuscript," Guérande replied, "but the local folklore suggests, if you read it from the appropriate angle, that plenty of other people have been into the caves in the past, although it's probable that not all of them have come out again. I seriously doubt that they've ever seen flameflowers, but they might have said they had, to make their boastful tales more interesting. If they saw even a few of the paintings... well, there's nothing else like them in the world, Auguste. No, that's wrong—there probably are, perhaps scattered all over the Auvergne, and the Alps and Pyrenees too; but no one else has found them yet, because they're so well-hidden. They're not so very far removed from the art-work that the Thierachians still make, for the most part, but they're certainly more mysterious... very old, and very nearly, if not actually, magical. They're *very* old, Auguste. There are many more bone fragments in the caves, of course—animal bones, mostly, like the ones you've just been looking at, some charred, some bearing the marks of stone tools. I've yet to find a reliable yardstick, but I believe some of the paintings to be tens of thousands of years old, although others have been retouched more recently. If their representations can be trusted...well, I suppose you'll see for yourself in a day or two, and perhaps you'll be able to tell me whether I'm mad or not."

"The Comte de Tibère might not have read *Telliamed*," I put in, thoughtfully, "but if he's old and stuck in the past, he must be very familiar with local folklore—more so that you, perhaps. He might not take peasants' talk of flameflowers very seriously, but he might be convinced nevertheless that there's *something* in the caves. If descriptions have been handed down of these paintings and carvings....there's a good deal of folklore in the Midi, if I'm not mistaken, that attributes residences in these mountains to the devil's minions. Much of it was probably invented in the days of the Cathar Crusade, but even so...and if the Bishop of Viviers really is an admirer of Simon de Montfort...we might be living in the nineteenth century, but there are Churchmen a-plenty in America who believe that that Devil is still very active in the world, and I dare say that French Catholicism is by no means free of such conviction. What you said about the Bishop's possible reaction to the mountain's murmurs, Dupin, doesn't seem so implausible any more...."

"You're suggesting that the Bishop might use the possible presence of the Devil's imps inside the mountain as a pretext for blocking its issues?" Guérande said, skeptically.

"No," I said, working through the idea as it occurred to me, "I'm suggesting that he might *really believe* that there's something diabolical under the mountain, and that the Thierachians are genuinely under its sway. Faith is a dangerous thing, Monsieur Guérande, and when recent Christian crusaders have found clear evidence of idolatry in America, they've been known to act in haste, and violently. Perhaps the Bishop has asked you to dine at the château because he wants you to show him the murals, so he can judge for himself what meaning they might contain—and if you refuse, he and his friars are probably perfectly capable of finding them for themselves."

"He mustn't be allowed to damage the artifacts," Guérande said. "We must prevent that, at all costs. I don't care what he believes—they're the most precious works of art on French soil, the Classical sculptures and Old Masters in the Parisian collections notwithstanding. At least the Thierachians know that I've treated everything within the caves with appropriate reverence. If the Bishop decides that they're idolatrous, and need to be smashed, imprisoned or painted over, the Thierachians *will* react, I'm sure of it—and God only knows where that might end."

"The unease has reached Paris already," Dupin said, pensively. "By chance rather than design, I seem to have become an ambassador of sorts. The Bishop did not seem to me to be an altogether unreasonable man, though—it's not impossible that we can come to some understanding with him, practically if not intellectually. We should at least, be able to discover this evening whether he is willing to listen as well as to talk. Opening a dialogue with the Thierachians might be even harder, though...."

"I need more time, Auguste," Guérande stated, bluntly.

"What I have already discovered might change our notion of the origins of humankind, but what I might still discover could change our notion of the origins of life. I need time, to continue my explorations."

"If you had appealed for help fifteen, ten, or even five years ago, Claude," Dupin said, with a hint of reproach, "you might have made your crucial discovery long ago. You had students of your own at the university, in Malet's day—you would have found the assistance you needed easily enough. You might even have asked Julie. You had no need to be so jealous of your discovery and so secretive in trying to complete it."

The choice of the term "jealous" was perhaps a trifle unfortunate; Dupin could, after all, have restricted himself to "secretive." Guérande was as sensitive as I was to the potential double meaning inherent in the word "jealous," as applied to things he had been keeping from Dupin for fifteen years.

"She's my wife," was all that Guérande said, perhaps in reply to the suggestion that he could have recruited her as a research assistant. Perhaps all he meant to imply, I told myself, was that he would never dream of subjecting his wife to the dangers inherent in subterranean exploration—but I didn't believe it.

CHAPTER TEN
DINNER AT THE CHÂTEAU

We set out for the château at six, in a carriage drawn by a pair of horses that seemed to me to be a trifle on the small side.

"To tell the truth," said Madame Guérande, when I commented to that effect, "we'd probably be safer being pulled by the donkeys, for the road around the crag is a poor one and the donkeys very sure-footed, even when fully-laden—but the horses are local, and well-used to the terrain. I only hope that the carriage will not be overloaded with four passengers, given that they're rarely asked to bear such a burden."

In fact, the horses coped very well with the spiral climb up the crag on which the château was situated, and I dare say that I would have had a comfortable journey had I only taken the precaution to sit on the side of the vehicle that traveled beside the wall of the crag rather than the side that overlooked the sometimes-sheer drop. I survived with only a few dire flutterings of the heat and mild vertigo, however, and consoled myself with the thought that if I retained the same position on the way down, I would not have to imagine the drop so close at hand in the pitch darkness.

We were ushered into what must once have been an authentic banqueting hall, complete with a minstrel's gallery, although there were no minstrels on hand and the dining-table that had been laid for six seemed very tiny, becalmed as it was in the middle of such a vast tiled floor. Obviously, the Bishop's stonemason monks had been relegated to the parlor where the servants ate.

The food was mediocre and the wine poor, but I was grateful to both, in that they saved me from paying any great heed to the conversation. The convention that serious matters are not to be discussed until the coffee is served evidently extends far beyond Paris, but it was equally evident, that evening, that it can cause considerable stress where Parisian urbanity is conspicuously lacking.

The Comte, I have to admit, did not seem conspicuously crazy. He made every effort to be polite, and to fulfill his duties as a host conscientiously. Indeed, I got the unexpected impression that he was at more odds with the Bishop than with Claude Guérande—or, at least, more at odds with the Churchman than with Madame Guérande, whom he had seated to his left, and to whom he made every attempt to be courteous, even charming. Aignan, who was seated to his right, the Comte seemed to be intent on ignoring as much as possible. That compelled the Bishop to spend much of the time in conversation with Dupin, who was seated to his own right. I was placed between Guérande and his wife, opposite Dupin, but no one was interested in me— which was perhaps as well, given the intensity with which my companions were studying their potential adversaries.

The Comte must have been over seventy, and had dressed himself as his father might have dressed while Louis XVI was still in his heyday, in a bizarre purple frock-coat, with an antique wig. Indeed, had he taken the extra step of powdering his face, he would have been a complete grotesque, but he was evidently resigned to his florid complexion. He could not have been much more than a child when the Revolution had broken out, but he had obviously had abundant time to absorb the attitudes and manners of the day, and probably felt a little slighted that no one had ever thought him worth guillotining. He obviously knew that Julie Guérande was the product of a very different era, having been born at the dawn of the Bonaparte's Empire, but that only made him try harder to impress her with obsolete gallantries.

If the Bishop was offended by the Comte's neglect, he showed no sign of it, but seemed genuinely interested in Dupin—not that he asked him any impertinently personal questions. Instead, he asked him questions about Paris, which he had visited on occasion, and its monuments, gladly sharing his own impressions of Notre-Dame, Saint-Sulpice, the Sorbonne, the Luxembourg Gardens and the Tuileries, with only the lightest spice of political enquiry.

Guérande was quiet, content to wait for the real purpose of the assembly to arrive, but he rarely took his eyes off the Comte, and did not seem to approve of the attention that Tibère was paying to his wife. Madame Guérande did not seem to mind overmuch, although she occasionally turned to me for momentary relief—hopelessly, as the Comte was always quick to reclaim her attention with comical imperiousness. It was obviously the first time that she had been to the château as a guest, although Guérande did not seem to be a stranger to the place, and I wondered whether the animosity that Guérande had inherited from his father and grandfather might have been laid to rest long ago if only he had recruited his wife to soothe the way to a reconciliation, in the role of peacemaker.

It occurred to me one again that the adorable Julie must have found a very sharp contrast between the exceedingly sheltered life she had been forced to live in the Ardèche and her earlier life as the peripheral star of Achille Malet's Parisian town-house. She might have been less lonely had she had more children, and sooner, but there had obviously been some slight difficulty in that regard, revealed in the extent to which both parents doted over Sophie, as well as the fact that she had arrived late in the marriage and had remained an only child.

Finally, the awkward formalities ran their course, and it was time to get down to brass tacks. The Comte could not suggest that the men withdraw, in order to leave the ladies to their own idiosyncratic chatter, because that would have meant leaving Madame Guérande on her own, so we stayed where we were, with Julie Guérande both present and eagerly attentive.

It was, inevitably, the Bishop who took the floor. "I consider myself to be here in the role of a diplomat," he told us. "My friend the Comte has acquainted me with his long-standing quarrel with the Guérande family—whose continuation seems to have become slightly absurd, given that it began in political disputes with the present Monsieur Guérande's father and grandfather. There has been resentment on the Comte's side, of course, in the context of the confiscation of his property by the local Jacobins in the wake of the Revolution of 1789, and he has long felt a moral entitlement to be considered Monsieur Guérande's landlord—but I have persuaded him that there are times when one simply has to accept the vicissitudes of fortune.

"He has long considered, too, that he ought to be acknowledged as the owner of the tract of land to the east of Monsieur Guérande's property, on the slopes of the hill known in the vicinity as Mont Dragon—which, so far as my own meager enquiries have contrived to ascertain, was thrown into a kind of legal limbo by the ill-drafted order of confiscation, having no permanent residents to whom title was effectively granted. Again, I have persuaded the Comte that there is no point whatsoever in trying to assert a claim to ownership through the existing tribunals, given that any such suit would be unlikely to reach a conclusion while he is still alive, and that his two sons, both resident in Paris, show not the slightest interest even in the remaining part of the estate. They are likely to sell the château itself once he dies, with all its possessions, however limited. In my view, these circumstances remove the basis for any significant dispute between the Comte and Monsieur Guérande, who might easily be reconciled with a little good will on both sides."

He paused. Everyone, I think, was waiting for a "but" or a "however." No one said a word.

"Indeed," the Bishop continued, "I believe that there might be significant gains for both parties were they to join forces against a common...nuisance, which the long-standing coldness between the families has allowed to fester unchecked. I refer, of course, to the so-called Thierachians, who have made it a habit to maintain a presence in the valley for several months every year, routinely holding larger gatherings in the spring, shortly after the equinox, and in the autumn, shortly before the equinox. That the Thierachians are pagans, and therefore devil-worshipers, is not in doubt...."

"If you will forgive me, Seigneur," Dupin put in, seemingly trying to match the other for unctuousness, "I'm a stranger here, and perhaps have no right to express an opinion, but I do beg leave to doubt that the Thierachians are devil-worshipers. Pagans, perhaps; vagabonds, certainly; but not devil-worshipers. From what I can gather, they are a mild-mannered folk who never cause any serious difficulty...."

"You're right, Sir," Tibère cut in. "You have no right to express an opinion, since you are not acquainted with the facts. If the Bohemians were merely common thieves, that would be one thing, but they are child-stealers, and that cannot be tolerated—and you, Monsieur Guérande, ought to be as anxious about that now as I once was."

Guérande seemed startled by that gibe, and Madame Guérande frowned.

"Forgive me, Seigneurs," Dupin said, again, "but I am familiar with that accusation, as a slander leveled at traveling folk everywhere. Child-stealing by Bohemians is nowadays commonplace as a conventional item of popular fiction—indeed, half the melodramas played out in the theaters of the Boulevard du Temple in Paris are dependent upon it for their plots, and even Victor Hugo did not consider it unworthy of use in *Notre-Dame de Paris*—but I find it hard to believe that it is anywhere near as commonplace in the real world, especially since the prevalence of the myth means that Thierachian encampments would be the first place searched by the agents of the law, if and when a child were to go missing."

"It's happened in my own family, damn it, less than a century ago," said the Comte, hotly, "and there are dozens more cases on record, as the Bishop has contrived to ascertain, by means of a disciplined search of parish records. If it happens less commonly today than it did in my grandfather's time, it's because the valley is no longer as populous as it once was—and that's because so many families moved out rather than risk having their own children stolen. This is history, not rumor, as the Bishop has proved—if only he would take proper heed of his own evidence."

"Is this true?" Guérande asked the Bishop, concerned now.

"It is true that I ordered a search of local parish records—which have, thankfully, survived in greater quantities than the records held in the Mairies of the region, which have suffered the ravages of our turbulent era. It is true, too, that I have found evidence of a worrying pattern of missing children, distributed over a century and a half, although it has been ameliorated in recent times. However...."

"My own family, damn it," the Comte repeated. "The damned Bohemians even had the nerve to steal one of my great-grandfather's own children. The camp was turned upside-down at the time, but not a hair from the poor boy's head was found—but that must be because they spirited him out of the valley before the searchers came."

The Bishop waited for him to finish, and then resumed what he had been saying: "However," he said, "I am inclined to agree with Monsieur Dupin that the reason the Thierachians were blamed for these disappearances owes more to legend than to evidence. As he has said, and my friend the Comte has confirmed, the first action taken when any such disappearance occurs, is always to search the local Bohemian encampments—and there has not been a single instance, so far as I can ascertain, when any child other than their own has been found in the possession of Thierachians or any other vagabonds. That they are devil-worshipers, in spite of Monsieur Dupin's objection, there is no doubt, but that they are child-stealers, there has never been any solid evidence. There is, however, evidence of a different sort, which might offer a more likely explanation of what happened to the missing children."

Suddenly, I realized where he was going—and so did

everyone else. Guérande and his wife both made as if to speak, but the Bishop was implacable.

"Throughout the eighteenth century," he said, "and long before, rumor circulated as to mysterious entities inhabiting the caves on Mont Dragon. Those rumors faded away at the end of the eighteenth century, more because of the after-effects of the Revolution than the intellectual Enlightenment proclaimed in Paris. For fifty years now, there has been less talk in the region about sleeping dragons and wondrous flameflowers—and that, I believe, is the reason for the decline in reports of missing children. I firmly believe, however, that many, if not all, of the missing children went into the caves, perhaps by means of openings through which an adult would have great difficulty passing, in search of the mysterious flameflowers—and fell prey to the dangers therein. I believe that Monsieur Guérande is in a position to confirm what I say."

"What!" The loudest exclamation was Guérande's, but his was not the only one.

The Bishop fixed Guérande with a steely stare, and said, in his most imperious tone. "Monsieur Guérande, have you, or have you not discovered human bones in those caves?"

The Bishop obviously knew that he had. The few items that Guérande had been willing and able to remove from the caves did, indeed, include human bone fragments. I had seen them myself, only a few hours earlier. His servants had seen them too—and had probably been far less cautious in identifying the bones as human than Dupin had been. They had talked; the rumor had spread.

"Only a few of the bones are human," Guérande stated flatly, "and they date back far beyond the eighteenth century, or the seventeenth. They are small, but...."

"Are you saying, Monsieur Guérande," the Bishop cut in, selecting his words like an expert advocate, "that there is no evidence of recent human activity in the caves."

"Activity, yes," said Guérande. "Thierachian activity, and the activity of people who might have been the Thierachians' remoter ancestors, or ours. The bones of eighteenth-century children, no."

The Bishop was not appealing to any kind of jury, and even his supposed ally, the Comte de Tibère, seemed to be against him on the specific point in question, but he continued regardless. "Can you say for certain," Aignan demanded of Guérande, "that none of the missing children went into the caves?"

"No, of course not," Guérande replied, "But...."

"I do not believe," the Bishop interjected, relentlessly, "that you, of all people, can afford that *but*. You have a small child of your own, and you should not be content with possibilities and probabilities. You should require certainty, as should all the other children in the vicinity—including, and perhaps especially, the children of the Thierachians. How many of them, I wonder, have gone missing while the nomads were camped here, without any report ever reaching the parish records or the civil authorities? Devil-worshipers they may be, but their children are born innocent of all but original sin, and are deserving of our consideration, given that we are good Christians. Those caves, Monsieur Guérande, need to be made safe. It should have been done a hundred years ago, but it was not. We have been fortunate these last fifty years—but you cannot be unaware that the tales of dragons and flameflowers have begun to circulate again, among the credulous people of the neighborhood, and that their renewal has invested them with a new glamour. Are you sure, Monsieur Guérande, that your own child has not heard them?"

That, I had to admit, was a very clever blow—and it struck home more accurately than the Bishop could have hoped, for Guérande suddenly turned to look at me, and to stare at me, as if a terrible thought had just occurred to him: a true one, alas.

He did not say anything to me. He turned back to the Bishop. "You can't seal the caves," he said, hoarsely.

"As a matter of legal entitlement," the Bishop said, "I believe that I can, unless you have sound documentation to prove that they belong to you rather than the Comte—which you cannot have, because no such documentation can exist. If you mean that I *ought* not to do it, then pray tell me why you are prepared to put your own daughter, and the children of a dozen or a hundred other men, at risk, simply for the sake of your vanity as a scientist, and the possibility of discoveries that you have not contrived to make in twenty years of searching?"

He was good—I had to give him that. Even speaking to a hostile audience, without any kind of claque to back him, he was quite an orator, and it was difficult to fault his rhetoric, however empty and insincere it might be. This was only a demonstration; he was merely giving us notice—politely, I suppose—of the extent to which appearances would be against Guérande if this were ever to be argued in public, or in a tribunal.

"There are artifacts of inestimable value in those caves, Monsieur Aignan," said Guérande, with a blithe disregard for titular etiquette, "not merely to science but to the nation."

"I'm prepared to give you time to bring them out," the Bishop said, presenting the very image of a reasonable man ever-ready to compromise. He must have known, or at least suspected, by virtue of what he had gleaned from local rumor, that there were painting on the walls of the caves, and carvings in the rock—idols all, in his view, and all the better for being immovable.

"It would be a sin to bury them," said Guérande.

"An interesting choice of words," the Bishop replied. "But sin, I think, is my area of expertise, not yours—and in my view, it would be a sin to allow the caves to remain accessible. We must think of the children, Monsieur Guérande, and must do our utmost to ensure that no other family suffers the kind of grief that still echoes in Monsieur le Comte's memory after a hundred years. What do you think, Monsieur Dupin?" He was evidently confident, in appealing to his cleverest adversary for a judgment.

"I don't feel competent to express an opinion," Dupin replied, smoothly, "having not yet seen the artifacts in the caves. If you will forgive my saying so, I'm not at all sure that you ought to condemn them unseen yourself. Might I suggest that we all go together to inspect them, once the way becomes clear—if Monsieur Guérande will consent to guide us?"

That was an obvious challenge, but I couldn't see that it had the potential to gain anything but a little time.

"I *am* curious," the Bishop admitted. He had, after all, visited the mouths of the caves earlier that day, and must have heard the sounds within the mountain. Obviously, he couldn't see that Dupin's suggestion could cost him anything but a little time—unless, of course, he failed to come back from the caves.

That, I thought, would be the worst possibility of all. If there is one thing in the world more scandalous than a possibly-abducted child, it is a possibly-murdered Bishop. Aignan was rightly confident, however, that we could not possibly mean him any harm. I wasn't so sure about the Thierachians, though, if they got wind of what he was planning to do.

Guérande seemed to be on the point of declaring that Dupin and the Bishop could both go to hell, and that he would keep the secret of the artifacts' location to himself, but he swallowed the impulse. He could see that it would do his cause no good, now that matters had reached their present state of crisis. We had been taken by surprise, and we had no ready answer. As Dupin had feared, there had been something we did not know—or, at least, had not anticipated.

I could not help studying Madame Guérande, wondering whether she might not already have been won over the Bishop's party—and whether, in fact, she might not have belonged to it all along, had she known exactly what flag it was flying. She said nothing, but did appear to be thinking hard, and there was no doubt that if she ever had to choose between Sophie and her husband's work, there would be no contest. Indeed, I suspected that if Guérande were ever faced with such a choice himself, and could find no other alternative, he would choose his daughter over his as-yet-incomplete discovery.

The journey home, in spite of the fact that it was all downhill and that I was not sitting directly above the disconcerting precipice, was far from being comfortable.

When we got back to the house, Sophie was still awake, in company with Madame Cormontaigne, waiting to bid us all goodnight. She could not have been disappointed by the enthusiasm of the hugs that her parents gave her, although she might well have picked up some contagion from their evident anxiety.

"Good night, Sophie," I said, when my turn came, bowing with careful formality.

"Good night, Monsieur Reynolds," she replied, casually ignoring my unprecedented invitation, perhaps because her parents were there, and would have thought her rude had she called me "Sam." She bid Dupin a polite goodnight too, and retired with all possible dignity.

I went to my own room shortly thereafter, and did not even attempt to read myself to sleep, merely lying down supine on the bed, content to listen no matter what the cost. In the event, the bravado and the lack of reading material proved unnecessary; after a few minutes of listening to the snoring of the dragon, I dropped off—but my slumber was fitful, full of sinister groans and hisses that my imagination must have magnified, if they were actually based on real sounds.

I dreamed about flameflowers, and dragons too—but in my dream, the eternally-sleeping dragon opened a baleful red eye to stare at me before belching fire, and when I tried to pluck a flameflower, the razor-sharp edges of its petals cut my fingers to ribbons. I listened hard, in the hope of hearing singing, or at least music—perhaps the harmony of the spheres—but there was just the rumbling and hissing of gargantuan breathing.

It was only a dream, though; when I woke up the next morning, my fingers were uninjured, and I actually felt somewhat refreshed.

CHAPTER ELEVEN
THE THIERACHIAN PERSPECTIVE

That morning, the Thierachians began to arrive. I had vaguely expected a huge company of caravans to emerge over the ridge at the north end of the valley in convoy, but that was not the way it happened. Caravans there were, but there were also carts, riders and pedestrians. Most of the new arrivals did, indeed, come over the northern ridge, briefly silhouetted against the sky before descending the shallow slope to the heath where they invariably made their camp, but others came from the south and the east. They came in small groups, not in long convoys, and when they reached their destination there was a great deal of fuss and hectic activity—fuss as people who had presumably not seen one another for months renewed their acquaintance and exchanged news, and hectic activity as they pitched dome-like tents of various sizes, established makeshift pens for various sorts of livestock, and converted a bare expanse of ground into a makeshift village in a matter of ten or twelve hours.

All day we watched them come, studying them from afar. By noon there were half a hundred, by sunset, we had lost count well in excess of two hundred individuals, more-or-less equally divided into men, women and pre-puberal children. Dupin, Guérande and I took turns to study them with the aid of Guérande's naval telescope. We were doubtless not the only ones studying them, and probably not the only ones equipped with such optical aids. Nor was the observation a one-way process, and more than once, while the sun was making its way from east to west across the southern sky, I caught glints of light that might have been lenses tracking over the upper floors of the house.

"The mass gathering will continue for a day or two," Guérande told us, "perhaps peaking at five hundred souls. In a week or ten days, however, they'll begin moving on again. The permanent camp that remains throughout the summer will number fifty or sixty individuals, but not always the same ones. They operate in shifts. While some remain here, small groups will spread out, most eastwards, trading for food and other necessities, and offering their services as laborers."

"Will people give them work?" I asked.

"Yes—not so much now, perhaps, but when July and August come, they'll help bring in the harvests in the more fertile valleys. The attraction of the towns has taken a considerable number of the younger men away from the locale over the last few decades, so the depletions suffered in the days of the *grand armée* have never been fully compensated. If it weren't for migratory labor, the farmers throughout the region would have a difficult task bringing in the harvest. The farmers all talk nostalgically about the good old days, when everything was much better organized, but those who were alive in pre-Revolutionary times were little children then, and nostalgia has tidied up the tales handed down to them. This was always relatively poor land, and the plain to the east was never the cornucopia that legend makes it. Anyway, the theory is that if people don't trade with the nomads and employ them at need, they'll simply steal more in order to supply their own needs. Livestock always goes missing—but it always does and always will, while there are foxes, lynxes and eagles abroad; the Thierachians are merely one more component of the expectable attrition of nature, not even the most gluttonous."

"And no one has ever tried to stop them gathering?" I said.

"I'm sure they have—perhaps time and time again, over the centuries. They haven't been attacked while I've been living in the house, but my father remembered troubles—skirmishes, at least, though not very bloody ones. My grandfather always said that there was no point in trying to make war on them, because they would always run away like cowards, but always come back, like the seasons themselves, and as unstoppably."

"I don't know how large the villages and towns to the east are," I observed, late in the afternoon, "but it seems to me that the camp is already the largest community for several kilometers around. They're capable of defending themselves against any mob raised in the locality—and easily capable of defending the caves against the Bishop's stonemasons, even if the bishop recruits an entire company of friars to support their endeavor."

"But that is what Lucien's friends in Paris do not want to happen," Dupin murmured. "You speak in terms of defense, but the Bishop will speak in terms of attack: monks engaged in work for the good of a community, with the blessing of the lord of the manor, assaulted and driven off by Bohemian devil-worshipers. Suddenly, the local Prefect's silly petition to the king, on Tibère's behalf, will become yet another tragically unheeded cry for help. In normal times, it would be reported one day and forgotten the next, but the Bishop knows full well that this is a time when everyone is hunting for pretexts to advance their political agendas, and any one might explode. Frankly, I do not see what I can possibly do that might prevent trouble, but Lucien will not forgive me if I cannot tell him that I have tried. Tomorrow, I shall go to the Thierachians' camp, and make every effort to play the ambassador."

"For God's sake don't tell them that you've invited the Bishop of Viviers to go into the caves with you in order to examine their ancestors' artifacts," Guérande said. "That's one thing we ought to do in the strictest secrecy, if we can—and for once, the natural hazards of the labyrinth aren't the only thing I'll be anxious about while we're in there."

"If we were to go in and not come out," I muttered, "that really would cause a stir in *Le Constitutionnel* and all its rivals. Not merely the murder of an ambitious provincial Bishop and orator, but that of a Parisian member of the Légion d'honneur."

"Then we had better be very careful of our footing when we make our expedition," Dupin observed. "It would be terrible if we were to fall or become trapped by our own carelessness, only to have the province and the nation up in arms against the innocent Thierachians accused of our murder."

In the afternoon, Guérande slipped out on his own, probably to inspect the entrances to the caves. He left us behind at the house. Dupin did not seem overly disappointed, and went for a long walk with Madame Guérande, perhaps to reminisce about old times that he probably missed as much as she did. I would have loved to eavesdrop, but I was conspicuously uninvited. Sophie was busy with her lessons, on which I did eavesdrop for a little while—somewhat to Madame Cormontaigne's annoyance, I think—but they were profoundly uninteresting, and I eventually went out for a short walk myself, choosing a direction at a distinct angle to the one I had seen Dupin and Madame Guérande take. I met no Thierachians, and the local people whose paths crossed mine all looked at me suspiciously and anxiously, as if unsure as to whether I might be a devil-worshiping Bohemian myself, in spite of my attire, and unsure as to how they ought to react if I were.

Afterwards, I explored Guérande's library, looking for something to read. I eventually selected a volume of Robert Hooke's on fossils, largely because it was in English—of a sort—and I felt a little homesick for my native tongue. I would gladly have read the latest issue of Le Constitutionnel instead, but there were no newspapers at all to be had in the shadow of Mont Dragon, let alone samples of the Parisian daily press.

Dinner was a slightly somber affair; anxiety seemed to have gripped the entire household staff, perhaps Sophie's governess most of all. Imported from Paris, she was a stranger in the neighborhood, and although she had been present when the Thierachians gathered the previous year, she knew that something was different this time. Everyone, it seemed to me, knew that *something* was different this time, even though few of them had any inkling of what the Bishop of Viviers' presence in the château actually portended. To give Aignan his due, though, he did seem to be correct about the recent resurfacing of old superstitions; the servants seemed to be gripped by a particular apprehension that I had seen before in people fearing to see ghosts. I put it down to the fact that the sleeping dragon seemed to be having something of a nightmare, for the house had shaken twice during the day, and there had been some very peculiar gurglings underground.

Dupin and I had not made any formal agreement with the Guérandes not to say anything in front of Sophie, but I was so well aware of the boundary that ought not to be crossed that I had actually avoided the child when her lessons ended, in case she asked me some question that I did not want to answer. Madame Cormontaigne, however, was no part of that tacit conspiracy, and evidently did not feel that the situation was one of those that ought not to be talked about at table,

"The servants are anxious, Monsieur," she said to Guérande. "I know better, of course, than to take silly talk of the dragon awakening more seriously than it deserves, but I wonder if you might have a word with them for Sophie's sake. It's bad enough that she picks up tales of dragons and flameflowers when we go to market, but to have it in the house...."

"No one in the house believes that there is a dragon under the mountain," Guérande said, dismissively. "They know full well what the explanation is of the hissing sounds and occasional rumblings heard at this time of year."

"But the explanation is less convincing when they can actually hear the sounds," the governess argued, probably with a good deal of justification. "I'm an educated woman, as you know, but last night, when I was in my bed...and if I remember correctly, the phenomena might well continue for another week. If it were only the distant noise, that would be unsettling enough, but the house quivered today more than I have ever felt it before, Monsieur....and it is sometimes harder, in the dead of night, to believe in the strange pressure of melting ice and running water than in restless dragons."

"It is impossible in all circumstances to believe in dragons, Madame Cormontaigne," said Madame Guérande, firmly. "You're correct, however, in your estimation that I ought to have a word with the servants. Sophie is at an impressionable age."

The little girl was sitting at the table, hardly being seen and not being heard at all, and I could not help meeting her eye at that moment. She remained silent, even making an effort to keep her face expressionless, but her eyes were saying clearly enough: "You see! I listen, but no one speaks to me. *Nobody tells me anything.*"

"Forgive me for saying so, if it is not my place," I found myself saying, without having formed any conscious intention to do so, "but it seems to me that Mademoiselle Sophie is old enough now to make her own judgment of market gossip and parlor chatter. She is being well-educated, I believe, and is therefore impressionable in the best sense of the word rather than the worst. If explanations were more frequently offered directly to her, they might be more effective."

It was *not* my place, of course, and certainly not my place to say any such thing in front of Sophie—who did not seem grateful for the intervention herself. The governess seemed offended, and so did Claude Guérande. When I looked to Dupin for moral support, I could not see any sign that it might be forthcoming—but it arrived nevertheless, from a different direction.

"You're absolutely right, Monsieur Reynolds," said Madame Guérande, "and I thank you for saying so. This house has been infected for far too long with the contagion of my husband's mania for secrecy. We ought to speak frankly to one another, and to Sophie, not only about this but many other things."

My gratitude did not ebb away, even when I realized that it was something she had probably wanted to say for a long time, and part of the reason why she had taken the decisive step of coming to Paris in order to invite Dupin to stay. Had I not made my remark, she would have found some other pretext. I could see Guérande writhing under the accusation, but he was quite uncertain, in the circumstances, how to meet it.

How he would have extracted himself from the confusion I have no idea, but he too was spared by an unexpected intervention, when a manservant appeared and said: "There is a gentleman at the door, Monsieur, asking to see you."

The house had no doorbell, or even an iron knocker; I assumed that the visitor must have rapped with his knuckles, discreetly enough to be inaudible from the dining-room.

It was presumably not unprecedented for the house to receive visitors, but it must have been unusual. Had it been a matter of routine, the servant would have had a better notion of how to introduce a visitor.

"Is it one of the Comte's men, or the Bishop's?" Guérande demanded.

"Neither, sir," the manservant replied, blushing as he realized his error. Belatedly, he held out a visiting card, which he had presumably been unable to read.

Guérande's eyes widened. "Monsieur Arnauld Lebrun," he read, not bothering to proceed to the second line of print. We already knew that Monsieur Lebrun was a man of law, apparently from Lyon.

Monsieur Guérande threw down his napkin. "I'll see him in the study," he said, flatly.

The servant hurried out to fetch the unexpected visitor to the study.

Guérande made no objection when Dupin and I stood up to follow him. Madame Guérande made as if to stand up too, but thought better of it, and sat down again with an expression of frustration on her face. Her own plans for the evening had obviously gone astray, through no fault of her little finger.

We reached the study first, and were lined up in front of Guérande's desk, facing the door, when the visitor was shown in. He was wearing a black frock-coat, like any lawyer about his business, but his feet were shod in sturdy walking-boots such as I had never seen in the vicinity of the Palais de Justice in Paris. His beard was neatly-trimmed, and his black hair carefully combed, but his sun-bronzed complexion seemed to be carrying an additional flush, as if he had come some distance and had not quite got his breath back. He was carrying a portfolio under his arm.

He bowed, formally, and said: "Thank you for receiving me, Monsieur Guérande. I apologize for the lateness of the hour, but there is a certain urgency about what I have to say to you."

"Your name is not unfamiliar to us, Monsieur Lebrun," Guérande said, with a slightly ominous edge to his voice. "These gentlemen are friends of mine from Paris: Messieurs Auguste Dupin and Samuel Reynolds."

Lebrun looked us both up and down. "Monsieur Dupin's name is not unfamiliar to me," he said, mechanically echoing Guérande's turn of phrase. "I'm delighted to meet you, Monsieur—and you too, Monsieur Reynolds."

"May I enquire as to the name of your client, Monsieur Lebrun?" Guérande asked. "We're aware that you have recently been to the Bibliothèque Nationale to consult the National Archives, searching for documentation relating to landholdings in this vicinity, but we do not know why."

Lebrun seemed slightly startled to be confronted with this knowledge, and cast a slightly longer glance at Dupin, evidently having heard mention of his reputation as a detective.

"I would be within my prerogatives as a man of law to claim the right of confidentiality," Lebrun said, with a faint smile, almost as if to parody the habitual manner of speech employed in his profession, "but I wish to speak frankly to you, and I hope that you will speak frankly to me, so I do not want there to be any unnecessary barriers between us. I represent the people that are probably known to you as Thierachians, Bohemians or Hescheboix, although none of those names is their own."

It was our turn to be startled. "You were hired by the Thierachians?" Guérande said, hardly able to believe it.

"No, Monsieur," Lebrun retorted. "I *represent* the Thierachians. I am not their hireling, but their ambassador. Perhaps I should also add that, although my name really is Arnauld Lebrun, insofar as the official records of the University of Lyon and other French institutions are concerned, it is not the name by which I am known among my own people."

"You're a Thierachian *and* a graduate in law?" Guérande still could not believe it.

"Yes, Monsieur. I don't mean to be impolite, but I do have a good deal to say to you, and if I read your expressions correctly, you have questions that you would like to address to me. Could we possibly sit down? I fear that city life has softened my muscles somewhat, and I am not as used to walking as I once was."

Guérande hastened to indicate chairs to all of us, which we arranged in a quadrilateral. He also rang for the manservant, and asked for a bottle of wine and four glasses. The man of law was correct; we did have questions that we wanted to ask—and we were eager, too, to hear what information he wanted to impart to us, with an altogether un-Thierachian frankness and urgency.

"You doubtless consider us to be a strange and secretive people," Lebrun observed, obviously feeling that some background might be useful before he got to the meat of his business, "and so we are—but I know that you are intelligent men, of a philosophical turn of mind, and I trust that you will be able to understand the reasons why a tiny population, adrift in a strange land, might feel obliged to maintain its insularity with great determination, lest it simply be absorbed, as so many other populations have been absorbed, into the mass of what are nowadays called Frenchmen. There were Thierachians in this land not only before the Romani came, but before the Franks came, before the Romans came, and before the Gauls came. Our race is older than yours—or so, at least, we believe—and we have tried to maintain it against the inevitable ravages of time. It would be ludicrous to claim that we have never imported foreign blood into our clans, but we have been careful not to allow that process to dissolve us within any of the races that have surrounded us.

"You see us as people who try to shut you out, denying and

defying your cultural influences, your religion and your laws, resolutely trying—sometimes in the face of great hostility and naked violence—to maintain our own customs and our own beliefs, and you are correct in that...but again, I ask you to try to see the matter from our viewpoint, and understand the reasons for that defensiveness. You call us vagabonds, which we are, and proudly, and you call us thieves, which we are, to some extent, as all men are—but no worse thieves than you, and probably no better, although we have our vanity in thinking ourselves better, as you do. You also call us barbarians and savages, however, which we are not. You call us ignorant, too, which we are not.

"We have our vanity, as I say, and perhaps we overestimate ourselves, as all men tend to do, but I honestly believe that there is some truth in our claim to know the world better than you do, by virtue of having the custom of traveling so widely through it, and having so deep a sense of history. We have no books, and no phonetic writing of the sort that comprises your repositories of knowledge, but we do have records of a sort—and I think you are aware, Monsieur Guérande, of how far some of those records extend into your prehistory, maintaining in symbolic value what they have lost in factual accuracy. We are well aware of historical and technological change in your society, as we have to be in order to face up to its ever-changing threats. Because, rather than in spite, of our determination to follow our own course through the ages, we find it convenient occasionally to place representatives in your midst, specifically commissioned to adopt your ways and to integrate themselves into your society, in order to be able to bring news of it back to our encampments.

"I am one such representative, groomed from early childhood not merely to become a city-dweller but, more specifically, to become a student of law. Increasingly, over the last hundred years, the weapons used against us by those of your people whose hatred has overflowed reasonable bounds have included written laws. Once, as you obviously know, your law, at least in parts remote from the capital of your fledgling nation, was largely a matter of established custom, but nowadays, national constitutions follow one another with bewildering rapidity, laws flood out of your parliaments in cataracts, and the letter of that law has become the principal justification for the wielding of swords and the firing of muskets. Our law is of a different kind, but it is your law against which we need to defend ourselves—and so, we have thought it prudent to explore it, and, in my own case, to obtain qualifications entitling us to practice it....even though we do understand how feeble, arbitrary and corruptible it is, even in your highest courts. You will understand, I hope, that I am not such a fool as to believe that it is a battleground on which I could fight with any chance of winning, any more than we could possibly win any other kind of battle against your enormously superior might.

"Now, having introduced myself properly, I would like to pass on to the specific matter that brought me here. Have you any questions before I do that?"

Dupin got in first, and went straight for the poor fellow's jugular. "Do your own people still regard you as one of them?" he asked. "Do you really have their trust to the extent of being able to represent them."

"The simple answer," Lebrun said, after a moment's reflection, "is no. They do not really regard me as one of them any longer, and I do not have their complete trust to the extent that I would like—but there are complications in that situation that you probably cannot appreciate. The more important thing is that I still feel, very deeply and passionately, that I *am* a so-called Thierachian, as well as a Frenchman, and that I am fully committed to doing whatever I possibly can to defend the interests of my people."

"Are you a believer in the Thierachian religion, then?" Guérande put in. "Or has your education in Lyon revealed any flaws in its credo?"

Lebrun tried to smile. "The subtleties of what you call Thierachian 'religion' would take weeks or months to explain," he said. "It has no credo, in the sense that the Bishop of Viviers attaches to that word, nor even any worship, in any sense closely analogous to Christian worship. The simple answer to your question, however, is yes. Nothing I learned while studying at Lyon has weakened my commitment to the beliefs of my people. I am, in terms of the Christian faith, a pagan—but not an idolater, and certainly not a worshiper of any principle of evil. We hold life in greater esteem than you do, I think—more sacred, in your terminology—and I think, too, that we have a better understanding of what life is than you do...even you, Monsieur Guérande."

Guérande seemed ready to debate that point, and I could easily imagine that the diversion might extend for a long way, but Dupin held up his hand to ask his old friend to be quiet—and such was his natural authority that Guérande obeyed.

"I would like to talk to you about these matters at length, Monsieur Lebrun," he said, "and if you will grant us your permission, I am sure that my friends would be interested to visit you at the encampment, in order that we might learn more. You came here tonight, however, with something specific to tell us. Perhaps you ought to do that now. It concerns the results of your research in the National Archives, I assume?"

"It does," said Lebrun, seemingly relieved to have got to the point at last. "I hoped to discover some clear indication of the ownership of the land on the eastern slopes of what you call Mont Dragon. I began that research expecting that there was strong possibility that the documents would be unhelpful and contradictory, having been issued at widely different times under different legal systems, and carelessly drawn up. Somewhat to my surprise, I found more consistency, and more accuracy, than I had feared. It was not easy, but I am reasonably sure that I could now set notarized copies of documents before a tribunal that would prove beyond a reasonable doubt that the land in question still belongs, as it has for hundreds of years, to the estate of the Comtes de Tibère. That does not apply to your house, Monsieur Guérande, which is clearly the property of your family in spite of attempts made by others to call that ownership into question, but you have no plausible claim to the land into which the caves open. The ownership of the deeper caves themselves might perhaps be debatable, but under French law as it now stands—until the next Revolution, at least—the superficial caves, including the ones in which you have made what you believe to be significant discoveries, definitely belong to the Comte de Tibère."

There was a moment's silence as we absorbed this news—which was not entirely unexpected, but was disappointing nevertheless.

"That does not seem to be good news for you, Monsieur Lebrun, any more than it is for me," Guérande observed, finally. "What do you intend to do with this information? Not that it matters, since the Comte—or, more accurately, the Bishop of Viviers—seems fully determined to act on the assumption anyway."

"First of all," said Arnauld Lebrun, now speaking with meticulous care, "I would like to know your opinion on that matter. My impression is that you are honest men, and that, even though you think this information is prejudicial to your interests, you would not be prepared to deny or hide it. My question to you, Messieurs, is this: if the documents copied in my portfolio really do demonstrate that the land belongs to the Comte de Tibère, will you accept that as a fact, and not seek to hide or avoid it?"

It was such a peculiar question that I sensed a trap of some sort, although I could not imagine what it might be. Guérande was wary too, but Dupin had no doubts. "I am prepared to accept your word as a man of law that the implication of the documents is clear," he said. "The truth is the truth, and I am not in the habit of denying it. If you intend to publish this information, I certainly shall not attempt to refute it dishonestly, and I cannot imagine that my friend Monsieur Guérande will do so either, no matter how much inconvenience it might cause him."

Guérande actually groaned—a hollow sound of which any ghostly dragon would have been proud. "You do not understand what is at stake here, Monsieur Lebrun," he said, "and I cannot imagine why you would want to further Tibère's cause, but Monsieur Dupin is correct. If you have proof, you have proof. If the Comte owns the land, and the caves...well, no matter what the consequences of that ownership might be, I am a citizen of France; I abide by its laws."

"Do you intend I publish the affirmation?" I asked, curiously.

"Not in any tribunal," Lebrun relied, coldly. "As I have said, I know better than to expect any justice there—but I have already published it, have I not, in making you party to it? I hoped, in doing so, that I could trust you, as honest men, and I accept your assurances that I can. No matter how many others might deny the truth, I believe that you will accept it."

"But no one will deny it," Guérande said. "It is what the Comte and Philippe Aignan want to believe, although the Comte has long feared opposition should they be forced to prove it. You probably do not know this, but they told us yesterday that they intend to act on the assumption regardless—publication of your documents will only prove that their legal ground is solid."

Lebrun smiled—rather wolfishly, I thought. "Forgive me, gentlemen," he said, with just a hint of mockery in his legally-educated voice, "but you seem to be laboring under a misapprehension. The man who lives in the château, and who is presently playing host to the Bishop of Viviers, is not the legitimate Comte de Tibère, and I have documentation to prove that, too—although it might not, alas, be documentation that that would satisfy a tribunal, in the face of determined opposition. Honest men like yourself, on the other hand....."

I remembered Madame Guérande having made some remark about the long-standing feud between the Tibères and the Guérandes being ultimately based in a claim to the title. "You don't mean that *Claude* is the legitimate heir to the title?" I said.

The same thought must have occurred to Guérande, because there was a hint of hope in his eyes—but it was very soon dashed.

"I fear not," said Arnauld Lebrun. "I mean that I am."

CHAPTER TWELVE
MYTH AND REALITY

Guérande clearly thought that the suggestion was preposterous, but Dupin merely nodded. He was wearing a wry smile,
of which Lebrun took note.

"Will you still take my word, Monsieur Dupin" the lawyer
asked, "As a man of law?"

"I'm inclined to do so," Dupin replied, "but I fear that your
anxieties are correct regarding French tribunals. The records
proving your direct descent from the Tibère heir who went
missing in the last century are, I presume, Thierarchian records,
which have no standing in any provincial Mairie or parish."

"They are, however, accurate," Lebrun said.

"You mean," I said, incredulously, "that the child whose
disappearance the Comte was complaining about last night
really *was* stolen by the Thierachians? He didn't come to harm
in the caves after all?"

"As a matter of fact," Lebrun was quick to put in, "he *did*
come to harm in the caves—which was where my people found
him, after mounting an intensive search...although one could
have forgiven them for not taking the trouble, after the rude
manner in which their own camp had been searched. The boy
was in a poor state by the time he was found—so poor that they
did not dare to hand him back, lest they be held accountable for
his injuries. That was wrong, I agree, but they were in fear for
their lives, and with good reason. So they kept him—and yes,
I am obliged to concede, as an honest man, that they *did* steal

him.

"I have no reason to doubt that my people have stolen other children in the past, in the strictest sense of the word, but I can assure you that the great majority of outsider children taken in by my people had been abandoned or maltreated by yours. It is, indeed, within the customs of the tribe to adopt new members, provided that they are young enough to be assimilated—taught our language, our customs and our beliefs as if they were our own—and there probably have been times when little children have been stolen in the truest sense of the word, perhaps in reprisal for acts of violence committed against our own babes-in-arms. I ask you once again, however, as honest and educated men, to look at the matter from our point of view, and understand what we do, even if you cannot forgive it.

"At any rate, there is only one case that is material to our present situation, and that is mine. I am the lineal descendant of the vanished Tibère heir, and therefore—according to your own law and tradition—the legal owner of Mont Dragon and its caves. I have no intention of trying to dispossess the usurper of the château, in which I have no interest, but the caves are a different matter. I could not claim them in a tribunal either, but what I would like, for the time being, is Monsieur Guérande's acknowledgement of my entitlement. As an honest man, I believe that he should be willing to accept it."

"On the basis of records I cannot read?"

"Just so," said Lebrun, sternly. "I can show them to you, and bring forward half a hundred witnesses who can confirm their meaning. They are all Thierachian, admittedly, and I know that many Frenchmen would consider them automatically untrustworthy on that account—but I hold you in higher esteem than to think you guilty of such sweeping prejudice. The proof is there; I can show it to you. The question is: will you accept it?"

Guérande was trapped, and he knew it. Eventually, he nodded his head, rather ironically, and said: "I believe you, Monsieur le Comte. The caves are yours—but what is in them, I must insist, belongs neither to you nor to me, nor to any other mere human, but to science. It represents precious knowledge, which requires the fullest possible exploration, and eventual publication. If you intend to deny that, then we are still at odds."

"Let us take things in order," Lebrun said. "We differ on this matter, it's true—but I believe that there is scope for discussion, and compromise."

"Given that we four are all honest men," Dupin put in, "I believe that you're right, Monsieur Lebrun—but I still harbor some doubts about your representative status, with respect to your own people, and there is also the Bishop of Viviers to consider. Do you know what he intends to do?"

"No," Lebrun admitted. "I had not thought that there was anything he could do, except bluster and preach."

Dupin told him, succinctly, exactly what the Bishop intended to do, and under what pretext.

Lebrun's expression clouded over. "That is serious," he admitted. "It is underhanded provocation, you think? He actually *wants* us to react violently?"

"I believe so," Dupin confirmed. "We are living in anxious and turbulent times, when men do not always behave in a way that history will see as reasonable."

Lebrun looked him in the eyes. "We have been in living in anxious and turbulent times for the last eight hundred years, Monsieur Dupin. I could say eighteen hundred instead...perhaps even eighteen thousand. You count the lulls between the storms as a kind of normality, but we see things differently—and I repeat that we are the ones with the more accurate appraisal of the broad sweep of history."

"We differ on that, too," said Dupin, mildly, "but we are honest and reasonable men, and might reach agreement through discussion. The question is, can you dissuade your people from giving the Bishop what he wants?"

The simple answer to that, I guessed, was: "I don't know," but Arnauld Lebrun was a vain man, in his way, and was not about to admit that. What he actually said was: "I can try."

"I gained us a few days," Dupin told him, "by challenging the

Bishop to go into the caves before condemning them. His vanity would not let him refuse. I hope that your people will permit that—although, in all honesty, I do not expect that anything can be gained thereby in the longer term. He is not a man to change his mind easily."

Lebrun stood up, abruptly. His own plans had obviously been derailed. "I need to discuss this with the elders," he said. "Will you come to the camp, tomorrow? We must, at least, try to make what alliance we can on our side—but I cannot make you any promises as yet."

"We'll come," Guérande promised. "As honest men, with open minds."

Lebrun tried to smile, but failed. He took his leave, more anxious than when he had arrived.

We went back to the dining-room table, in order to salvage what we could of the meal. Sophie had been sent to bed, and Madame Cormontaigne had also retired, but Julie Guérande was waiting for us, in no mood to be kept in the dark.

Guérande gave her a brief account what Lebrun had told us.

"And you believe him?" she said, skeptically.

"Why not?" he countered. "Even if I didn't, it's hardly in our interests to challenge him—and I've been trying to open communication with the Thierachians for years. Thanks to the Bishop, we're now tacit allies, and there's a possibility that we shall become real allies."

"Not if the Thierachians do resort to force to prevent the Bishop blocking the entrances of the caverns."

"They might not have any reason to do that, if they know of points of entry that the Bishop doesn't," Guérande said, hopefully. "Although he'll find it easy enough to find the ones I know about, as Monsieur Dupin has pointed out, it's possible that I can find others, with or without the Thierachians' help. It's possible, too, that the Bishop can be persuaded to hesitate— or, at least, that the Comte can be persuaded to withdraw his backing from the action. Lebrun thinks, perhaps rightly, that it would be difficult to persuade a tribunal of the reliability of the Thierachians' records—but if Lebrun can teach Monsieur Dupin enough of their script to allow him to act as a translator and a potential witness, the threat of such an action might be enough to persuade the Comte to retreat—and without the permission of the notional landowner, the Bishop's license to act becomes dubious."

"Is he correct, Auguste?" asked Madame Guérande, drawing a rapid scowl from her husband.

"Quite possibly," said Dupin. "Did you talk to your daughter before you sent her to bed?"

"I asked her what tales she had heard about the mountain, and assured her yet again that there is no dragon sleeping beneath it."

"What did you tell her about the flameflowers?"

"The flameflowers? It's the dragon that she's afraid of, not the flameflowers. I did tell her that there was no such thing, of course."

"Perhaps I asked the wrong question. What did *she* tell *you* about the flameflowers?"

"Vague nonsense. They're said to be exceedingly precious, and magical. They're said to be products of the dragon's fiery breath, capable of movement when newborn, although they settle into immobility when they become flowers. They sing, too, in some of the tales, although not everyone can hear their song—like the chirping of bats."

"The details are all commonplace folkloristic motifs," I pointed out.

"Indeed," said Dupin. "Stubborn beliefs, in which storytellers still delight, in spite of the advent of the Age of Reason."

"That doesn't mean that there's any truth in them," Guérande said—but Dupin looked at him skeptically, as if to suggest that Guérande was the last person who ought to deny the suspicion of some truth behind the rumor.

"No, it doesn't," Dupin finally admitted, "but it does suggest something about the nature of belief, and it serves to remind us of one interesting fact that we learned from Monsieur Lebrun that passed without comment at the time."

"That the Tibère heir did go into the caves, presumably of his own accord," I put in, eager to claim the credit for the insight. "Do you think he was looking for flameflowers?"

"We must presume that he was looking for *something*," Dupin said, "and that the lure was strong enough to counter his fear of waking the dragon. The Bishop might have had a hidden agenda when he set out to compile his statistics, but they do speak for themselves, as he contended. It *is* possible that more children have gone into the caves, over the years, in search of flameflowers...just as it is more than probable that Monsieur Guérande is not the first adult to have done so."

"Is that true, Claude?" Julie Guérande demanded. It had suddenly occurred to her, I think, that there might be more than one reason for her husband's secrecy with regard to the object of his assiduous research in the caves—that he might simply have been embarrassed to confess that he was chasing the substance of local superstition and children's nursery tales.

"Yes and no," Guérande replied, defiantly as well as reluctantly. "No, I'm not searching for frozen dragon's breath—but yes, I am searching for something depicted in the cave-paintings. Perhaps it doesn't exist—perhaps I'm misinterpreting what I see, and perhaps what the ancient artist was depicting was merely a product of his imagination, a whom of his own superstition—but the animals are real, and while there's a possibility...."

"A possibility of what?" his wife asked, sharply, when he failed to finish his sentence.

"A possibility of confirming his theories," said Dupin, softly. "First and foremost, of course, Claude is searching for more artifacts, and more bones. Like Boucher de Perthes, he's exceedingly eager to find more human remains in company with ancient chipped flints and charred animal bones— stronger evidence for the existence of humans far more ancient than Bishop Ussher's Adam. But he also thinks that there's a glimmer of hope—a literal glimmer—of finding evidence of another creation, another evolutionary sequence, never wiped out by the kind of life to which we belong because it's protected within the bowels of the earth: the creation based on heat rather than light; the creation that makes light out of heat rather than heat out of light."

Guérande shrugged his shoulders, resignedly. "I gave you all the pieces of the puzzle, Auguste," he said. "I knew you'd put them together—but don't judge me until you've seen the paintings. Time hasn't done them any favors, but they're still visible... and legible. When you've seen them, you'll understand. God, I haven't quite lost hope yet that even the Bishop of Viviers might understand, once he sees them—if he can squeeze his paunch through the narrower passages."

Dupin patted his own paunch, although he had several inches of girth to spare over the Bishop. "Children have an advantage in that regard," he murmured. "Smaller frames...as well as keener ears."

"Do you think that flameflowers sing songs like the sirens of antiquity then?" said, Guérande, with a slight sneer to which he did not seem to me to be entitled.

"Unfortunately," said Dupin, with a sigh, "I already know that the sirens of antiquity were real, and I cannot discount the possibility that the rumors of singing are as firmly based as the tales of precious flameflowers...if there is, in fact, any truth in the latter."

"I will have a close watch kept on Sophie," Madame Guérande said, cutting short any debate.

"That might be a wise precaution," Dupin said. "The possibility is remote...but sometimes, remote possibilities should not be ignored. When we go to bed tonight, let us try to listen with an open mind, not merely for the dragon's breath, but for the strains of temptation."

He was being whimsical, I knew, but I also knew that he was being serious. Who could blame him? Claude Guérande had been going into the caves every spring and summer for twenty years and more, to study images that he had first discovered as a boy. The Thierachians came here every year, in their hundreds, and had apparently been doing so for centuries, perhaps thousands of years. And all of them were secretive about it, as if compulsively. I did not doubt that they all had conscious reasons for behaving as they did, which seemed perfectly reasonable to them...but as Dupin had said, sometimes, remote possibilities should not be ignored.

I was still looking forward to going into the caves, however, to see Guérande's artifacts. If I too were to be enthralled as a result...well, I had experience with sirens, and things far worse. Eventually, even the hardest skeptic learns to trust in luck—or destiny.

CHAPTER THIRTEEN
THE THIERACHIAN HERITAGE

Logically, my third night in the bosom of the dragon should have been easier than the second. I should, by then, have grown quite accustomed to the noises from underground. Dupin's whimsical suggestion that we should all try to listen to them more closely was not advice that I intended to follow. I wanted to sleep, in preparation for the next day, when we would certainly be confronting the Thierachians, and perhaps, if the way had cleared, making our first foray into the caves in Guérande's company.

For that good and sensible reason, I made every effort to screen out the distant hissing and the groaning, and to ignore the occasional ghostly tremor that brushed the house as lightly as the flicker of a butterfly's wing.

One of Dupin's favorite sayings was that consciousness is a refuge. What he meant by that—assuming that he knew what he meant, and was not merely hazarding a hypothesis for subsequent investigation—is that consciousness operates as a filter, protecting our self-awareness from things that a raw, untutored mind might find difficult to bear. If that is true—and I believe it with all the conviction of which my heart is capable—then consciousness is a good and frequently-effective guardian; indeed, were it not such a good guardian, I would never have got into the habit of making the notes on which this and other narrations are based, for if I had not written some of these incidents down while they were fresh in my memory, thus secreting and securing them, I believe that that they would have been gradually erased from conscious memory, or at least reduced to the status of distant dreams, capable of stirring a slight frisson of anxiety but not of troubling faith in the normality of the lived-in world.

Perhaps, I sometimes think, it would have been better not to have made those notes—and better, too, not to have gone back to them at an interval of several years in order to reconstitute the experiences as they were lived and felt. That is probably what a sensible man would do, seeking to take advantage of the guardianship of consciousness and the refuge it provides— but I, like Auguste Dupin, am one of those individuals severely infected with contradiction by the imp of the perverse. That was not a contagion I picked up from Poe, who shared a similar affliction; it was what drew me to Poe in the first place, and him to me. Perhaps, since I had begun my association with Dupin, it had become something of a *folie à deux*, but neither he nor I was able to regard it as folly, and I remain convinced to this day that Madame Guérande was right in her estimation that we were good for one another, and needed one another's society.

Had we be born Thierachian, or stolen by them while out minds were still raw and untutored, we might have had an *entire* society...but I should not get ahead of my narrative.

Consciousness did indeed contrive to keep the dragon at bay while I went to sleep on that third night—but when consciousness has contrived to nullify itself in order to rest from its efforts, even an adult mind becomes exposed to strange influences. Most dreams come from within us, but not all. Some are visited upon us by whispers and tremors from without, and the mere fact that those whispers and tremors are simple natural phenomena, including those generated by complex interactions of water and fire, does not mean that they cannot take on meaning.

What I dreamed that night was not a nightmare, nor was it a prophecy, although it seemed like both. The unconscious mind cannot predict the future any more than the conscious mind, for the future is yet to be made by our actions, rational and otherwise, but it can imagine it—and in imagining the future the slumberous mind cannot help but reflect our deepest fears.

What I dreamed was that one of Georges Cuvier's Epochs of Nature was about to end, and that the surface of the Earth was about to undergo one of its periodic upheavals: an apocalypse in which strange beasts would emerge from the earth and the sea, and the sky would change its face, and angels of death would run riot in the world, brining in a harvest of souls with their fiery blades—and there would be a Judgment.

Yes, there would be a Judgment, before the throne of Creation, which would determine those species that would survive, and flourish in the world to come, and those that would be condemned to the oblivion of rock, as petrified phantoms, faint, incomplete and broken.

It was not a personal Judgment; I was not involved as any individual self of any sort, but merely as a tiny atom in the flotsam of humankind—a species condemned and doomed, unable to survive the ordeal, in spite of all its science, art and music. Our failure was nothing of which we had need to be ashamed, however, for it was far more basic than any matter of mere intellect, rooted in the most elementary processes of nourishment. It was the sun that had judged our entire tree of life to be defective, and had transferred the loyalty of its light to another, better adapted to the spectrum of its emissions, with a kind of vital spark that was gifted with a greater zest and sense of purpose.

I could not see that new tree grow, or even display a tiny shoot, but I participated in the withering and decay of our own, the humiliation of its demise, and the bleak awareness of its loneliness. There was a bitterness in the knowledge that it might have done better, not only in terms of the failure of its own internal harmony, but in terms of its failure to reach out, to communicate in some fashion with the other trees of life making up the universal forest.

That, I felt, had been in some strange way *my* purpose,

and *my* failure, for which the censoriousness of my cowardly consciousness had been responsible.

It was only a dream—and that vague description of its content and emotion was all that I was able to write down before active consciousness, guided by the morning sunlight, brought a conclusive end to its ephemeral empire. I knew, though, even as I began the dutiful work of forgetting it, that it was significant. Significant of what, I did not know, but I knew that it reflected or portended *something*. Not the end of the world, of course, or even the Epoch, and perhaps not the end of anything at all—but something....

"Did you have bad dreams last night, Monsieur Reynolds?" Madame Guérande asked me, when we all sat down to breakfast.

"I did," I confirmed. "I fear that I have not yet accustomed myself to the agitations of the neighborhood, although they are certainly no noisier than the night traffic in Paris."

"You are not at fault," the lady assured me. "I have never known the stirrings so urgent in the twenty years and more that I have lived here. I think I would have had nightmares myself, had I been able to sleep at all."

"It must be the weather," Guérande opined. "The southerly wind is uncommonly warm this year, and the thaw has been faster than usual."

"Are you sure that it is not an increase in the heat diffusing from below?" Dupin asked him.

"Perhaps that is a factor too," Guérande conceded.

"I slept quite well," Sophie put in—and only brought the ghost of a frown to her mother's face for having spoken without first being spoken to.

"That's good," her mother said.

"Did you dream at all?" Dupin asked her, curiously.

"I believe so," the little girl said, scrupulously, "but as soon as I awoke I forgot what I had dreamed. It was a pleasant dream, I think. Strange, but pleasant."

Dupin nodded, as if in approval—but I knew him well

enough to know that he was ruminating some exotic possibility. Trust him, I thought, to find something ominous in the child's forgotten but pleasant dream, and to pay no heed at all to my echoing nightmare, a window to which had been cemented in my consciousness by my note-taking habit. I said nothing about the content of my dream, however. How could I, in front of the child?

I said nothing about it, either, when Guérande, Dupin and I set off for the Thierachian encampment to keep our appointed tryst with Arnauld Lebrun. We walked in silence, all three of us somewhat weighed down by anticipation. None of us knew what we might be told by Lebrun, as a spokesman for the tribal elders, but all of us were eager for whatever enlightenment the man of law might care to provide about the secret beliefs and folkways of the nomads—and we were a little apprehensive too.

Guérande had been to the camp-site on numerous previous occasions, and had been received placidly, if not hospitably, but his questions had never been answered. Many, if not most, of the adult Thierachians spoke French as well as their own language, but that did not prevent them from refusing to understand what they did not want to understand, nor from lapsing into incomprehensibility when they did not want to be understood.

This time, however, the visitors did not wait for Guérande to come into their midst. Lebrun came to meet him, to intercept us a full hundred meters short of the nearest cart in the ragged ring that formed the rampart of the improvised village. He had four men with him; they were all older than him, but they let him take up a stance ahead of them.

I could tell, as soon as we were within twenty meters of Lebrun's position, that something was wrong, but I had no idea what it might be. The four elders did not seem angry or aggressive, nor did they seem frightened—but something was on their minds. Lebrun did not seem angry or aggressive either, but he did seem anxious and apprehensive.

For a moment, I thought that they intended to hold conference there, in the open, forbidding us entry to their camp, but they were only observing some kind of etiquette. There were no introductions by name, and no handshakes or accolades, but we and the elders exchanged formal bows, and then the five Thierachians led the three of us, with all due dignity, to the center of their encampment, where there was a damped-down cooking fire, and a circle of chairs established nearby, around a wooden table. There was a large metal kettle on the table, still producing vapor at the spout, and eight cups.

We were shown which seats to take, positioned so that there was an alternation of elders and strangers—with Lebrun, for this purpose, seemingly classed as a stranger. The lawyer was stationed between two elders, as Dupin, Guérande and I were. Guérande was seated opposite Lebrun, while I was to his left and Dupin to his right.

There were men and women busy with various tasks around us, but the only child I saw was a girl of approximately the same age as Sophie, who poured the liquid from the kettle into the cups, and then distributed the cups, with considerable care, serving the strangers before the elders.

It was a infusion of some sort, but not tea. It was slightly bitter, but not altogether unpleasant. I sipped it cautiously, as did Dupin and Guérande, and then looked at Dupin in search of an opinion. He made no signal, even with his eyes, but I thought I detected a certain suspicion in the way he held the cup, and I resolved to drink as slowly as I could without seeming impolite.

The elders did not seem impressed by our wary eagerness to make ourselves agreeable. The girl brought bread, then, on a wooden tray. The bread was already broken into morsels, which she distributed. The elder sitting to my right nudged my elbow to attract my attention, and then made a show of dipping the bread into the infusion before taking a bite. I thought that he might have made less of a pantomime of it, but followed his example half-heartedly and rather gingerly. He laughed—whether at the mere fact of my compliance, or some awkwardness in my performance, I could not tell. His teeth were yellowed, but not by nicotine. The Thierachians did not smoke or chew tobacco.

Eventually, we got down to business. The elders indicated that Lebrun, as their appointed spokesman, should take the floor. Thus far, they had only spoke in their own language, and their utterances had been few in number. The man of law soon made up for that, though; he was obviously a trained orator.

"Before I attempt an explanation of the situation," Lebrun said, "I am obliged to issue a warning. It would be exceedingly dangerous for you, or for anyone else, to go into the caves tomorrow, or within the next few days. It would be dangerous, too, for the Bishop of Viviers to set his men to work at the entrances. At the very least, you must wait, and you must do your best to persuade him to wait—until next year, if possible."

"Will you try to stop us, if we refuse to heed your warning?" Guérande asked, flatly.

Lebrun almost laughed—indeed, I think he had genuine difficulty suppressing the laughter. "No," he said. "But I cannot promise that we will come to your assistance, should you need it."

"Do you think, then, that this is the year that the dragon will finally wake up?" Guérande asked, with a slight sneer in his voice.

"There are no dragons in our tradition," Lebrun said, "but if I were to translate our understanding into the crude terms of your fairy tales, yes, the dragon will become active this year, perhaps as early as tomorrow—and you should not try to pretend that you do not think so too. You know full well that it is time for an awakening. Mr. Reynolds!"

Startled, I said: "Yes?" For a moment, I thought he was going to consult me about my nightmare.

"I have read that there are certain plants in the Americas—desert plants, I believe—that come into bloom only once in a hundred years. Is that true?"

I had read the same thing, but I had never seen any such evanescent flower, nor could I have named any of the relevant species, in Latin or English. Lebrun was obviously not looking for a negative answer, however, and obviously had some further analogical point to make, so I simply said: "Yes, it's true."

"Even on the world's thin surface," Lebrun said, "life works to many different timescales. There are insects whose adult forms endure for less than a single day, while certain parrots are said to live for two hundred years—but all of surface life is linked, fundamentally, to the cycles of the day and the year. Your astronomers have recently discovered that it is not the sun that travels around a stationary Earth, but the Earth that orbits a Sun that is also moving; that is, however, a modification that the traditions of my people would consider irrelevant. For us, the Earth remains the center of our world and the universe spins eccentrically around it. For us, the concepts of *above* and *below* do not have the same significance they had for your ancestors, even before your astronomers complicated the issue. For us, *above* and *below* are seen primarily as different poles of creation, different directions on the axis of life. For us, life from above—the life whose seeds have rained down upon the Earth and the sea ever since time began—reflects in its nature the hectic whirl of the universe, the fundamental cycle of the day and the longer cycle of the year.

"In the traditions of my people, life on the surface of the earth, including the oceans, is all ephemeral in nature. The difference between a plant that flowers every year, or flowers once and then dies, and a plant that flowers once in a century, and lives for hundreds of years, is trivial, just as the duration of a human life is trivial, like the flickering of a tiny and unsteady star. Do not bother to tell me that the stars are really suns, some more massive and bright than our own. I know that, thanks to my education in Lyon; but I also know that, when I look up from the surface of the world where I walk, they are tiny and unsteady, and their light is very, very, faint.

"The life beneath the earth—perhaps, in your terms, what the traditions of my people only mistake for life, but perhaps what even you would be forced to recognize as life, if ever you witnessed one of its brief awakenings, and survived—is very different in the timescale of its actions. In the core of creation that is the center of the Earth, and the center of the universe, the processes at work know nothing of days and lights, or years, or human generations, or the lifetimes of civilizations. They are adapted to a very different scale of events, in which our days are but seconds and our years minutes, and even ephemeral life-times are to be measured in centuries or millennia, while life-times permitting the dawn of thought and dreams are measured in tens of millions of years—and the greater evolution of life, its change and its progress, in billions of years. Life in the core of creation, unlike life at the periphery, is long, and it is slow.

"Your people—by which I mean all the civilizations known to your history, except ours—have always tended to place your gods in the sky: the sky from which the seeds came, and still come, that give birth to surface life. If you retain any conscious-ness at all of the life in the core, you make its underworld an abode of darker gods or evil spirits, and sometimes of your own dead. I dare say that such fantasies are explicable—and they certainly do not want for attempted explanations, in your so-called Age of Enlightenment. We have no gods, as such, for we have never imagined creators in our own image, or the image of any other kind of creature; in our way of seeing, that would be paradoxical. We are, however, aware of the life above and the life below, and of the rare points beneath the surface of the earth where those two kinds of life sometimes come close enough, not quite to touch, but to influence one another.

"In our eyes, you—by *you* I mean all the people who are not *us*—have misunderstood and perverted the legacy of that influence. That is vanity, I do not deny. By virtue of my educa-tion in your ways, in deference to your supposed wisdom, I will even admit that we might conceivably be wrong in believing that our understanding is superior to yours in all respects—but I believe, nevertheless, that we understand what will happen here soon far better than you do. There is life beneath our feet—a very long way beneath our feet, in normal times—whose exten-sions come closer to the surface in certain places and at certain times than others. It never reaches the surface—but sometimes, it reaches out toward it, not to *touch*, but perhaps to *hear*, as if it were placing an ear against a closed door. Perhaps, in its own temporal terms, it does that very frequently, curiously and eagerly—but not in our terms. In our terms, the merest possibility of the very slightest sensory exchange only occurs once in every few decades, and the possibility of any genuine revelation perhaps once in every thousand years...or perhaps never, if what we take for revelation is mere delusion.

"At any rate, my people listen. If the name by which we call ourselves were translated into your language, it would be something akin to *listeners*, or perhaps *watchmen*. We travel the world, visiting places where listening is possible during a propitious season, always hoping to find more. It is our nature, and our duty. Perhaps, to be strictly accurate, I should say that our children listen, for adults grow less sensitive with time, even as they grow wiser in trying to determine what the life in the core of creation is saying to our children: what it is trying to tell us, and what is trying to learn from us—for the songs have changed, very slowly but markedly, over the millennia. What we hear now is not the same as what our remote ancestors heard in the high plateaux of Asia.

"We call ourselves the first humans, and perhaps we were, but I have learned enough in your world to know that, even if humans first awakened in the mountains of Asia to the voices of the Underworld, there must have been semi-humans of a sort before them, and apes of a sort before them. The milieu that gave birth to us was not even the cradle of human consciousness and intelligence, in all probability—but it was the nursery in which that intelligence first heard the songs of the life below, and the listeners found their vocation.

"There is no dragon sleeping beneath this hill—but there is *something* there, and if what is about to happen is not really an awakening, it is something like an advent of consciousness, which appeals in mysterious ways to our own consciousness. Something is already reaching out: something unimaginable to you, and perhaps also to us. Something is about to happen, tomorrow or in the few days thereafter, that has not happened for a very long time, although there have been lesser events of the same sort, providing us with premonitions.

"The elders believe that this is our business and ours alone, and that your people should not interfere, but they will admit, if pressed, that they have no moral right to deny revelation to others, especially to others who can hear the song—and they are honest men. They will not use force to prevent you from entering the cave tomorrow, Monsieur Guérande just as they never have never sought to prevent it before—but they want me to warn you that all the deposits you have made in the cave, of equipment, potable water and light-sources, in preparation for this year, will not help you when...there is no way to express this in your language that accurately reflect ours, but you have your own folklore derived from the song, so I will put it in your bastardized terminology: *when the flameflower blooms.*"

CHAPTER FOURTEEN
THE THREAT

That was a lot to take aboard, and Dupin obviously wanted to take his time doing it. He was thinking hard, looking down at the cup into which he had not dipped any bread, and which still seemed to me to be almost full. I had stopped sipping too while concentrating on what Lebrun was saying.

I looked at the four elders, who were putting on a fine show of impassiveness, as if they did not understand what Lebrun was saying on their behalf—but I did not doubt that they could speak French themselves, and knew exactly what he was telling us. If they were not taking part, it was not because they were unable to do so, but because they believed that their silence would have a greater effect on us than their speech. That they were striving for an effect of some sort, I did not doubt—but if they hoped that this strange revelation would deter us from further exploration, they obviously did not know us at all.

I was quite prepared to let them try, though. I was curious to hear more of the secrets they had been keeping from the rest of humankind since time immemorial.

Guérande wasn't so patient. "Are you trying to tell us that you think there's going to be some kind of volcanic eruption?" he asked.

"Absolutely not," Lebrun replied. "Indeed, I believe it to be impossible that any such eruption could happen here, or anywhere else where the life from the core extends toward the surface. Beneath this location, the central fire is controlled—I will not say *consciously* controlled, because that might be a step too far, but controlled nevertheless. That is not what you have to fear."

"Then what do I have to fear, given that I'm sure that I know these caves as well as anyone in your camp?" Guérande demanded.

"Physically," Lebrun told him, "what you have to fear consists of very ordinary threats: falls, broken limbs, getting lost, becoming stuck...and bad air too. Mentally, the disorder and disarray that make falls and broken limbs, getting lost and becoming stuck considerably more likely."

"Hallucinations?"

"If that is the label you prefer to apply to them, yes: hallucinations. If you go into the caves tomorrow, this week, or even this year, you risk going mad. Every year, you risk going in never to come out again, but this year, the risk will be far greater—and I think you know that already, Monsieur Guérande. You are not one of us, but your repeated expeditions into the cave have brought you closer to us. You have been anticipating this event for years, as we have. You know that it is about to happen—as your wife must too, else Monsieur Dupin and Monsieur Reynolds would not be here, would they?"

When Guérande did not answer that challenge, Lebrun followed up with another question: "You first went into the caves as a child, did you not?"

"What of it?" Guérande demanded.

"I first went in as a child myself," Lebrun told him. "It is the same for all our children. Sometimes we take them. Sometimes, we leave them to find their own way. This year, they will find their own way—and we shall try to recover those who do not come back of their own accord. You are not one of us, Monsieur Guérande, and never can be, As Monsieur Dupin has cruelly pointed out, there is a sense in which I am no longer *one of us* myself, and never can be again—but the song is within both of us nevertheless, and we can never be rid of it, for it exists on a far more extended time span than our petty lives.

"All that you and I can do about that, Monsieur Guérande, is to be careful, lest it kill us—for whatever you might imagine, within the framework of your scientific curiosity, the discovery you are so very anxious to make, and feel that you have been on the brink of making for so long, is already beyond your reach. When you were a boy, the life of the core was too distant; now that it is finally coming closer, you are no longer a boy—but whoever and whatever you were, you could not find the thing you are hoping to find, because what is actually there is very different. Were you to see the flameflower bloom at close range, it would very likely kill you...and if it did not, it would surely disappoint you. So, I implore you, do not go into the caves this year—or ever again, if you can help it. It is not merely our land, legally as well as morally, but our *world*...and even we cannot always survive there."

There was a slight pause before Dupin spoke for the first time. "As an honest man," he said, dryly, "you do realize, do you not, that everything you have said to us is more likely to increase our determination than to diminish it?"

I remembered what Lucien Groix had said about curiosity killing cats, in spite of their nine lives, and Dupin's occasional tendency to *barge in*.

Lebrun shrugged his shoulders. "I do realize that," he admitted, "but those on whose behalf I am speaking are not convinced of it, for they do not have the understanding of civilized perversity that I have gained in the course of my education, and I have a duty to them as well as to you. Monsieur Guérande is a captive of his birthplace, I know—and I suspect that if you and Monsieur Reynolds were not good friends, who will feel duty bound to lend him your assistance, Madame Guérande would not have appealed to you. I understand your sense of duty, and your temptation too—but it is still my duty, as an honest man, to warn you that there are dangers confronting you that you do not and cannot understand. For the sake of your souls, if you insist on going into the caves tomorrow, or any other day thereafter, *be careful*. I will come to help you, if I must, but I am not at all sure that those on whose behalf I am speaking will come to help me, let alone you. And if you honor your invitation to the Bishop, you must be very careful indeed of his welfare— and you must do everything possible to ensure that we are not blamed, if he does not come out again. Even if you could bear the sight and sound of the flameflower, which I doubt, I cannot believe that the same is true of him, or any Churchman."

"I promise you that we will do our best to keep him safe," Dupin said, "and will make it clear, if anything does go wrong, that your people are not in any way to blame..

"I will make you the same promise," Guérande was quick to add.

"You must have a great many questions," Lebrun said. "I will do my best to answer them, consulting the elders at need. The elders will help, as and when they feel the need, but I beg you to be patient, for translation is a difficult business."

Guérande already had his mouth open—he, at least, could think of half a hundred questions, and I suppose that I could have thought of dozens myself once I had made a start—but Dupin cut in brutally before anyone else could speak.

"No," he said, curtly. "We have no questions to ask. We thank you very much for your generosity in giving us the explanations that you have supplied, and perhaps, when we have talked about it among ourselves, there will be questions that we want to ask—but for the moment, we must leave."

All four of the elders attempted to make some comment, aiming their remarks at Lebrun.

"I'm sorry," said the lawyer from Lyon, "but as you can see, the elders would consider it rather rude if you left just now. It was, as I'm sure you appreciate, a major decision for them to invite you to the camp and sit down in conference with you. You really ought to appreciate the honor, and show them a little more deference. Surely you owe them that?"

"Perhaps so," Dupin replied, rising to his feet, "but the fact is that we have urgent business elsewhere, It's necessary that I speak to the Bishop. I issued my challenge to him without understanding what I was doing. I need to withdraw it, and persuade him not to go into the caves, if I can."

"Perhaps Monsieur Guérande and Monsieur Reynolds could stay a little longer," Lebrun suggested, evidently perceiving that he could not bend Dupin's determination.

"I think not," said Dupin. "I have one question, though, that I would like to ask you now, Monsieur Lebrun. Do you have children?"

Lebrun pursed his lips, but answered regardless: "Yes—two."

"Are they at home, in Lyon?"

"No," Lebrun retorted. "They're at home, *here*." It seemed to be a slightly sore point, perhaps because his own people no longer considered that this as their home, or his.

"Will you introduce us to them?"

Lebrun met Dupin's stare boldly enough, but the elders were no longer capable of maintaining their stern pose of impassive authority. They were exchanging glances in which there was more than a hint of consternation.

"No, Monsieur Dupin," Lebrun said, finally. "We do not allow our children to speak to strangers. We are very protective of them."

"Then you understand my sense of urgency. We had not realized how much danger Monsieur Guérande's daughter might be in—but I think I do, now. Thank you again for your hospitality, but we must go now."

If Guérande had been hesitating, he was not hesitating any longer. He practically bounded to his feet, and I was not slow to follow him. We took our leave as politely as we could contrive to do—which, in the circumstances, seemed rude regardless— and then we left the camp, with hundreds of eyes upon us.

"Do your really think that Sophie is in danger?" Guérande asked, as soon as we were out of earshot of the camp.

"Not if she is maintained under careful surveillance," Dupin said. "Your wife and Madame Cormontaigne are already doing that, I think. She should be safe enough."

"Are you really in so much hurry to see the Bishop, then?"

"I do believe that I ought to talk to him—but no, there's no urgency on that score, unless he makes a sudden move of his own accord."

"Why such haste, then?"

"First of all, to avoid drinking any more of that infernal tea."

"But Lebrun and the elders drank far more than any of us, and it all came out of the same kettle. How could it possibly be poisoned?"

"They had no intention of poisoning us—but I suspect that they were trying to tranquilize us, and perhaps make us a little somnolent. Lebrun was trying to tantalize us, too, with his vague but intriguing account of his people's beliefs. He wanted us to ask questions. The most revealing thing of all in what he said, however, was his careful and continual repetition of the word *tomorrow*. He warned us and implored us, not once but repeatedly, not to go into the caves tomorrow, or at any later date—and he knew, as he readily admitted when accused of it, that the likely effect of what he said was to make us do exactly what he was asking us not to—*exactly* what he was asking us not to do."

"You mean," I said, "that he was actually trying to suggest that we *should* go into the caves tomorrow....or any later date. Not *today*...or tonight."

"He has been the one, all along," Dupin said, "with the greater sense of urgency. He and his people have a very acute sense of the timing of this strange crisis, and whether they have the slightest real understanding of *what* is about to happen or not, I am prepared to believe that they have a fairly clear idea of *when*—as we would too, had we been better able to accomplish what I suggested that we attempt to do last night, and listen for something beyond the snoring of the imaginary dragon."

"You want to go into the caves today, then?" Guérande put in. "I'm not even sure, as yet, that the way is clear." He did not seem at all unhappy about the prospect, though—indeed, he seemed positively eager. His stride was lengthening already.

"If we want to have any chance of seeing the flameflower

boom—or whatever phenomenon it is that Lebrun was prepared to dress up in that twee phrase—I think it might be as well to start soon: this afternoon, perhaps, if we can make our preparations in time. If we were to leave it until tomorrow, however early, we might be too late to reach the heart of the mountain in time—which is, I think, exactly what Lebrun and the Thierachian elders wanted to happen."

"But they've tranquilized themselves in the process," I pointed out.

"The elders never had the slightest intention of going into the caves," Dupin said. "That's not their job, any more. The Bishop, I suspect, spoke more truly than he could possibly have suspected when he asked us how many Thierachian children had gone into the caves over the years, never to come out again and never to have their disappearances noted in any parish record. Perhaps he is also right in his belief that the entrances ought to be blocked up, in spite of the artifacts sheltered within, in order to save future Thierachian children from the same risk. But before then....if there is a chance that we might see something, no matter what, that will not be accessible to human eyes again for a thousand years, I think we ought to do our utmost to take advantage of the opportunity, don't you?"

"Absolutely," said Guérande. "I knew that I could rely on you, Dupin."

But this, I could not help thinking, *is exactly what Madame Guérande was and is relying on Dupin to prevent*. Suddenly, the adorable Julie's little finger seemed a very weak reed indeed. How could she ever have thought it capable of competing with the machinations of the dragon under the hill?

"We could have learned more, though," I reminded them. "Just a few well-judged questions...."

"No," said Dupin, "I don't believe that we could. I'm even prepared to suspect that the information Lebrun just laid out as a lure might be a tissue of lies, intended to conceal rather than explain the Thierachians' true beliefs—perhaps intended to appeal specifically to our own prejudices, our own presumptions. Even if it was deliberately deceptive, however, it was a mask that had to be fitted over superficial phenomena that we can perceive as well as they can, and it's not impossible that the explanation they've concocted is more accurate than the one they're still trying to keep secret."

"You believe, then...," Guérande began—although he really should have known better.

"It's not a matter for belief," Dupin snapped. "All we have— and I suspect that we're not at any great disadvantage in relation to the Thierachians, in this regard—are fancies and hypotheses. Of one thing, and one thing only, can we be reasonably certain: that something very unusual, anticipated for a very long time by those sensitive to its timescale, is likely to happen tonight or early tomorrow morning. If we want to be close enough to it to experience it as fully as we can, we need to hurry."

"Do you discount what Lebrun said about the danger, then?" I asked.

"Of course not," Dupin replied, trying hard to match Claude Guérande's generous stride, but failing miserably. "I'm convinced that the danger is very real—but I won't shirk it, given that the opportunity is likely to be unique within my life-time."

"Good man!" said Guérande, slowing down slightly in order that Dupin and I could keep up with him. "I wouldn't have thought that of you, you know, in the old days. You weren't so bold back then."

"Not nearly bold enough, I think," Duping muttered, in a tone that was not even intended for my ears, although I contrived to catch the words.

Dupin did not think it necessary to ask, but Guérande turned to me then and said; "Are you with us, old man?"

Old man! I thought. *Old man! Is that a gesture of friendship, an insult or a challenge?*

"It's my duty," I told him, brusquely, with a sarcastic edge to my voice. "In Madame Lacuzon's absence, who else is there to protect Dupin from the effects of his own intemperance? And he might not be the only one I'm obliged to protect, for, if my eyes don't deceive me, the Bishop really has made the sudden move that Dupin half-anticipated."

What I meant by that observation was that the Bishop was now clearly visible on the threshold of the Guérande house, having evidently been inside, awaiting our return. He had the same two Dominicans with him as before, but this time he was wearing a heavy ceremonial crucifix on his breast, supported by a chain around his neck, and he was carrying a leather-bound book.

"If I were a gambling man," I said, "I'd lay odds that the Bishop dreamed about the Devil last night—and now is in haste to perform an exorcism, before he seals his supposed lair."

There are times, as I almost said, when even the hardest skeptic begins to trust the luck, or intuition, of his guesses. They are, however, very rarely the times when he wants most ardently to be proved correct.

CHAPTER FIFTEEN
THE DESCENT

The Bishop was, indeed, intent on performing an exorcism, and the gleam in his eyes was that of fanaticism as well as faith. He had, indeed, had a dire dream, vivid enough to be counted—in his estimation, at least—as a revelation and a divine command.

"Something is happening, Messieurs," he declared, evidently in no mood to be contradicted. "I feel it; I know it. Whether you will consent to guide me or not, Monsieur Guérande, I am determined to go into the caves. I was summoned here for a purpose, without my quite knowing what it was at first. Now I do know, and must fulfill my mission. The Devil is abroad in this land, Messieurs, and not for the first time in recorded history. It is my duty to oppose the Father of Lies, and I shall not shirk that duty."

"It will be dangerous," Guérande told him, frostily.

"You have no idea how dangerous, Monsieur Guérande. I know that you will not be grateful to have a man of God with you, but you do not understand the true nature of your peril. I am here to save you from the forces of evil, whether you know it or not."

"I am not in need of salvation," Guérande told him, "and your presence would only slow us down, inhibiting our scientific research."

"On the other hand," Dupin said, placing his hand on his friend's arm, "it might be safer for all of us if we were to stay together—and we cannot prevent the Bishop going where he will."

"We can't," Guérande muttered, "but the landowner might."

"It's too late now to open that kind of discussion," Dupin said, curtly. "Tomorrow, or next week, perhaps...but for now, we must make our preparations." In a louder voice he said: "Monsieur Aignan will not mind waiting, I hope, while we gather equipment and supplies. If the Devil is there, I'm sure he won't mind waiting for *him*—Churchmen are, after all, the tastiest morsels of all so far as the dark collector of souls is concerned."

The Bishop scowled at the casual irreverence, but he did consent to wait for us. He was sufficiently intimidated by the caves to want a guide, if he could obtain one. He consented to come back into the house for a while and sit down in the drawing room.

There were other delays, of course—but Madame Guérande was not as furious with Dupin as I had expected. Indeed, she seemed reconciled to the fact that her husband could not be kept out of the caves, and rather glad of the fact that he was not going alone.

"Bring him back safely, Auguste, I beg you," she murmured, when she was sure that her husband could not hear her. She too seemed glad to find Dupin a little bolder now than he had been when she first knew him—although I could not tell how deeply she might regret the fact that he had not been bolder then.

"I shall do my utmost, Madame," Dupin replied, politely.

In fact, there was not very much in the way of gathering to be done, as Guérande had made is preparations in the house while waiting for the thaw, and had already taken the opportunity the day before to add extra ropes, helmets and safety-lamps to the pile. All that still needed to be freshly prepared and packed was food.

Even so, I noticed as the tools and instruments were distributed that Guérande had only made provision for three. I had observed that Brother Xavier and Brother Michael were carrying lanterns, and had bulging pouches at their waist, but they were markedly undersupplied by comparison with us.

"They have God on their side, and church candles," said Guérande, when I raised the possibility of offering them extra equipment. "What need do they have of hand-axes and stout ropes?"

And so we finally set off, a not-entirely-disunited party. As we began to climb the slope I saw Sophie and Madame Cormontaigne watching us from the window of the improvised schoolroom. I waved, but neither the child nor the governess replied. Guérande was too preoccupied to have noticed. Guérande, I knew, must have given the strictest instructions to his wife and staff that the little girl was to be very closely watched, les her habitual goodness lapse and some strange whim take possession of her.

In spite of the thick vegetation, we must have been clearly visible from the Thierachian encampment for long period of time as we scaled the mountain slope, but I could not see any sign of activity there suggestive of the possibility that anyone might come after us.

I did wonder briefly, whether Lebrun might have anticipated Dupin's cleverness, and made provision for it in advance, planning all along to encourage us to make our expedition today instead of postponing it until the morrow, but I decided that I was crediting him with to much slyness and subtlety, even for a lawyer trained in Lyon.

Guérande led us, at an uncompromising stride, to the topmost of the three openings he had already shown us—the broadest of the three, and the one easiest for adults to penetrate, at least for a short distance. Once we had negotiated the first steep slope and the floor of the tunnel leveled out, we would have been in pitch darkness but for the lamps. We had lit three. Guérande, in the lead, was carrying one. I was carrying the second, positioned in the middle of the file after Dupin. Brother Xavier, behind the Bishop, was carrying the third. It took me a little while to realize that Brother Michael was no longer with us.

"You've left the other friar to guard the entrance?" I said to the Bishop.

"It seemed a wise precaution," Aignan replied, a trifle sarcastically. "He will wait all night if necessary—but if we're not back by dawn, he will summon help from the château, and from the Thierachian camp, if they're willing to provide it."

"They told us that they would make no promises in that regard," I said, "but I think it was a stratagem, aimed to dissuade us. They will come, if need be, as they once did for the elder brother of your friend's ancestor—the true Comte de Tibère."

"What do you mean?" Aignan demanded, sharply.

I told him what Lebrun had told us about his researches. It helped to distract me from the difficulties and anxieties of the descent—for we were descending by degrees, as well as moving closer to the heart of the mountain. The path that Guérande had marked out was tortuous, but he had no need to be distracted by any blind alleys or unprofitable side-turnings. He knew where he was going; we had only to follow. There were narrow passages, and passages where we had to crawl, but there was a road of sorts.

Talking to the Bishop did not prevent me from taking note of the markers than Guérande and others before him had scored into the rock at various junctions, but their meaning seemed clear enough and they did not require overmuch mental effort to learn. Because talking seemed to be doing me more good than harm, I continued. By degrees, I told Philippe Aignan *everything* that Arnauld Lebrun had told us, including what he had said in the camp that morning. I refreshed my own memory in the reportage—gladly, because I had not yet had a chance to write any of it down.

Whether Aignan was as grateful for the opportunity to listen as I was for the opportunity to talk, I could not tell do it, but I dare say that it gave him abundant food for thought. He had more difficulty than any of us as we walked, crawled and occasionally clambered. I can only suppose that he listened to it all with a firm determination not to believe a single word about the Thierachians' supposed beliefs—and perhaps rightly so—but the news that he had been correct about the fate of at least some of the children whose names he had collected was sufficiently flattering to command conviction, and I judged that he had some difficulty rejecting the tale of the true Comte out of hand. The Thierachians' account of subterranean life and the blossoming of the flameflowers might be mere nonsense to a man whose conception of the world had been framed and limited by the Bible, but tales of stolen children and missing heirs were as plausible to him as they were to the audiences flocking into the cheap theaters of the Boulevard du Temple.

While I was telling my second-hand story, we heard numerous sounds, from above as well as below, much louder than those that were to be heard in Guérande's house—but here, for some reason, they seemed much more obviously the sounds of water running and rock creaking. Now that we were inside the imaginary dragon, they were no longer suggestive of breathing or even of a rumbling gut. They were just sounds—to me, at least. I did not enquire of the Bishop of Viviers as to whether he heard them as the muted threats of the Devil Incarnate.

The way had been eased considerably by the work that Guérande had done over the years, installing footholds and handholds, and even ladders to make awkward slopes negotiable. The Thierachians had not made any attempt to destroy or sabotage his work—perhaps because they were glad of it themselves. There was no ice in evidence, and not much water, although many of the walls and floors were damp, and we passed by several vertical trickles that doubtless made up streams further down. There were several places where I had to squeeze myself through exceedingly narrow gaps, including at least two that I thought the Bishop would be unable to pass—but with a little pulling on my part and a good deal of shoving on the part of the wiry stonemason, we succeeded in maintaining the number of our party.

Guérande took the trouble to explain, even to the two clergymen, the meaning of the various guide-marks he had placed whenever there as a junction in the tunnels, in order that he would not lose his way. He also pointed out other scars in the rock, which were not his, but seemed to serve the same purpose.

"Made by the Thierachians, no doubt," he said. "How long ago, I would not care to guess."

"For the guidance of their children," the Bishop muttered, disgustedly, having evidently absorbed that part of my narrative if not much else.

"Perhaps," I said, "but I'm not sure that the children come this way. There are, as you have doubtless observed, paths to two further entrances than the one we used, but which children could scramble through. There might be a more direct way than this to where we are going."

"This one certainly seems labyrinthine," aid the Bishop. "I long ago lost track of the direction in with we are headed, in terms of the compass, although there is no doubt that we are making our way downwards. We must be deep within the hill by now—and it's becoming fearfully hot."

"It's warmer than usual," Guérande admitted, "especially for the time of year. Be careful along this ledge—I've no idea how deep the cleft alongside it is, but it's not one in which I'd care to fall." By way of illustration, he dropped a pebble into the gap. We heard it bounce of the wall three times before it stopped tumbling—but even then, it could have been caught in some cleft rather than falling as far as it might have done.

Nobody fell—but we clung so close to the wall of the ledge that our hands and clothing were covered with black slime. There was nothing alive down here, so far as I could tell, but organic debris was washed down from the soil on top of the hill as the rainwater leached away, and wherever there was trickling water, it seemed muddy. Evidently, it was filtered by porous rock before it made its way out again in the form of spring water.

Finally, Guérande stopped, and said: "This is the first of the painted caverns." It was a simple statement, but he did not need to add any more.

It was the first time we had come to a sizeable chamber, where there was a flat floor on which a dozen people could have stood in relative comfort, and two reasonably flat walls. Where the walls were not flat, the projections of rock had been chiseled: not exactly sculpted, but at least engraved.

Everywhere the lamplight fell, there were images: images of animals. There were horses and bison, deer and shaggy cattle, hares and goats. Many were whole, seemingly moving in herds, but some were only partial: images of heads, for the most part. I searched for human figures, but could not find any. The paintings were, I suppose, primitive, but not in the sense that they were mere stick-figures, or that their limbs were wrongly articulated, as one often sees in drawings of horses and cattle made by modern children. The most remarkable thing about them, however, was the coloring: reds, blacks and browns, artfully shaded, which might have been even sharper once upon a time, but had now faded and blurred somewhat.

It was the colors that suggested, strongly, that the paintings had been renewed and repaired over time, for some of the pigment-layers were clearly overlaid on others. The retouching had not been compelled by fading; although time had certainly taken a toll on some of the images, they were so rarely subjected to illumination that light had not had sufficient opportunity to weaken and dull the dyes. Nor, so far as I could tell, had the extra layers of pigment been added by way of correction or improvement of the imagery; there did not seem to be any conspicuous development in the sophistication of the images. Indeed, it seemed to me, judging purely by intuition, that the later contributions to the cluttered and confused murals had been made purely and simply for the sake of making a contribution, of becoming part of an enterprise extending over centuries, millennia, and perhaps tens of millennia.

There was no water here; the cave was perfectly dry—but it was not quite as hot as some of the corridors we had recently come through, and the heat seemed to be in the air, not the rock itself.

It was the Bishop who voiced the obvious question. "Why? Why here, of all places? Why so far away from the surface?"

"The probability is," Guérande told him, "that they made similar artwork in a thousand other places, nearer to the surface and out in the open too—but the paintings exposed to the atmospheric weather and the seepage of water did not survive, even for a meager human lifetime. Perhaps their location here does have some additional mystical significance, but I suspect that this was simply the one place where the images were able to survive. I think it might have begun as a kind of schoolroom, where the children of nomadic hunters could be taught the arts they needed, in peace and seclusion—secretively, to be sure, but straightforwardly. Over time though, utilitarian functions acquire ritual elements, which are gradually embellished by the superstitious imagination."

I wasn't at all sure about that hypothesis. The "schoolroom" was a long way inside the mountain—too far, surely, to be convenient. The Bishop was even less happy with it, perceiving the tacit insult to the rituals of his own faith.

"I do not believe," Aignan stated, flatly, "that the Thierachians began sending their children into the mountain to be educated here as hunters. That's preposterous."

Guérande would not budge. "Perhaps they had to come this far to find exactly the right conditions of dryness, temperature and protective darkness required for their artwork to last. The ancestors of the Thierachians thought in terms of long periods of time, remember, at lest fictitiously. However much falsehood has been incorporated into their traditions, the traditions in question certainly aspire to longevity—and if I'm right about these pictures being tens of thousand of years old...."

"Then they must indeed be the work of the Devil," the Churchman told him, "And my work is to oppose him, with the Lord's help."

"There's more," said Guérande, ignoring the Bishop's assertions as if they were no more meaningful than the inarticulate noises of the mountain. "Tread carefully, I beg you—and for Heaven's sake, don't touch. Whether my estimates of their antiquity are accurate or not, the careless thrust of a thumb or a boot could still spoil something priceless."

There was, indeed, more. There were many more animals, individual and in groups, including much larger and more elaborate "engravings" in the ancient volcanic rock. There were human figures too, among the animals in the second chamber—again, not stick figures, through hardly portraits of a similar sophistication to those the street-artists of Montmartre will make for you in a matter of minutes. There were strange faces, of small men, often naked but sometimes wrapped in furs—but it seemed to me that there were no women, unless some of the children represented were girls. There were probably as many children as adults, although it was not always easy to tell the two categories apart. It was not easy to see what the humans were supposed to be doing, if anything, except for a handful wielding club and spears, seemingly threatening running animals. They, at least, were plausible images of hunters, perhaps bolstering Guérande's hypothesis.

Beyond the second chamber, however, the depictions became more peculiar. There were dots and streaks, approximate circles and ragged asterisks, but I could not make head not tail out of their order, if there was any order to them. I could not believe that they were an attempt at writing, however crude, for there was no obvious trace of attempted pictographic symbolism or vertical or horizontal alignment. Perhaps there was raw material for a story there, but I could not see it. There was color on the walls here too, but no longer organized in such a way as to replicate colored objects, like animal hides.

There were many bones accumulated in the corners of the third chamber, neatly sorted into various heaps—the careful work of Claude Guérande, I assumed. There were sticks with traces of pigment still evident on the frayed ends, but they had to be recent. There were flints too, and some evidence that the flints had been used to chip or break the bones, but they seemed to be simply more of the specimens we had seen shelved in Guérande's cabinet of curiosities. His selection seemed to be a representative sample, as one would expect of a careful collector and analyst.

In the fourth and smallest chamber there were more dots and streaks, but there was much more color, including one vast complex swirl in the center of the largest flat space on the most nearly-vertical wall. It was dull now, but it did not take much imagination to wonder whether its yellow and white pigment had once been much brighter, making the whole disk glow, even in the worst kind of tallow candlelight imaginable.

"It's the Sun," said the Bishop—which was, I suppose, better than the judgment that it was the face of the Devil.

"It's a flameflower," Dupin corrected. "Not drawn from life, I presume, and perhaps not even from memory—but that is what it must surely be intended to represent."

"I agree," said Guérande. "Given what we heard this morning, even making no assumptions regarding its sincerity, it must be a flameflower."

The bishop was skeptical, in spite of my repetition of the bizarre tale we had been told that morning. "It is the Sun," he repeated, softly. "And who could blame the artist, for thinking longingly of the Sun, in this dark and dismal place?"

"Not so dark and dismal," I said. "Have you noticed, Seigneur, that the groaning and hissing has almost died away. Perhaps it is still being produced closer to the surface, enough to make Guérande's house an apparent abode of phantoms still, but here, we're insulated from it. Here, it's dry, and quiet, and tolerably warm. Our lamps are not so very bright, it's true, but this is by no means darkness, and I find it a rather friendly place—no abode of the Devil, to be sure, not Hades either. This is not Hell, Seigneur."

Aignan looked at me in puzzlement, as if he were surprised to find that he no longer felt the anxiety and peculiar urgency that had driven him to seek the place out, armed for an exorcism. At least, he no longer felt them quite as strongly—but if he had the same intuition as I did, he knew that the truce was a temporary one, born of this special location. This was not the location for which the Thierachian children had been aiming, else they would be here. If we hoped to see the flameflower, we had to go on—and I knew that we would go on, and that the Bishop's suspicion that we were drawing closer to the Devil's throne might well return in force.

While the Bishop and I were looking at one another, peering in the uncertain lamplight in search of some light in one another's eyes, Dupin was saying to Guérande: "What you need to bring down here, my friend, is photographic apparatus. like that recently developed in Paris by Daguerre, the use of which is becoming quite a craze. Far better than any drawing or verbal description, that will give your *mémoire* the force it needs to take the Académie by storm. That is what we must do: we must transport as much photographic apparatus as we can from Paris, and take as may daguerreotypes as possible."

"We?" Guérande queried.

"I'm trying to help you, Claude, not steal your thunder," Dupin insisted. "It will be, as it has always been, your *mémoire*, your discovery, your triumph—but photography is the means you have been waiting for, to make accurate reportage possible. Magnesium lighting is tricky, but with a little assistance, you might do what it has not been practicable for you to do alone."

They too, I noticed, seemed to have lost their earlier sense of urgency, their earlier restlessness.

But we are here how, I thought, *and no longer need to be enticed.* And then, as an afterthought: *Except that we are only here, in a relatively safe place, to which a road of sorts has been contrived. There is much more, and deeper, and if we are to have any hope of seeing the flameflower bloom, we must go further.*

"How much further have you explored?" I asked Guérande.

"Hundreds of meters in several directions," he said. "I've found some marks, and left many more, but when we go on, we must be very careful. The hollow core of the mountain, where the chimneys are, along which lava once flowed in the very distant past, is not so far away. I have not been able to attach ladders to the most intriguing shafts. If any of you have any doubts about continuing, now is the time to turn back."

The Bishop assumed that the invitation as addressed to him, but the temporary ebbing of his anxiety had cut both ways, and he was not a man to back down from a challenge. "I'm no cosseted cleric, relaxing in the quietude of a cloister," he said to Guérande. "Nor is Brother Xavier. We are here to take the fight to the Evil One, if he dares to reveal his presence, and I am determined to do that. Lead on, Monsieur Guérande."

Once again, we arranged ourselves in single file, and set forth with due concentration, listening for Guérande's instructions. Now, however, there seemed to be marks in both branches of every junction, and I was no longer sure that I would be able to remember which ones held the key to a successful return, if I had to make my way alone.

"This is the most promising of the paths, in my opinion," Guérande told us, "though not the easiest. We'll be on the threshold of uncharted territory soon enough."

"Given that you're the only one who has a chart," the Bishop muttered, "that will make little difference to the rest of us." He muttered in order that his voice should not echo, for when Guérande called back to us his voice sometimes rebounded eerily from near and distant walls, occasionally distorted so that the French words seemed transformed into some barbaric tongue.

As the Bishop stopped speaking, however, we heard an echo that was not his voice, nor Guérande's, unless it was extremely distorted. It was shrill and it was plaintive, although no words could be made out at all.

I stopped, and the Bishop almost collided with me. I felt his hand on my shoulder as he steadied himself. It was trembling.

"It's not the Devil," I whispered, fearful of echoes myself. "It's a child—a boy—and although his speech is Thierachian, I have no doubt that he's calling for help."

"You're right," said Dupin. "And we must provide it, if we can."

CHAPTER SIXTEEN
THE DEPTHS

It was not easy to follow the direction of the cries for help, whose echoes made them deceptive, but Guérande had spent so much time in the caves over the years that he was sure of himself even in passages where he had never set foot before— not that he was able to stay upright for much of the time. The Bishop's difficulties became extreme, but he seemed reanimated now, not so much by any Christian determination to help a child in distress but by the sharp renewal of anxieties and obsessions that had been momentarily lulled. He squirmed and he squeezed, and tolerated some rude shoving by Brother Xavier, but he got through the worst of the narrows, and seemed genuinely disappointed when we came to an abrupt halt, confronted for the first time by a seemingly-insuperable obstacle.

We found ourselves at the top of a sheer cliff, which extended into seemingly-illimitable darkness. The cries for help were clearer here, coming from directly below, but rebounding repeatedly from an invisible wall that must have been at least twenty meters away. The cliff extended upwards as well as down; it certainly seemed to be the wall of a deep well inside the mountain, which had once reached a crater that time and the weather had rounded off. It was by no means neatly cylindrical, but it was a shaft of sorts.

For the first time, as we peered into that abyss, unfathomable by our light and perhaps by our imagination, I wondered whether the cries of the child might be a hallucination, akin to the breathing of the non-existent dragon, or a lure, tempting us to out destruction by appealing to our compassion.

Perhaps, I thought, there was no child in need of succor. Perhaps there was nothing but that dark gullet, extending in serpentine fashion all the way to the Earth's hot core, into which no human could safely descend, and from which none could ever return.

Dupin, who had moved a little way along the ledge to shield himself from Guérande's lantern, said: "I think I can see a light down there. They have a lamp of some sort. It is not so very far—although I cannot tell, of course, where they are on a substantial floor, or merely a ledge like this one."

"They?" Guérande queried, after a pause, belatedly taking note of Dupin's exact terminology.

"I think there's more than one voice, although they are taking turns to call out. Their lungs seem sound enough, so it is possible that they're calling out on behalf of a third party. I think there's a group, perhaps a company of children there, gathered for the same reason that we have come here: in the hope of seeing the flameflower when it blooms."

No one ventured to correct him by alleging that we had only come to that particular spot in response to the cries for help. We knew where we were, and why we had come. We were no longer in the haven of the painted caves. Our journey was in a new phase now.

I no longer knew what I felt, or ought to feel. This was alien territory.

Brother Xavier had knelt down, and had lowered his lantern over the edge of the precipice. "It's very steep," he said, "but not quite vertical—and there are clefts and spurs in abundance. I have no fear of heights, and I've climbed walls sheerer than this one. I think I can get down."

"You don't know that," Guérande said. "Our lanterns are better than theirs, but nine-tenths of the drop is invisible from here. You have no idea what you'll find lower down."

"I smell brimstone," the Bishop announced.

He was right. There was indeed a faint odor of sulfur rising up from the deeps, along with a distinct updraft powered by heat below, presumably renewed by air sucked into the shaft from clefts life the one that had brought us to the ledge, connected by labyrinthine paths to the outside of the mountain.

"There's not enough to make the air dangerous," Guérande said. "The greatest danger in cave-complexes like this, once trapped water has drained away, is accumulated carbonic acid gas—but that can't build to hazardous levels at this level when there are shafts like this one to drain it away. The organic detritus washed down by the melt-water doubtless forms methane somewhere down below, but that can't rise up either, in sufficient quantity to be dangerous, even in an updraft like the one in his shaft."

"If you will give me the use of your longest rope, Monsieur Guérande," said Brother Xavier, "I'll go down. I should do it alone, for it might need all your strength to pull up the children—especially the one who is injured—and perhaps to help me climb back."

"It's not a child," the Bishop stated, flatly. "It's an imp of Satan, luring us to our doom." He was perfectly serious, and there was no doubt in his voice.

I wished with all my heart that I had no sympathy with what he said, but a similar thought had occurred to me, without the clothing of Satanism. I too doubted that that voice was really that of a child—but I did not lend the Churchman any support. As usual, I looked to Dupin for a decisive opinion, and took his silence for a denial.

The Dominican was a mere artisan monk, and Philippe Aignan was the Bishop of Viviers; the difference in status between them was immense, and must have been considerable even before they took Holy Orders—but the humble stock from which Xavier had come before he was renamed Xavier was stubborn, commonsensical and confident. "It's a child," he stated again. "A pagan child, no doubt, but a soul in peril. I'm going down."

"I'll go," said Guérande.

"You won't, Monsieur," the Dominican said, firmly. "You might have been crawling around these caves for years, but you haven't climbed as many walls, or sat on as many ledges as I have. This is no cathedral, but a wall's a wall and a fall's a fall. Once I know what the situation is, Monsieur, we can decide what to do next, but until then, it's vital that we only risk one of our own party, and the one most likely to make the climb successfully. That's me—but I'll borrow your little helmet-lamp if you won't mind, for I can't carry this larger one."

I could not consider the helmet-lamp a reliable instrument, although I knew that coal-miners had been using them for years when they needed free hands and could not place lanterns on the floor in such a way as to light their work. The demand for coal had increased so vastly with the advent of the steam engine, and its application to ocean liners and railway locomotives, that progress in the design of such lamps had been necessarily rapid.

Guérande wasted no more time in futile debate; he gave Xavier the end of our longest rope to tie around his waist, and made arrangements on the ledge to pay it out slowly and securely. The Dominican put on the helmet with the lighted lamp, and immediately began his descent, having already scouted out the best available footholds. Within a matter of seconds, he had disappeared.

The Bishop was already muttering prayers, with his hand pressed to the crucifix on his breast—a crucifix that was now soiled and scarred, having suffered the ravages of our journey. He no longer had the missal he had been carrying when we set off, having abandoned it *en route* as an unnecessary inconvenience, but I had no doubt that he could remember the formulae of exorcism, if he felt the need to pronounce them.

The cries for help had died stopped once the children below had realized that help was coming. We did not understand Thierachian, but they understood at least a little French, and had heard our reassurances gladly.

We did not have long to wait. Xavier called up to us within

a few minutes that he had reached the ledge where the children were. It was a ledge, he told us, his voice echoing up the well, but a broad one, and the continuation of the shaft was much narrower and not so nearly vertical as the section he had just negotiated. There were four children there, two boys and two girls. One of the girls had fallen badly, but she had injured her wrists and hands more severely than her ankles and knees. Xavier told us that it might not be necessary to pull them up, and that with his assistance and better light, they might be able to retrace their own route more easily than ours...eventually.

"What do you mean, *eventually*?" Guérande demanded, shouting down into the pit.

"The others want to wait," Xavier said. "Even the one who is hurt doesn't want to go back before...whatever they are waiting for. They want assistance for the injured girl, but they don't want to go back—not yet."

He had listened while I was telling the Bishop what the Thierachians had said to us, I knew. Nobody had told him anything, but he had listened. He knew what it was that the children had come to see—and he knew, too, what Philippe Aignan was convinced that they would actually see. He was a brave man—but at least he had confirmed that the children were real, and that they were, in fact, merely children.

"Is it safe to come down?" Guérande asked.

"Better not, Monsieur," Xavier replied.

"I asked, *is it safe*?" Guérande demanded.

After a moment's hesitation, the Dominican replied: "Yes, Monsieur, if you're agile—but you must be very careful, and you must deploy your ropes wisely."

"He's right, Claude," said Dupin. "Better not."

"Shut up, Auguste!" Guérande spat out, with a sudden and most unexpected explosion of bile. "You have no voice in my decisions, no matter what Julie might think. I should never have given her permission to hare off to Paris—but I wanted her out of the way, for once. I never imagined that she would return so rapidly, or that you would ever consent to come. This is not your affair. Go back, I beg you. Take your friend and the Bishop with you. There's nothing for any of you here. *This is mine.*"

Dupin, for once nonplussed, could find no reply—not, at least, until Guérande had fitted a second helmet-lamp to his head and disappeared over the edge. I could not tell whether he had deployed his ropes wisely, but I suspected not. Nor was there a third helmet-lamp in the equipment we were carrying, although I had observed at least two in the deposits we had passed on our journey, and thought that I could find my way back to the painted caves if necessary.

"Damn!" said Dupin, quietly. "This is what Julie wanted me to prevent. I've failed her."

For a moment, I thought he might start climbing down himself, leaving me to look after the Bishop—or *vice versa*—but he was not that foolhardy. First, he needed to think: to weigh up the situation, which had developed thus far with too much momentum, even in the intervals in which it had lacked urgent haste.

"Is something going to happen soon?" I asked him, softly, although I knew the answer. I didn't require confirmation, but I did want to hear his voice. I didn't know what to feel, and I thought that his patient, rational and wise voice might help me. I wanted to feel secure, at least in the prison of my own consciousness, and I thought that he might be able to shore up those walls—and perhaps work a tiny miracle on the Bishop's behalf, if Aignan were still amenable to reason.

"We must assume so," Dupin replied, as if struggling for his own security through the medium of speech. "I cannot tell what, and I'm certainly not prepared to take what Lebrun told us at face value, but whatever the phrase might mean, I'm prepared to believe that the metaphorical dragon is going to awake and the literal flameflower to bloom. We might have to wait for a few hours yet, but the awakening will happen, and *something* will bloom, soon enough."

"A breach in the boundaries separating us from the worlds that fill the emptiness?" I suggested.

"Possibly," Dupin assented, "but it's possible, too, that Claude and the Thierachians are correct, and that there are seeds of life within the Earth as well as on its surface, some of which have lain dormant there since the planet coalesced from the nebula that once surrounded the nascent sun. If so, those seeds might indeed have their own evolutionary thrust built into them, producing a system of life very different from the one that has colonized the oceans, the land and the atmosphere. If so... however peripheral the phenomenon might be that we might be privileged to witness, it might be very remarkable."

"Do you really believe that?" I asked him.

"It's not a matter for belief," he told me, inevitably. "It's purely hypothesis. But if there really are seeds of life drifting in space, as Huygens, Tiphaigne de la Roche, Montlivault and others have suggested, which sow the depths as well as the surfaces of planets as they form, there is no reason why there should not be many different kinds of seeds, and if the principle of pleni-tude holds in distributing universes through empty space, and life throughout those universes, there is no reason why there should not be evolutionary stories unfolding everywhere, in the hot cores of worlds as well as on their cool surfaces."

"Even to the extent of the evolution of mind?"

"Especially to that extent," he said. "One thing we cannot doubt is the mental effects that have afflicted this mountain and valley, both recently and in the distant past. That, we can feel, even as newcomers—perhaps *especially*, as newcomers. That something is reaching out to us, by means of something we construe as sound, for want of any better analogy, we know. It cannot speak to us; perhaps it can do no more than make us feel a vague and essentially incoherent disturbance, but we do not know of what it might be capable, in moments of rare effort—and I understand why Claude is so eager to find out, no matter what peril he has to brave. I shall be deeply sorry if I fail Julie—but I would be equally sorry, now, were I to fail him. He was my friend, once. He still is, in spite of everything."

"Do you intend to follow him, then?" I asked, fearfully. I

did not think that I was capable of descending the cliff, and the thought of being trapped on a narrow ledge with the Bishop of Viviers, in the grip of religious mania, was not attractive.

"I'm not at all sure that I can," Dupin admitted. "The spirit would be willing, if the flesh were not so weak, but I'm not a man of action. That Dominican is a brave and good-hearted fellow, though—a great credit to your Church, Seigneur."

The Bishop had, of course, been listening to our conversation, although how much of it he had understood I could not tell.

"Brave he is," he muttered. "I warned him—but I doubt that he has the strength of soul to withstand the Devil. The flesh is, indeed, weak, Monsieur Dupin. But my soul must be strong enough, now, to meet its crucial challenge. Creation was not what you imagine it to be: like Pascal, Voltaire and all the rest, you have been Devil-led into an intellectual maze far darker and crueler than this filthy labyrinth. Creation was the work of God, and only God can preserve us now. We are deep in the Devil's clutches, but I, at least, have nothing to fear, for I have the might of the Lord in my soul and my hand. The Devil is near; I can smell him and I can feel him—but I am ready for him."

Dupin did not scoff. He merely said: "I'm glad. Do what you can, Seigneur, and what you must: but be ready, I beg you, to do your utmost to save your flesh if, perchance, the Devil defies your divine authority."

The lamplight had deteriorated, in both the oil-lamp that I was holding and the candle-lamp that the Bishop had taken from Brother Xavier. Both were in need of renewal. Even in the yellow gloom, however, I could see that the Bishop's face was taut and drawn, and that his eyes were wild and blazing: that something was within him less simple than fear or terror— something that was, as Dupin had said, reaching out for all of us, gropingly, not even knowing what we were, or whether we could respond.

Perhaps it was to Aignan's advantage, I thought, that he could put a name to it, however incorrect and inappropriate the name might be. I could not, and I suspected that my own face and my own eyes were gradually developing those same symptoms of distress, but I had other advantages—not as well-developed as those which Dupin, the greatest magician in Paris, had at his disposal, but advantages nevertheless. I had not only heard siren songs before, but had accompanied them with stolen fingers and a borrowed mind, which had left their inevitable residue in the murky depths of my memory.

I was by no means sure that I could watch the flameflower bloom with impunity, even at a distance, but I was sure that I could do what Dupin was asking of the Bishop, and exert the last resources of my mind and flesh in saving my life thereafter.

Dupin knew that. He whispered in my ear: "We must save him if we can. Lucien would want us to try."

"Was Groix in love with Julie too?" I asked, on impulse. "Whether he was sent to the salon as a spy or not, did he fall victim to her flirtatiousness? I asked him, but he would not tell me."

"How should I know what is in another man's secret heart?" Dupin replied, with a trace of bitterness. "He's a married man now, just as Julie is a married woman. Neither is entitled to regret."

But Dupin was not married, and surely never would be, now. Was he entitled to regret? I knew that he would not tell me, if I asked—and how could I possibly know what was in another man's secret heart, any more than I could know what was in the secret heart of a world, inaccessible to any kind of life belonging to the delicate dendrite extended in time between monad and man?

"The dragon," Philippe Aignan said, in a low voice, as he changed the candle in his lamp, "is the Devil. The symbolism is as old as the Church, and probably older. He seems to sleep, sometimes for centuries, but while he sleeps, his dreams are echoed in the human soul, and he wakes from time to time, to extend his grip—but he shall not have mine. Mine is consecrated to the Lord; I am his warrior, like the saints of old. I wear their spiritual armor, and I wield their spiritual sword. Heretics you may be, and idolaters too, but I will not desert you. When you see what the fiery swords of the militant angels can do, you will come back to the fold. Trust in me, my children, and I will protect you from Lucifer the prideful, the bringer of hostile light. I will protect you from Satan the Father of Lies, the enemy of innocence, and all his vile imps."

I had renewed the oil in my own lamp while he was speaking but I was by no means satisfied with its glow, which still seemed uncommonly jaundiced, and more than a trifle sickly. Reflexively, I put out my hand to touch the wall, to make certain of its support. It had felt warm before, but it was hotter now, as if feverish. It no longer felt like rock at all, but more like flesh: not delicate flesh, like that of a child or a woman, but hard, callused flesh, like the hand of a stonemason or some other practiced artisan. It was hard and horny, but it felt alive, not throbbing with the beat of an animal heart, but quivering, with some mysterious kind of protoplasmic surge.

"It's beginning," I said to Dupin.

"It's been beginning for years, and for centuries," he said, calmly. "Nor will it end for a long time yet—perhaps the lifetime of the planet, even if that is to be measured in billions of years. But it's changing, as all living things change. It's reaching some kind of existential climax, as all living things do. It's playing its part in the surge of evolution, its communication of the urge to improvement, the urge to feel."

He reached out as he spoke, and took my hand—as much, I think, for his own need as for his perception of mine. At that moment, we both needed society—but when we both reached out to take the Bishop's hands, he would not join our triangle. He was standing up on the ledge, staring out into the eerie orange gloom, and he began to chant, in Latin. His exorcism had begun.

I knew that it wasn't going to work, in any literal sense, but I hoped that it might be enough to save his soul, now that he was evidently in need of some sort of salvation.

For myself, I tried to wedge myself as securely as I could

into the angle of the ledge and the wall, unafraid now to image it even as a draconian claw, or a cranny in some monstrous fire-breathing throat—and I prepared to watch the flameflower bloom, or at least to listen as its murmur grew loud, whether it could tell me anything I could understand or not.

CHAPTER SEVENTEEN
THE FLAMEFLOWER

Would the experience have been different if the Bishop of Viviers' rite of exorcism had not mingled with its sensations? I don't believe so; that frantic babble was merely a trivial complication, an attachment whose sounds and meanings had no connection with the heart and soul of the alien Creation—at least for me.

It would be far too simple, and frankly incorrect, to describe the experience as a dream, although I understood when I wrote it down then, and I still understand now that I am trying to make it more exact, that it will inevitably seem like a dream to any reader who might one day come across it, long after I am dead. For what it is worth, though, I was fully conscious throughout—perhaps more conscious than I had ever been before...unless consciousness really is a mere refuge and nothing more, intended simply to shut things out that might harm the ability to reason.

I would not dream of disputing Dupin's opinion, of course: consciousness *is* a refuge, which really does filter out much that our intelligence does not need, and perhaps could not bear; but it is not *only* a refuge. It is an instrument too, and a powerful one: *the* instrument of intelligent inquiry.

Consciousness has only five senses at its disposal, in ordinary circumstances, and perhaps it has no more than that even in extraordinary ones, but if the latter is the case, consciousness certainly has the possibility of extending its senses in extraordinary circumstances: of hearing things that the drums and bones of the inner ear cannot normally transmit; of seeing things that the retina of the eye is not normally capable of registering; of touching things that fingers cannot normally caress; of discovering tastes of which the tongue is normally incapable of savoring; and of smelling perfumes that the nasal membranes cannot normally translate into beautiful or noxious sensation. Perhaps consciousness needs assistance to do all that—I am, in fact, certain that it does—but there are multiple sources from which that assistance might come, which do not all participate in the same kind of strangeness.

First of all, the metaphorical dragon finally awoke—but that was something of an anticlimax, for its wakefulness was no more closely akin to our wakefulness than its sleep had been closely akin to our sleep. It had no eyes to open, no dreams to dispel. It did, however, have breath of a sort to expel, in a kind of long sigh, that might well have had regret in it, but certainly had relief—for it had been held in suspension for years and centuries, and a span of time much closer to forever, within the narrow conceptual frame of quotidian human consciousness.

The dragon sighed; exhaling air richer in carbonic acid gas and countless trace elements than the open air we generally breathe, even in spring. There was sulfur in it, and perhaps other toxins, but there were perfumes too, some richer than any nectar, and there was nothing calculated about its faint toxicity. There was nothing *hostile* in that fiery breath, nothing intended to burn. It was merely breath, no more than a sigh; it was not even truly plaintive, although it was difficult for human ears to hear it in any other way.

My ears, at least. I can't speak for the Bishop, or even Dupin. Nor can I speak for the children on the ledge below, whose ears were so much keener than any adults: the children who listened, even though no one could tell them anything.

There was a sense in which, because they had better ears than the rest of us, this was their task, their duty and their opportunity, while I was merely an eavesdropper—but there was a sense, too, in which the mere fact that they were better equipped to hear was not enough to justify thrusting upon them a responsibility that was, in truth, a adult responsibility. More than that, it was a responsibility of science and logic, of consciousness at its most ambitious. The children could hear, but they could not possibly understand. There was, therefore, a sense—the most important sense of all, in my view—in which theirs was not their task, their duty and the opportunity at all, but Claude Guérande's task, and duty, and responsibility...and mine too, and, most of all, Dupin's. No matter how ill-equipped we might be by nature and maturity to apprehend the flameflower, we were the ones to whom it might, perhaps, communicate something worthwhile...and perhaps *vice versa*.

I believed that, whether it was a matter for belief or not, and I prepared myself to meet the challenge in my own way, as the Bishop of Viviers was preparing himself to meet it in his, and Auguste Dupin in his.

And the challenge materialized.

The metaphorical dragon awoke; the not-quite-unreal dragon breathed—and nothing happened, for a moment or two. How long those moments lasted in real time, I have no idea, but it was long enough to become disappointing, at least to my expectant consciousness. Perhaps that was because the fire of the breath was so ethereal, and so pale...at first.

But legend had the right of it, at least insofar as my ever-Romantic mind was ready to perceive and decide. The dragon's tentative breath, its possibly-plaintive sigh of relief, really did give birth to a flameflower...perhaps I should be representing it in the plural, but I shall maintain the singular...and the flameflower was the Main Event. I was not as close to it as I might have been, but I was close enough, and even at the range from which I was able to contemplate it, the flameflower was not anti-climactic at all.

Its substance came up the chimney, from a very long way down, rising on the updraft as a wisp of vapor might, but it was not vaporous. Perhaps it was solid, like one of those wisps of spidersilk that drift in the air, sometimes bearing a tiny spider, or a light gossamer-winged plant-seed, or a fungal spore, but it might have been some alternative state of matter that cannot long endure near the surface of the Earth—not because the conditions are any more brutal there than they are in the hot, pressured core of the planet, but simply because they are different.

At any rate, it came up, at first, in a long thin stream, more akin to the spider silk than any of the other analogies that occurred to me, but it began to weave itself while it was still some way below us, and I had to abandon my snug angle in order to get a better view of it.

I lay flat on the ground, prone, and edged my way forward until I could look down into the hole. The distance was deceptive, obviously, because I had seen the spider silk even while I was huddled against the wall, and had seen it begin to curl and coil and fabricate itself even before my careful fingers reached the rim of the precipice and my head peered over. Even so, the heart of the flameflower was beneath me, and a long way down. If Brother Xavier, Claude Guérande and the Thierachian children were looking at it too—as I supposed they must be—then I imagine that they too were lying prone and peering over the lip of the abyss, looking vertically downwards, not into the literal center of the Earth, but most certainly into the actual core of creation. They were closer; I could only hope that they were not *too* close.

The flameflower, although made of something more like flame than flesh, was not the color of any Earthly flame or flower. Indeed, its most essential property, so far as the sense of sight was concerned, was that its colors were none of those pertaining to quotidian sight.

Although Isaac Newton labeled seven colors in the visual spectrum, because he considered seven to be a magical number replete with mystical significance, the common opinion is that there are only five that qualify as distinct, orange and indigo being mere fringe effects—but just as there are people possessed of perfect pitch, who can hear nuances in music to which the rest of us remain deaf, so there are people possessed of finer sight who can distinguish more than five true colors. There are animals, too, which can see at least a little way beyond the edges of Newton's spectrum, into the infra-red and the ultra-violet, although no one knows what colors they see there. Perhaps, just as children can perceive the piping of bats, they can see those additional colors, but lose the ability as they grow, as they lose so much of the inherent magic of the world.

There are, at any rate, more colors than five, and colors very different from the five with which were are familiar and their intermediate admixtures. With the right assistance, the mind can perceive them, although the retina of the eye is normally insensitive to them. The flameflower might have been as many as half a hundred colors, or perhaps no more than a dozen—the children on the ledge below, I think, *must* have seen more than I could, just as their ears were far more sensitive to the song of the dragon and its breath—but in terms of its multitudinous coiling colors, the entity was, even in the sense that my crude vision could perceive it, as spectacular as it was unexpected.

Was it beautiful? Could I compare it to a rose, or a lily, gilded or ungilded, or some heraldic device merely symbolic of floraison but striking in its symmetry?

I don't know.

I don't know that the standards of beauty my eyes had been educated to observe were appropriate to fire's creation. The flameflower was magnificent, certainly; it contained a world, or worlds—but it was probably too strange, too alien, to be merely beautiful. It was beyond the reach of such adjectives as that.

On the other hand, and however paradoxical it may seem, its scent was definitely sweet, and luscious, and slightly heady. Perhaps its scent had more in common with Earthly perfumes than any of the aspects that appealed to the other sensory apparatus of consciousness had in common with their analogues.

Yes, there was brimstone in it, but not in an offensive way. If you have ever melted sulfur, and seen the delicate lemon yellow fluid that precedes the ugly viscous brownish liquid that succeeds it, you might care to imagine the familiar reek of sulfur as that viscous, slightly offensive stickiness, while the sulfurousness that was a component of the flameflower's multitudinous scent was the more delicate, more ethereal phase.

Were the other components—those I thought of as a cocktail of nectars—literally intoxicating, even hallucinogenic?

I don't believe so.

When I say that they were "heady" I don't mean that they were befuddling, like the fumes of various alcohol, acetates and other miscellaneous distillates produced by latter-day alchemists, or the "laughing gas" with which Humphry Davy is said to have delighted and inspired Coleridge, Keats and other Romantic poets. The scent, however complex it might have been, was an *honest* scent, a scent that did not seek to distort or deceive consciousness, but merely to appeal to it.

Perhaps there was something plaintive in it, as there seemed to be in the dragon's sigh, but I'm inclined to believe that much, if not all of that, was a projection of plaintiveness in me... although I could not imagine then, and cannot now, what I had to feel plaintive about, having never, so far as I could remember, loved and lost, or loved at all.

If the scent of the flameflower was sweet, however, its taste was not. I do not mean that it was bitter, sour or salt, but that it brought some sensation—*apparently* via the tongue—that was very unfamiliar.

There was something metallic about the taste, I think, and something hot, but it was not like dipping my tongue into molten iron or silver might have been, if such a thing were physiologically possible. The flameflower only had a flameflower taste— there was nothing to which I could easily compare it—but it did have a distinctive taste: a taste that was, in its own strange way, appetizing, and, in an even stranger way, memorable.

Scent is sometimes said to be the sense most closely connected with memory, most conducive to sudden reminiscence, but either that judgment is mistaken or flameflowers do not obey the rule, for it was the *taste* of the flameflower that awoke something in my consciousness akin to echoes of memory. Not *my* memory, to be sure, but memory in some vaguer sense: memory that could reach back beyond the meager history of my own consciousness into a much deeper well of time and experience.

I remembered, vaguely and briefly, having been an apelike creatures learning to walk on a vast savannah, and before that, a smaller primate in the branches of a forest, and before that, something like a squirrel, and before that, something like a mouse, and before that, a lizard, and a frog, and a fish, and an infinite number of worms, and perhaps even a monad.

The last sensation must surely have been an illusion, for a monad can no more secrete memories—even those that a tiny worm might be imagined to have—than a spore drifting in the infinite vacuous wilderness of empty space.

Except, of course, that the vacuum of space is not really empty, and seeds drifting there, in the ultimate dormancy, might be subject to more complex combinations of subtle force and phantom presence than mere humans could ever imagine.

I certainly could not remember Creation—how could anyone?—let alone a time before Creation. I could no more see God, or his absence, than I could remember not being a bird, or a spider, or a starfish, or a barnacle, or a rose, or a bracken-leaf—none of which I numbered among my ancestors, and none of which were in any wise contained in the taste of the flame-flower.

I think I vaguely regret the unmemory of the bird—and, strangely enough, that of the spider—but that is something that afflicts me now, and did not then.

It was not all comfortable though. There was the touch.

Before I looked down into the abyss, toward the core of Creation, I was very much aware of the rock beneath my prone body, and even more aware of Dupin's right hand, clutching my left. Indeed, I felt that hand as a kind of anchorage, not so much to the physical world to which I belonged as to the social world: the world of companionship, of unloneliness—and on that account, I considered it very precious, and vital to my well-being.

I would never have let go of that hand, and I am utterly convinced that Dupin would not have let go of mine, either. I pitied the Bishop for preferring the grip of his golden crucifix, and not because the crucifix had been stained and scarred as we wormed out way into the dragon's entrails. I have never had a bad word to say against the Jesus of the gospels, who appears to have been the most admirable of men, in spite of all the crimes that his unworthy worshipers have committed in his name, but I would not have traded any human hand in the world for the effigy of his martyrdom, at that or any other moment.

I did not let go—and neither, I am sure, did Dupin.

Nevertheless, the grip was broken—not wrenched apart, or dissolved, or subjected to any other physical process, but simply canceled out.

The flameflower was not a jealous entity, nor a possessive one, but, in order to touch us, it apparently had to detach us from any other touch. That included the touch of any other human hand—or, for that matter, the symbolic touch of Christ embodied in a crucifix. It also had to detach us from the touch of the dragon's flesh, or that of the rock of the mountain. Its touch was incompatible with any rival solidity, any rival caress.

How fearful the children must be! I thought. *And yet, how privileged they would feel, if only they understood....*

The creature from the depths of the world did not drop me, and I did not float; indeed, I was held more securely than before in the bosom of the flameflower, and held *up*, in way that seemed very unexpected indeed on the part of such a chthonic entity—although I suppose, in retrospect, that it was not merely reaching for the surface that it could never attain, but for the void beyond that surface: not for the stars, as such, but for the essential core of a different creation, the antipodean pole of its own.

I felt the fabric of the flameflower all around me, not like a spider's web at all, in spite of the way it had begun its odyssey in exotica, but more robust and more insistent. It was not an affectionate caress, any more than it was an angry slap or a belligerent punch, but it was forceful, in a way that made me feel claustrophobic and pressured. I could breathe perfectly well, although I could not feel my own lungs pumping or my own hart beating, but I nevertheless felt trapped, like a fly in mystical amber, or a flaw in a magical gem.

I did not belong in that grip, and I knew it. I felt a deep, instinctive desire to get out—but there was no way out. I did not struggle—at least, not consciously—but I did move. I know that now, because of what happened later, but I think I was aware of it even at the time. Was the movement the result of some reflexive twitch of my own, or did the flameflower actually carry me?

I don't know.

I suspect the latter, because I know that not everyone who went into the mountain that day came out again, and that not everyone who did come out came out in the same physical state that they went in, and no bones were ever found of the people who did not come out. I have no idea what happened to them, and I have no idea whether it was the fault of their own unconscious reflexes or the unconscious carelessness of the dragon's progeny.

I only know the facts—but I suspect that the people who were lost were carried off, and were simply *not put back*.

I was carried off too—though not, I think, with any purpose—but I *was* put back. I was not put back exactly where I wanted to be, or in any very convenient location, but I *was* returned to the familiar realm of touch, eventually.

I would far rather have been returned to the touch, and the clutch, of Dupin's hand, but wherever he was carried, it was in another direction. He eventually came back too, though, whole and entire....but I shouldn't get ahead of my narrative, because there is one sense as yet unaccounted for, one more channel of communication by which the flameflower was able to reach out, not merely to me, and not merely to the people inside the mountain, but to people further away, in the valley, and perhaps even atop the crag where the false Comte de Tibère clung like a leech to his false heritage and a past that never really was, even before the Revolution.

I heard the flameflower sing.

Had I had the slightest inkling of its language, I might have grasped a little of what it was singing, but as matters stood, I could barely comprehend the music accompanying its song.

Is music a universal language? Some people think so, I know, but others point to the seeming strangeness of Japanese instruments or Peruvian performance, and say *probably not*. Perhaps it is not a matter for belief, but I tend to the former opinion. The general case does not really matter, though; the point is that I did feel some sort of harmony, some sort of empathy, with the flameflower's song.

As I listened to that song, I began to comprehend why the Thierachians came back, year after year, in the hope of hearing its faintest echoes when the sleeping dragon stirred, and why they had roamed the world throughout the epochs of their history, searching for other locations where snatches of it might be heard, even at risk to themselves and their children. And I understood, too, why the children, who had keener ears than their parents, probably able to hear the whispering of bats as well as coarser and more melodious sounds, were the ones who came into the mountain, and were permitted to come, whenever that song was able to sound a little more distinctly, a little more...I should not say meaningfully, for that would be a guess too far, but more intimately, in a more *heartfelt* fashion.

One day, the Thierachians presumably hoped, their children might be able to understand the words of the song, and discover what it was that the entities of the alternative Creation had been trying to say to them—to us, and to anyone or anything that had ears to hear—since the Earth first condensed out of the solar nebula, insensibly clutching the seeds of its eventual inner life.

I wanted to join in that song, but I could not. Perhaps Philippe Aignan wanted to join in too, but was equally incapable of making himself heard. I doubt that a Thierachian adult could have done any more—but I believe that some, at least, of the Thierachian children were able to add their voices to it, in chorus. For some of them, at least, the communication was two-way.

They sang, and they were heard. More than that; they sang, and something *listened.*

I listened too, to the song of the flameflower and to its human answer. I did not understand either component of the experience, but I knew that there was a harmony of some sort between them, and I felt—in no doubt, at last, as to what I *ought* to feel—that there was something infinitely precious in that brief and tentative harmony. The Creation at the world's core could not quite reach the surface of the Earth, let alone the infinity beyond, but just for a moment, once every thousand years or so, it could reach *us*: humankind...or, to be strictly accurate, our children, stolen or otherwise.

I was carried off, as I have said, by the flameflower's touch, its grip. Perhaps I traveled a few meters, or even a few hundred meters, in space—but I travelled much further on the metaphorical wings of song. It was through the sense of hearing that I undertook my true journey into the core of Creation: a journey that could have no terminus, of course, even at the metaphorical equivalent of Chalon, but which would have been undertaken with a deal of effort, and a deal of hope, had any been required.

I cannot reproduce that song, or the notes of its music. They were not the notes of our Pythagorean scale, and the mathematics underlying them were not our mathematics. And yet, at the very edge of my perception, I can still sense their reverberation in my eardrums, the bones of my inner ear, and in my soul. The song does not trouble me, in the way it apparently troubles the Thierachians, but it will never leave me either.

I could not speak for Dupin, let alone the Bishop of Viviers, but I think that it was innate in them too, from that moment on, quiet but not impotent, barely heard but never to be forgotten.

Contact between our Creation and the other is possible; there is no doubt about it. Communication is possible; there is no doubt about that, either. Mutual understanding, on a conscious level—as opposed to mere heartfelt sympathy—might take another million or billion years, and it will surely not be human beings who finally achieve it, but when the flameflowers touch the minds that that will finally reach that understanding, those minds, under the spur of exotic taste, will still remember us....

At least, I hope they will still remember us. Perhaps they will remember birds, or spiders, or perhaps they will only remember worms, or monads, if monads can be remembered at all...but whatever the case may be, they will remember *something* of our vast and hectic tree of life. Our Creation will survive, long enough not only to hear and touch the other, but to understand it, to empathize with it and perhaps—who can tell?—to love it. Evolution will take care of that, with a little assistance from our urge to improvement, our determination to be better than we are...or if not ours, that of some cousin species with a greater talent for self-improvement.

The heart of the world is, after all, not so very far away... closer even than the Moon, let alone the Sun, or the stars, or the distant nebulae that are continuing the Great Work of Creation elsewhere and everywhere.

CHAPTER EIGHTEEN
THE RESCUE PARTY

When I returned to myself, I was alone and in the dark. I did not wake up, because I had never been asleep. I saw the flameflower retreat and fade; I lost the taste and smell of it: I felt its grip upon me relax, and heard its song became fainter and fainter and fainter, although it never died away completely.

The dragon was silent, though. The mountain was inert. I groped around in every direction, hoping to lay my hand on a lantern. It would not have mattered had its wick gone out, or even if its reservoir of oil had been exhausted. I had a tinder-box, and safety-matches, and a wax candle.

When I could not find a lamp, I lit the candle, and found a niche in the rock where I could wedge it in an upright position, in order to take stock of my situation. The good news was that I was no longer precariously perched on a ledge above a precipice. The bad news was that I was in a cave I was certain that I had never seen before, which had two very narrow exits, neither of which was marked with any kind of a scratch to indicate a direction I might usefully take.

I was lost. I did not know which way to go, or whether either way would be negotiable for a person of my bulk.

I knew that I had to make a choice, because the candle would not last forever, but I sat there for a few moments studying its flame, trying to read the air currents by means of its flickering and the drift of its smoke. I do not know what I would have deduced from the direction that the smoke was drifting—

whether to follow the current or to go toward the apparent source of the air-flow, but I did not have to.

Lantern-light suddenly flooded one of the two narrow issues, and someone came through, walking calmly and purposively.

It was the very last person I expected to see.

"Have you seen my father, Monsieur Reynolds?" Sophie asked, with scrupulous politeness. "I've been searching for hours, but I can't find him."

I looked behind her for companions, but she had none. She had come alone—presumably because her mother would never have given her permission, had she asked. In spite of the vigilance with which he had been watched, the little girl had contrived to get away.

"Hours?" I queried. "Did you see the flameflower, then?"

"No," she admitted, "but I heard it."

"Did it touch you?"

"I don't think so."

"What time was it when you set out?"

"About noon. I slipped away after my morning lessons. Everything was confused, and Mother was busy with the Thierachians and the monks. Everyone's searching—but more for the children and the Bishop, so far as I could tell, than Papa. Nobody asked me, or told me anything, so I came on my own. Nobody will mind, if I can find my father. Do you know where he is?"

"No," I said. "Dupin, the Bishop and I were together when the flameflower bloomed, but we became separated when it touched us, and I suspect that we're all lost. If anyone can find his own way out, though, it's your father. He went to help some children. With luck, they weren't separated, and the children will be able to show him a way out, even if he can't find one on his own." It sounded better, I thought, to say that he had gone to help the Thierachian children, even though I wasn't entirely sure what his motives had been. I wasn't surprised to learn that we had been inside the mountain all night and half of the following day, even though I'd lost track of the time.

It took a moment or two for another thought occurred to me. "Are you sure that you can find your way back?" I asked her.

"Oh yes," she said. She showed me a piece of chalk in her hand. "I made my own marks. Better to be safe than sorry."

She was staring at me, and I knew why. There was a conflict going on inside her between desire and duty, purpose and obligation.

I was having a similar conflict of my own. How could I possibly let her go on, knowing what the dangers were? How could I even go on with her, knowing what her mother would say? And yet, I ought to look for Dupin.

In the end, I said, very tentatively: "I'll help you look for your father, Sophie. I need to look for my friend—Monsieur Dupin."

"Monsieur Dupin is looking for my father too," the little girl told me.

"Have you seen him?" I asked, sharply.

"No," she said, "but I heard him. Didn't you?"

I didn't understand. "Where did you hear him?" I asked.

"I was in my room. Mother told me that it was a dream, but it wasn't. I don't know where he was, exactly."

"What did he say?" I asked, utterly confused.

"He didn't *say* anything. He was singing—with the children. I might not have made any noise, but I was singing. He might not have been making any noise either, but he sang as well. I heard him."

I had not been able to sing with the children. Nor, with my adult ears, had I been able to hear Dupin singing with them—but if Sophie had heard Dupin join in with the song, I was prepare to take her word that he had. He was, after all, a very exceptional man, even if he was no wizard.

"The Bishop heard him too," Sophie put in, apparently unsure that I believed her.

"The Bishop?" I repeated. "*The Bishop* joined in the song?"

"No—he was too busy with his own chanting. But he could hear Monsieur Dupin, and the children—I'm sure of it. Mother says that I dreamed it, but I didn't. I couldn't see, but I *could* hear. It was real, even though she couldn't hear it. I want to find my father—I think he's hurt, but he's not dead. I can still hear him. And Monsieur Dupin's looking for him too."

"Can you find them, do you think?" I asked her, quite ready to believe that she knew the secret of the labyrinth.

She was holding the lamp up, so that its light fell on her face. She was still staring at me, with a slight expression of perplexity. "Perhaps," she said. She didn't move, though. She just continued looking at me.

"It's all right," I assured her, although I knew that I had to take her back to the surface, to her mother. "I'll help you. You'll be safe with me."

She shook her head slowly. "I can't," she said, as if speaking to herself. "Now I've found you, I ought to show you the way out. I need to help *you*. If I can, I'll come back to look for my father—but if there are people at the entrance, they probably won't let me."

She wanted me to know what she was giving up, in order to obey the call to duty that was instructing her to help me. Perhaps she wanted me to volunteer to follow her chalk marks on my own, and let her continue her search, or perhaps she wanted me to insist that I would go on with her, deeper into the mountain, in search of Dupin and her father—but she wasn't hopeful. She knew, deep down, that I couldn't let her do that, any more than the people waiting at the entrance could let her do it. We each had a duty, to make sure that the other was safe before going on. She was right; now that she had voiced the issue, I could see that she was right.

"Thank you, Sophie," I said, eventually. "It pains me to admit it, but I needed rescuing. You've done that I think. I'm sorry that I'm not your father."

"It's not your fault," she observed, although she didn't seem entirely convinced.

She was as good as her word. It took a long time, but she guided me out, to the same entrance by which I'd entered the caves. We passed half a dozen Thierachians on the way—not without difficulty, given the narrowness of the passages. I didn't know any of them; they weren't elders. They were parents, anxious for the children they had sent forth, perhaps foolishly, to see and hear what they could no longer hear and see themselves.

There were people waiting by the entrance, as Sophie had feared: Brother Michael, one of the Thierachian elders, and Julie Guérande. The lady might have hugged me if she hadn't been so enthusiastic to imprison her daughter in her arms, but she tried hard to thank me through her tears.

"You're mistaken," I said, dutifully. "It wasn't me who rescued Sophie, but she who rescued me. I'm only sorry that it was me she found, not Claude. Is there any news of Dupin?"

"Not yet," Brother Michel told me. "You're the first of your company to be found."

"Brother Xavier is a very brave man," I told him. "The Bishop too, after his fashion. I truly hope that God protects them."

I wanted to stay by the entrance, or at least somewhere on the mountainside, to wait for the others to emerge, but I was utterly exhausted. I hadn't slept a wink for more than thirty hours, and had not slept well for many hours before that. In response to everyone's urging, I went back down the slope with Julie and Sophie, in order to wait in the house.

The Bishop was carried down on a stretcher by two friars a little while later, exhausted but uninjured. I hastened to ask him whether he had seen anything of Dupin since the event had begun.

"No," he said. "When you and he fled, I faced the Devil alone. I have looked into the fires of Hell, and have seen the Devil."

I doubted that, but I didn't contradict him. "Did your exorcism work?" I asked, curious to know what he believed that he had experienced.

"It did," he said. "I sent the fires of the Inferno back into the bowels of the Earth, and the Devil with them—but the victory was not really mine. God sent a choir of angels to help me in my hour of need, with Christ himself at their head. He it was who extended his merciful hand, and saved the world from catastrophe. He did not come to save me, I suppose, but to save the children. Pagans they might be, but...the Lord, it seems, considered them worthy of salvation."

Sophie had told me that the Bishop had heard Dupin's voice, as she had. I believed, now, that he had heard Dupin's song too... but that he had interpreted the voice in the light of his own prejudices, and his own desires. I was not about to argue with him; it would have been unwise as well as unkind.

"You must be proud," I said, a trifle ironically—and more than a trifle thoughtlessly.

"Pride is Satan's sin," he reminded me. "I have conquered pride. I have seen the army of angels, with Christ at their head, but I am not proud. I am humble. I know now, what humility is worth."

I looked into his eyes, and remembered them as I had seen them in the depths of the mountain, ablaze with fanaticism. They were not ablaze now, nor even aglow with the faintest ember of reckless ambition. Whether he knew it or not, the flameflower had carried him off, not to the gates of Pandemonium but to somewhere closer to its own fiery but unadversarial bosom. The song was within him still, and in him, it really had taken on the form, and the significance, of an angelic anthem. He was not the same man that I had seen before.

I wondered, as he looked at me, whether I was the same man that he had seen before—but I did not invite him to make any comparison.

I left him to rest.

Julie Guérande was waiting for me outside the room where the Bishop had been placed.

"Does he have any news?" she demanded.

"We were separated from your husband before we were separated from one another," I told her. "Aignan was alone with his particular hallucination—but he has survived, with a little help from his faith. Claude was better equipped than any of us to withstand the experience. He'll come through it, I'm sure."

"*What* experience?" she demanded.

"We saw the flameflower bloom," I told her. "It does not mean to be harmful—quite the opposite, in fact—but I can imagine how it might seem disturbing to the unprepared. The Thierachian children are prepared, I suppose, after a fashion—but all six of our party were armored, one way or another, Claude and Dupin most securely of all. I have come through it; so will they. Your husband will doubtless tell you what he experienced when he returns, and anything I described would seem like a mere dream...as, perhaps, it was. Sophie can tell you more, I think. Don't be angry with her for trying to find her father."

"How can I be?" the lady complained. If she was angry with anyone, it was Claude Guérande—but it was also Claude Guérande for whom she was most fearful. She loved him.

"Don't be angry with Dupin, either," I said. "He did what he could—and I suspect that he will not come out of the caves until your husband has been found. He feels that he owes you an obligation, and will not rest until it is fulfilled."

"I could always get him to do what I wanted," she said, softly. "I could always get every last one of them to do exactly as I wished. It was unfair. I took advantage—but what choice did I have, as a mere decoration, a pretty bauble to decorate the arena of my father's genius?"

"It was not wrong for you to take advantage," I told her, "especially of Dupin. That is how he sees his role in life now. If no one took advantage of him, he would be bereft. You have no idea how delighted he was to reply to your appeal." It was flattery of a sort, but it was probably not untrue—and in any case, she didn't believe me.

"You're very kind, Mr. Reynolds," she told me. That too was flattery, and probably not true.

I was direly tempted to go to bed then, and make an attempt to sleep, but excited noises outside told us that someone else was being brought down to the house from the mountain. We ran out of the front door of the house and around to the side opposite the barn.

Whoever had been recovered was being carried down on a stretcher borne by two slow-moving Thierachians, and there was a long lapse of time before we could obtain information as to who the casualty was.

It turned out to be Brother Xavier. He was in good spirits, but in need of a bone-setter. When he finally arrived at the front door I inspected his bruises and his broken leg carefully, but the fracture did not seem to be serious. Wherever he had fallen, it was not into the abyss from which the flameflower had risen. He had been closer to the creature than I had, but he had been armored by his intelligence, his kind heart and his faith, perhaps better than the Bishop.

"They brought the injured child out first," he said. "She is in no danger—but I fear for some of the others, who have not yet been found."

"Do you know what happened to Guérande?" I asked.

"I fear not," the Dominican replied. "He was with us when…it happened, but afterwards had disappeared. You saw it, did you not, Monsieur? You heard the children singing?" He seemed anxious for confirmation that he had not simply suffered a hallucination.

"Yes, I heard and saw," I said. "The Bishop believes that he looked into Hell, but was saved by a choir of angels. That is not how I interpreted what I saw and heard, but I have no intention of arguing with him. Each to his own."

The stonemason looked at Madame Guérande, and then at me. "He's the Bishop of Viviers," he said, in a carefully neutral voice. "It's not for the likes of us to contradict a man of his standing in the Church. I bear him no ill will. If Heaven really thought it necessary to send a choir of angels on a rescue mission, he is surely the one they would have come to aid. Personally, I have no idea what it was that I saw, and would be glad of a little enlightenment, when Monsieur Guérande is found."

I knew that he had said that for the lady's benefit and did not take offence.

"You must stay here until the bone-setter comes," Madame

Guérande told him. "You cannot possibly go back to the château."

"Thank you, Madame," the Dominican said.

Once the friar was comfortable, I decided that I would not retire while the vigil was still in progress. Julie Guérande and Sophie needed someone a trifle sturdier than Madame Cormontaigne to keep them company, and I doubted that I would really be able to sleep while Dupin was still missing.

The mother was considerably more agitated than the daughter, although Sophie did risk saying at one point that she ought to have turned back as soon as she was sure that I could find the entrance, even if it meant giving me the slip.

"Dupin will find him," I told her.

"I know," she replied. "And he will be able to show Monsieur Dupin the way out."

That was blind guesswork, of course. She was no longer hearing things—but it was good guesswork, for that is exactly what happened. Dupin found Claude Guérande, in the end, and Guérande, although hardly capable of unassisted locomotion, was able to indicate to Dupin which route to take in order to reach a place where the Thierachian searchers found them.

Arnauld Lebrun was with the party who eventually carried Guérande down, just as the sun was setting. Dupin was still able to walk, albeit a trifle unsteadily. I offered him my arms in case he wanted to collapse into them, but he did not—mercifully.

"Are all the children safe?" I asked Lebrun, when I was sure that Dupin was only tired.

"No," the man of law said, flatly. "Three hurt, four still missing. We'll keep searching—all week, if necessary. You should have done as we asked and stayed out of it."

"I disagree," I told him. "I wouldn't have missed it for the world—and I can't help resenting the sly way in which you tried to dissuade us."

He shrugged his shoulders. "I'm a Thierachian," he said, "and a lawyer—if any such combination is really possible." To get past his embarrassment he changed the subject, nodding in the direction of the group clustered around the recumbent Guérande and the seated Dupin. "Guérande will live," he declared, "but he might never be the same man again. You and Dupin were a little further away, as I understand it?"

"True," I admitted. "I'm unhurt and, I think, unaltered—and Dupin has proved himself in harsher ordeals than this one. The Bishop was badly shaken, but he too has found a way through it."

"Is he still of a mind to block the tunnels?" Lebrun wanted to know.

"I don't know—but I think he might be a little more tractable now than he was before. He has had a vision...and he is too sincere a man not have been deeply affected by it. Would you like to see him?"

Lebrun hesitated, but then said: "Perhaps later. I must get back to the caves."

"I'll find out what his intentions are," I promised. "I'll bring word to the camp if I can obtain any solid information."

"Thank you," he said, mildly surprised by my willingness to help, after his chicanery of the previous day.

"Good luck," I said, as he turned round, and went back to help with the search.

I hadn't asked Lebrun whether he'd seen anything himself because I knew that he hadn't. It wasn't his place, according to Thierachian tradition. He had heard the song, though—perhaps not as clearly as Sophie, but he had heard it. I doubted that he had heard Dupin's part in it, though, any more than I had. That was going to be our secret—unless the Thierachian children had perceived his participation, and were able to convince their elders of the fact.

I went to speak to Dupin.

"You fulfilled your obligations, after all," I observed. "To your friend's wife, and to Lucien Groix too, it seems. The Bishop is unharmed, and seems to have interpreted his experience in a manner that will not trouble the peace overmuch—not that I believe for a moment that Monsieur Groix really cares about that."

Dupin looked at me a trifle strangely, but he was extremely weary. "What do you mean?" he asked.

"Groix doesn't give a fig about provincial bishops and would-be heresy-hunters," I said. "He just wanted to insert himself into your mission of mercy—to maintain a phantom presence within it, even though the adorable Julie had left him out of it. He was jealous."

Dupin could not even muster a faint smile. He had known that, I think, since the moment when I had told him that Groix had come to call, and he had asked: "Was he alone?"

"Lebrun says that Claude might never be the same man again," I observed. "What do you think?"

"The Thierachians are exceedingly jealous," Dupin reminded me, "of their arcane secrets, and of their supposed understanding of the truth that underlies them. They tried to forbid us a glimpse of their precious flameflower, simply by virtue of that jealousy, and having failed, are eager to believe that we could not stand the sight—but we could, could we not? Claude was badly bruised, and certainly shaken up, but he has been anticipating a discovery of some sort for half a lifetime, and he has the mind of a true scientist, as logical as it is inquisitive. He has accepted the cost of his curiosity gladly; he will recover, and he will be still be the same Claude that he always was, beloved by his wife and daughter—as he certainly ought to be."

"You sang," I said, baldly, not specifying that I only had the information second-hand.

"Did I?" he said. "I tried, with all my might—but I could not tell whether I had succeeded. If I did join in the song, in any effective manner, I cannot calculate the result. I heard no response, alas."

"Aignan mistook you for Jesus, leading a choir of angels," I told him.

Dupin shrugged his shoulders. "Perhaps Jesus was really there," he said. "How can I tell? My attention was focused in a different direction."

He had not changed at all—but he had always been secretive, in certain matters. Eager as he was to share his wisdom with his consultants on matters they brought to him, and willing as he was to use me as a sounding-board for his thoughts in progress, there were certain things that he always kept entirely to himself. I knew that this would be one of them: that no matter how much I told him about what I had seen when the flameflower bloomed, he would not reciprocate in any detail, any more than he would ever confess to me or to anyone else in the world what feelings he had once harbored with respect to Julie Guérande.

I went to bed then, and to sleep. I slept until late the next morning.

Three more days were to pass before the Thierachians finally gave up on the two children who were never found. We saw Lebrun every day, but he would never tell us what he believed regarding the missing children's fate, nor how many others the Thierachians had lost to the caves in previous years. We saw the Bishop every day too, when he came to visit the Dominican, for whose injury he felt a certain responsibility.

"Were the effects of your exorcism conclusive, do you think?" I enquired, delicately, when I thought it was safe to raise the issue.

"I believe so," he told me. "I have heard no diabolical whispers since. It was not easy, but the Lord gave me strength and lent me the assistance I needed. I have looked into the very mouth of the Inferno—but I survived. I'm sincerely glad that I enabled you and Monsieur Dupin to escape unscathed, and that Guérande was not mortally wounded."

"Do you still intend to seal the caves?" I asked, tentatively.

He thought about it for a long moment, and then said: "I shall consult with the Hescheboix in that regard. If what you say is true, and the land really is theirs...well, I'm an honest man, and I shall do my best to convince my friend Tibère that there may be a need for compromise. I shall advise him not to pursue any attempted legal action against Guérande."

"A need for compromise between the Church and pagan idolaters?" I queried, in mild surprise.

He looked at me long and hard, and finally said: "Yes, even that." His exorcism might or might not have worked, in terms of his own interpretation of what he had seen and felt, but he was definitely not *quite* the same man that he had been before experiencing the flameflower's quasi-miraculous touch. A seed of tolerance had been planted in his soul, or at least roused from dormancy and caused to germinate there.

Claude Guérande was in bed for a week, and by the time he got up again Brother Xavier had been taken away in order to recovery his health in a priory. Claude had not needed the flameflower's glow to trigger the development of any tolerance, so he did not seem to have been changed in that fashion, and he still loved his wife and doted on his daughter, so there really was no conspicuous change in him, in spite of Lebrun's prediction—although, from the viewpoint of Madame Guérande, he seemed to have returned to an old self that she had very nearly lost. She credited Dupin with that, although he modestly denied any responsibility at all.

And that, in essence, was the end of the story—a happy ending, for those of us on the surface. Was it happy, too, for the emissaries of the other Creation? I would certainly like to think so. I would like to think that for them, too, potential confrontation had been averted, that down there as well as up here, the doctrine of "live and let live" held gentle sway, and would survive even when their next Revolution came around.

As I write this now, nearly ten years after the events in question took place, Claude Guérande has still not presented his *mémoire* to the Académie regarding the cave-paintings of Mont Dagon, or the bones discovered in the same locale. Whether he ever will, I cannot tell, but I doubt it. He still makes his annual pilgrimages into the caves, according to Madame Guérande's occasional letters, and he still thinks that there might be further discoveries to be made there, if he only persists—but he is no longer anxious, feverish or obsessive, merely methodical and unhurried.

Sophie is in her twenties now, but she still lives at home, and has only deigned to visit Paris twice, for brief vacations. She told me when I last saw her—very briefly—that she is quite content where she is, and that she still listens, even though no one is yet inclined to tell her anything.

All the vague threats of disturbance that had hung over the valley before the dragon's brief awakening vanished once it sank once again into its slumber. The people of the region are naturally secretive, and naturally placid; when the anticipated Revolution actually arrived, in 1848, and when the *coup-d'état* of 1851 turned the clock back yet again, there was no hint of terror, red or white, in the vicinity of Mont Dragon.

Dupin was, of course, correct in the belief that he could claim no credit for any of that, any more than I could. We had merely been privileged to be witness to something strange, and wonderful, and to lend a little society to a man in temporary need of it.

So far as I know, Dupin never saw the adorable Julie again. How deeply he regretted that, I cannot tell. I never heard him mention her in the presence of Lucien Groix, and never heard the ex-Prefect mention her to him—but sometimes, when they were together, I could not help studying them carefully, wondering whether they had a little more in common than seemed likely to other eyes.

The secrets of the hearts of men may be jealously sealed, like the secrets of the heart of the world, but sometimes, they reach out of their own accord, and make themselves sensible, albeit in an inarticulate fashion. And we evolve—and, if our inner efforts are successful, make progress.

ABOUT THE AUTHOR

Brian Stableford was born in Yorkshire in 1948. He taught at the University of Reading for several years, but is now a full-time writer. He has written many science-fiction and fantasy novels, including *The Empire of Fear, The Werewolves of London, Year Zero, The Curse of the Coral Bride, The Stones of Camelot,* and *Prelude to Eternity.* Collections of his short stories include a long series of *Tales of the Biotech Revolution,* and such idiosyncratic items as *Sheena and Other Gothic Tales* and *The Innsmouth Heritage and Other Sequels.* He has written numerous nonfiction books, including *Scientific Romance in Britain, 1890-1950; Glorious Perversity: The Decline and Fall of Literary Decadence; Science Fact and Science Fiction: An Encyclopedia;* and *The Devil's Party: A Brief History of Satanic Abuse.* He has contributed hundreds of biographical and critical articles to reference books, and has also translated numerous novels from the French language, including books by Paul Féval, Albert Robida, Maurice Renard, and J. H. Rosny the Elder.